Praise for
ART, WINE, and

If you'd like to live in a world of fine art, grand cru wine, French chateaux, Ferraris–and mystery–Tana Boerger has created a treat for you. *Art, Wine and Crime,* is like one of the soirees hosted by her appealing protagonists, Lord and Lady Crosswick. It's sophisticated, entertaining, and over before you want it to be.

Robert Cullen,
Former international correspondent and
author of four acclaimed thrillers,
including the New York Times
Notable Book of the Year, *Soviet Sources*

How marvelously Tana Boerger weaves mystery and intrigue through the glamorous French high life, the beaux arts, and the elite world of wine in *Art, Wine and Crime.* She continues the fast and thrilling ride of Philip and Genevieve Warwick, this time through wide Parisian avenues and historic vineyards of Bordeaux. This second book in the *Lord and Lady Crosswick* series is exhilarating, insightful, and stylish from start to finish—especially with a glass of grand cru in hand.

Vidya Vijayasekharan,
Artist and art historian

A Lord and Lady Crosswick Mystery

ART, WINE, *and* CRIME

Tana L.H. Boerger

Copyright © 2023 by Tana L.H. Boerger

All rights reserved. No part of this publication may be reproduced, distributed, or transmitted in any form or by any means, including photocopying, recording, or other electronic or mechanical methods, without the prior written permission of the publisher, except in the case of brief quotations embodied in critical reviews and certain other noncommercial uses permitted by copyright law.

Altta Publishing
2 The Pointe
Sanford, NC, 27332

Printed in the United States of America

Paperback ISBN: 979-8-9873285-5-2
Hardcover ISBN: 979-8-9873285-3-8
Ebook ISBN: 979-8-9873285-6-9

First Edition

*To Cody and Stella,
you inspire me every day.*

ART, WINE, AND CRIME

ONE

THE PLANE PLUMMETED toward earth with a searing whine and thunderous shudder of the fuselage. These could be their last moments before slamming into the ground and exploding into a million bits. Tears stung her eyes, but Genevieve was calm, dead calm.

"Lord and Lady Crosswick, brace for impact," Captain Bruni barked over the intercom.

With their heads between their knees, Genevieve and Philip locked on each other's gaze. If these were their last moments, they would cherish each other until they perished in a ball of flames.

She stretched toward him, brushing his lips with hers. Philip's hand cradled the back of her head, pulling her to him and firming what was probably their last embrace. Each could feel the other's taut muscles and prayed their combined strength might ease the plane to earth.

And then, the jet engines roared back to life, their thrust pressing Philip and Genevieve back into their seats. The front of the plane nosed up. Outside the window, the horizon leveled.

"What the hell?" Philip gasped under his breath.

The hum of lowering landing gear filled the cabin with a glorious moan.

"Lord and Lady Crosswick." They could hear Captain Bruni's smile and relief through the speaker. "It appears our engines had a change of heart and have decided to take us into Paris rather than smashing us into a farmer's field. We shall be on the ground shortly."

Overcome with relief, Philip and Genevieve's whoops and whistles bounced off the walls of the Bombardier jet. Still gripping Genevieve's hand, Philip brought it to his lips and kissed each knuckle.

She croaked a laugh, tears streaming down her adrenaline-flushed cheeks. "That's quite an entrance into Paris," she said, glancing down at her trembling hands.

"After what we've been through since September, all I wanted was a few calm months in France." Philip shook his head. "This does not bode well."

Lights flashed, sirens screamed, and three ambulances clustered in front of the General Aviation Terminal at Paris-Le Bourget Airport, waiting for the Warwicks' jet to ease to a stop. Unsure what to do next, Genevieve and Philip didn't move, didn't release their seatbelts, barely breathed.

After what seemed like an eternity, the cockpit door opened. Filling the doorway with his tall, broad-shouldered frame, Captain Francesco Bruni paused before he entered the owners' cabin.

"Well done, Captain Bruni." Philip mopped his brow with a crumpled linen napkin left from lunch. "What the hell just happened?" He motioned for the captain to sit in the seat across from him.

Bruni hesitated, then sat. In his lilting Italian accent, he began. "Lord, Lady Crosswick," he said, hands clasped between his splayed legs, his handsome face pale from strain, "until the mechanics investigate, it's difficult to say what caused the flameout, but I wouldn't—"

"Flameout?" Philip interrupted.

"This term is often used for any failure in a turbine engine, but its technical meaning is a power loss not associated with mechanical failure. In this case, though the engines stopped, we were able to restart them."

"For which we are grateful." Genevieve reached out and touched the captain's sleeve, her eyes still sparkling with tears of relief.

"If it wasn't mechanical, what could have happened?" Now that the unthinkable was behind them, Philip wanted answers.

Captain Bruni cleared his throat, his gaze riveted on Philip. "Lord Crosswick, the problem could have been caused by a number of things: birds flying into the engine, a compressor stall, or…" Bruni glanced down at his interlaced fingers, looked at Genevieve, then back at Philip. "Or perhaps water in the fuel. If we find that is the problem, there will be serious consequences for whoever is responsible."

"I don't understand. How does water get into the fuel?"

"Under normal circumstances, it does not. I don't want to speculate, but we're scrupulous about testing before we refuel, so I would say if that turns out to be our problem, we need to find the person responsible."

Philip ran his hands over his face. "Are you saying if the

engines stalled because of water in the fuel, someone intended to make that happen?"

"As I stated, I don't wish to speculate. I shall work with the authorities to uncover the problem and, I assure you, we'll discover what happened. Please, leave it in my hands. You will have a report as soon as possible. And now, Lord, Lady Crosswick, your car is waiting to take you home. I would suggest you do your best to enjoy the rest of your day."

Through the window, Genevieve saw a silver Rolls Royce Ghost at the ready. She unsnapped her seatbelt and gave Philip a nudge with her shoulder. "Philip, if there's nothing we can do here, we should go."

"I guess we'll leave you to it, Captain Bruni. And again, thank you." Philip extended his hand, a rare gesture for an earl to a member of his staff. Without hesitation, Bruni gripped Philip's hand.

With the door open, cold January air rushed into the cabin, chilling Genevieve's cheeks as she walked forward. She stood at the doorway, felt Philip next to her and laced her fingers through his. "Here we go again," she said.

He felt his phone vibrate. It was out of his pocket and at his ear before the second ring.

"Tell me," he demanded.

Silence filled the line.

"Tell me." This time he whispered through clenched teeth.

"Sir," the caller's voice cracked. The caller cleared his throat and started again, his cockney accent thick. "Sir, I did it, but the pilot was able to restart the engines."

He yanked the phone from his ear and smashed it against the wall.

Henri, their driver, maneuvered the Rolls through midday Paris traffic with the skill of a Formula One driver. Exiting from A1 onto Boulevard Périphérique, Philip and Genevieve could see Sacré-Cœur in the distance, regal atop Montmartre like a queen on her throne.

As the ring road made a graceful sweep around Montmartre, Genevieve smiled. Releasing her seatbelt, she cuddled close to Philip and prickles of excitement began replacing the terror of the morning. "Remember our ride through Paris on the quad last year?"

"Do I?" Philip gave Genevieve a sidelong glance that said, are you kidding me? "That was one of the greatest travel adventures we've ever had."

Genevieve recalled mounting an ATV at 5:00 a.m., Philip driving, Genevieve's arms wrapped around him from behind. She tested the GoPro on top of her helmet, and then for the next two hours, they roared through Paris, their guide leading the way, the wide, empty boulevards all their own. Just before sunrise, at the foot of Sacré-Cœur's extravagant stairs, they drank mimosas, ate croissants still warm from the baker's oven, and toasted the sun as it rose over the Basilica's glowing dome. It was an experience to remember.

Now, as Montmartre faded into the distance and the warm glow of the memory vanished, the reality of their brush with disaster came flooding back. "How are you feeling after our near-death experience this morning?" Genevieve asked as much to explore her own thoughts as to take Philip's emotional temperature.

"I'm grateful we didn't die." His wan smile confirmed he was still shaken.

"You're not alone. But I have to say I'm shocked at how serene I was when I thought we were going to crash. The thing that went through my mind was I'm here with Philip and the kids are well taken care of." Genevieve squeezed Philip's hand. "I was okay."

He leaned into Genevieve and kissed her forehead. "While you were totally Zen as we plummeted toward death, my mind was racing trying to figure out if someone was trying to kill us. That's how suspicious I am of everything and everyone, after what we've just been through in England."

Genevieve nodded her agreement. "What a rollercoaster our lives have been since our phone rang that Sunday morning." She closed her eyes, a whirlwind whipping through her mind: an inherited title, a huge fortune, and a maelstrom of murder and mayhem. She shook the thoughts away, grateful for the calm they had been living for the last three months in Wilmingrove Hall, their historic family seat near York.

As if he could read her thoughts, Philip sighed and leaned back in his seat. "I'm looking forward to exploring our Paris apartment," he said, and Genevieve smiled at the thought of their French inheritance, still as yet unvisited due to the upheaval in England.

When the car stopped in front of a wrought iron gate, they were not disappointed. Henri rolled down his window, smiled into a camera, and punched in a code on the digital pad. A pretty chime sounded, the gates lumbered open, and the car eased onto the stone driveway of their grand château in the middle of Paris.

"Of course," Philip said with a hint of awe. "What else would we expect?"

Genevieve craned her neck to peer up at the elegant Belle Époque building.

Though she had seen photographs of their Paris property, she was still impressed. "We own the entire building, is that correct, Henri?" Genevieve squinted, trying to see the small windows on the top floor.

"Oui, countess. Welcome to Maison de Laney, your home." Henri stopped in front of the arched doorway, swept out of the driver's seat, and opened Genevieve's door in one smooth motion. Philip waited for Henri to come to his side of the car. It had taken some time to become accustomed to having so much done for him, but at last, he was beginning to enjoy the perks of his position.

The chauffeur swung Philip's car door wide. "Merci, Henri," he said, nodding his appreciation.

As Genevieve and Philip walked up the stone path to the

entrance, the double glass and wrought iron doors parted. There to greet them stood Parisian perfection. Almost as tall as Philip and every bit as lean as Genevieve, Madame Morier, their chef de ménage, commanded the gateway to 22 Avenue Foch. At forty-five, she was all French demeanor and style. Her chiseled features were as elegant as a Degas statue.

"Whoa," Philip whispered to Genevieve without moving his lips. "Stylish or what?" He nodded at her French uniform of casual but sophisticated, thoughtful but thrown on.

"And *the scarf*," agreed Genevieve, her gaze drifting to the long, elegant neck where grey and black silk was tangled to perfection. Arrogance wafted from Madame Morier like an expensive fragrance.

Usually the most elegant woman in the room, Genevieve felt as dowdy as a washerwoman. For a moment, she longed for the warmth of stout, sensible Mrs. MacIntosh, their housekeeper at Wilmingrove Hall.

"Lord and Lady Crosswick. Bonjour et bienvenue." Madame Morier's thick chestnut hair swished at her chin with beveled precision, and her eyebrows arched into severe, straight bangs as she waited for a response from her new employers.

Genevieve decided there was nothing to do but rise to the occasion and replied to Madame Morier in her best French, saying that it was a pleasure to be here: "Quel plaisir d'être ici."

"S'il vous plaît, entrez." Madame Morier motioned for them to come in, making the Warwicks feel privileged to enter their own home. She switched to flawless English with ease: "I understand you had a difficult landing."

"Oh, no, madame." Charm poured into Philip's smile. "It wasn't difficult to land. It was just difficult to land without all of us dying."

Genevieve snorted a laugh, and Philip grinned at his wife. Nonplussed, the housekeeper could do nothing but shake her head and study her two employers with a judgmental stare.

Genevieve giggled a bit more, then said, "Madame Morier, I assure you we haven't lost our minds. We're just relieved that today we cheated death."

"Allons-y." Still baffled by Philip and Genevieve's casual regard for their dire experience, Madame Morier mumbled something under her breath and led them through the grand marble hall. "Why don't we go into the salon?" she tossed over her shoulder. "Perhaps a Scotch is in order."

Genevieve felt like an errant child as she and Philip followed their housekeeper. She caught Philip's eye and made a snooty face. In return, Philip flashed a stern look and shook his head.

Halfway along the fifty-foot foyer, they slowed to a stop. Philip's head pivoted back and forth. Genevieve circled in place, disbelieving. The realization hit them both: they were walking through a gallery of masterpieces, all of which belonged to them. Two O'Keeffes, a Kline, a stunning collage by Motherwell, a small Monet tucked into a recess, and a charming Andy Warhol screenprint of Mickey Mouse filled the corridor with creative energy. Philip and Genevieve looked at each other, then back at their collection, their eyes lingering over each canvas.

Madame Morier entered the grand salon and turned to speak to Lord and Lady Crosswick, but they were nowhere to be seen. When she walked back into the foyer, the two stood rapt, enthralled by the collection.

"My lord, my lady, you must stay with me," she snapped.

Intimidated by her tone, Philip and Genevieve obeyed and followed her into a room that glowed from the winter sun. Three sets of French doors lined the far wall. An enormous Frankenthaler canvas in blues, whites, and splashes of pink and rose dominated one end of the salon, while a massive fireplace had pride of place at the opposite end.

"Madame!" Genevieve strode the length of the room to the vibrant canvas. "I can't believe we have a Helen Frankenthaler. How long has this canvas been hanging here?"

A slight smile pulled at the corners of Madame Morier's mouth, as if surprised that the American recognized a great painting when she saw it. "It has been here as long as I have, countess, and I have been the head of Maison de Laney for more than fifteen years. You enjoy contemporary art?"

"Lord Crosswick and I value all periods and genres, but we both have a passion for modern art."

"I have an advanced degree in Art History and did my master's thesis on how the CIA used Jackson Pollock and other contemporary artists in the cold war." Philip seldom talked about his academic accomplishments, but, much to his surprise, he felt the need to impress Madame Morier.

"Hmm." Madame Morier hummed a mere flicker of acknowledgement. "Vraiment?" she said, splashing Scotch into three faceted glasses and handing one to Philip. "Then you will appreciate the paintings throughout the house. The head of your foundation, Lillie Langdon, keeps a close eye on your collection."

"That does not surprise me." Philip accepted the glass with a nod, amused that the house manager was joining them for a drink. "We spent time with Lillie when we were in London. She has a real passion for the foundation's work and for the museums. What about you, Madame Morier? Are you an art lover?"

She gave an arrogant flick of her head. "Of course, my lord. I love all beautiful things. After all, I am French."

"Naturellement, art, beauty, and the French go hand in hand," Genevieve said. As she walked back to the other end of the room, she admired the carved moldings nestled high up where plaster ceilings met silk-covered walls. Her steps were cushioned by a thick carpet of vivid color, which, overwhelmed by the Frankenthaler painting, she had not noticed until now. "Madam Morier, this carpet looks like a piece designed by Pierre-Josse Perrot, but that's not possible, is it?"

"I am surprised, my lady. Few outside the arts and antiquities world would recognize his work. And, sadly, this is not one of his originals. When the 12TH Earl repurchased Maison de Laney, returning it to the House of Crosswick, he commissioned the carpet a la Savonnerie. Though it is not 17th century, it is still beautiful and quite valuable."

"It's stunning." Genevieve accepted the tumbler Madame Morier held out to her, and the three clinked glasses.

"To beauty," Madame Morier said. "If you would like a tour of Maison de Laney, we shall do that now before you dine."

Though Genevieve would have enjoyed a quick shower, she was anxious to learn about their Parisian château. "I'd love that," she said, with a sweet smile she hoped would woo madame.

"If you'd like to be seated," she motioned to her audience of two to sit, "we can start here, in the grand salon. I'm sure you know nothing of Baron Haussmann, the Préfet of Seine, the man tasked with executing the reconstruction of Paris."

Not appreciating Madame Morier's condescending tone, Genevieve plucked up an arrogance of her own. "Of course, we know about Haussmann," she said.

Not bothering to suppress a smirk, Madame Morier said, "Vraiment? Perhaps I should not have assumed you were unfamiliar with his work, but I believe few Americans know about his extraordinary contribution to Paris."

Annoyed by madame's insinuation, Genevieve said, "The Opéra Garnier, the Opera House, is one of our favorite buildings in the world and it's very close to Boulevard Haussmann."

"Are you referring to the Palais Garnier?" Madam Morier raised one eyebrow.

Feeling foolish in her feeble attempt to impress Madame Morier, Genevieve waved her hand and mumbled, "Um, never mind."

Until now, Philip had been entertained watching the parry and thrust between Madame Morier and Genevieve, but he had questions. "Am I correct that, when the 9TH Earl of Crosswick inherited this property from his wife Charlotte Chaubert's family, the first thing he did was name the house Maison de Laney for his family?"

"Oui, my lord. Well done." She honored Philip with her first smile since they arrived.

"The 9TH Earl is one of my favorite distant cousins in my newly discovered family tree. His first name was also Philip." He flashed his most charming smile back at Madame Morier, and a flicker of approval crossed her face.

Genevieve watched the evolving interaction between Philip and madame, feeling more like a third wheel with each exchange.

Madame Morier set her glass down on the table next to her and crossed her legs. "The 9TH Earl spent ten years in Paris during Baron Haussmann's thrilling renovation of this decaying city. Though the earl was a titled Englishman with a substantial allowance, he loved the gritty side of Paris, befriending painters and spending his time in the ateliers of artists who were about to revolutionize the artistic world—and he began collecting."

"She's missed her calling," Genevieve thought begrudgingly. "She's a natural docent."

The room darkened as clouds raced across the sun, then brightened again as they streaked off to cast shadows elsewhere.

Madame Morier's energy began to build. "Lord Crosswick was awed by the artists' willingness to risk everything to follow their passion. Dedicated to acquiring works from friends and only works he loved, he began buying small pieces, reflecting daily life in Paris—a gathering in a bar, a bridge bathed in late-afternoon light, a flower past its prime. He was wild for the works of the Impressionists. He couldn't resist the beauty of the spontaneous brush strokes and ever-changing light covering these canvases, and soon, the pace of his acquisitions sped up dramatically."

Mesmerized by the captivating raconteur, Philip leaned forward, not wanting to miss a word. "Would you say my cousin was a patron of these Impressionists?"

"I would say oui," Her broad grin reached her eyes. "By the time he left Paris in 1870 to return to England, he shipped forty-two crates from Paris to Wilmingrove Hall, each containing six or eight paintings. He had, indeed, become a collector and, as a result, a patron in the true sense of the word."

"What about Charlotte? When did she and Philip meet?" Genevieve loved to hear stories about Charlotte Chaubert. The more she learned about the Countess of Crosswick, the more she liked her.

"Ah, Charlotte." Madame's smiles came easily now as she spoke of the Laney family. "They met two years before he went back to England. As the story goes, he was smitten, and she was not. He pursued her. She thought he was a soulless Englishman trying to buy affection from the artists he befriended. But, as she grew to know him, she succumbed to his charm, his elegance, and his passionate heart."

Genevieve watched the color rise in Madame Morier's cheeks and saw a flicker of affection in her eyes. "I do believe madame has a crush on Philip's long-dead cousin," Genevieve thought.

The house manager took a deep breath before continuing. "Lord Crosswick's most cherished acquisition was the beautiful, talented artist with whom he had fallen in love, Charlotte Camille Chaubert. Charlotte was a twenty-four-year-old free spirit with a fine pedigree. Philip's parents approved of her immediately and were relieved that their thirty-three-year-old only son was settling down at last. Philip and Charlotte were married at St Paul's Cathedral on September 7, 1871, with Charlotte's family in attendance. Though the townhouse in Kensington was their primary residence, they loved spending time in Paris and entertaining their creative friends here at Maison de Laney."

She drained the last of her Scotch, put the glass on the coffee table, and said, "Come with me."

Philip and Genevieve followed Madame Morier into the foyer, down the hall, and into a cozy room.

"This is your study, my lord." She walked to a painting over the fireplace. "And this is your cousin Philip and his beloved Charlotte."

The three of them gazed at an Impressionist work in soft blues and greens. A couple sat on a garden bench, surrounded by a soft halo of sunshine. The man leaned forward, captivated by the beautiful young woman. With her chin tilted down, the mademoiselle looked up at him through her lashes, a soft smile at the corners of her mouth. Almost closing the distance between them, their hands rested on the bench, just a whisper from touching. It was an exquisite homage to love.

"This was their engagement portrait," Madame Morier said, her hands folded in front of her and her head cocked to the side.

Philip leaned close to the lower right-hand corner of the painting. "B. M.; Is that Berthe Morisot?" His mouth hung open. He couldn't tear his gaze from the signature.

"It is," Madame confirmed. "Venez avec moi." Again, she directed them to follow her, and, like two obedient students, they did. They walked through the dining room to the two sets of doors at the far end.

"See the blue bench?" She pointed into the garden.

"That's the bench in the painting!" Genevieve cried. Overwhelmed at the idea that the portrait of the two lovers had been painted in this garden, her eyes stung. "I feel as if I'm in a dream." She looked at madame, her eyes glistening. "Madame Morier, though Philip and I are adjusting pretty well to our new roles as the Earl and Countess of Crosswick and all that it means, it's still staggering to realize we are responsible for so much heritage and so many treasures."

Madame Morier stared at her employer for a moment. Genevieve thought she was about to say something kind, but instead, she stiffened, said, "Allons-y," and forged on.

Two hours later, Genevieve sat in a picture-perfect petite salon. Challenged by their housekeeper's sublime French style, she had worried too much over what to wear for dinner and had changed clothes several times before coming down. At last, she decided on grey wool pants, a matching cashmere sweater and grey suede ballet flats. Understated but chic, she thought. When she was drying her hair, Genevieve smiled at the fact that she and Madame Morier had similar haircuts. At least, Genevieve thought, the cosmopolitan head of their household couldn't fault her hair!

Earlier, she had enjoyed the engaging, knowledgeable Madame Morier and had begun to think this woman was going to be a welcome ally as she and Philip navigated the complicated world of French society. And then, warm madame had vanished, and the cool, arrogant house manager who had greeted them upon their arrival reappeared. It was perplexing, to say the least.

She pulled her thoughts from Madame Morier to the straight line of perfect bubbles rising from the stem of her Champagne glass, breaking the surface and tickling her nose as she sipped. She had tried to wait for Philip, but after fifteen minutes, she could no longer resist the pretty pink call of the Widow Clicquot. As she savored the soft finish on her tongue, she stared into the fire crackling on the hearth. Scenes of the day floated through her mind, and she played the happy conclusion over and over. She closed her eyes and blew a little puff of air from her cheeks. She and Philip seemed to live a charmed life. From the time they met, Philip, about to finish his master's degree in art history, and she in her second year of law school, they had been lucky, indeed. And now, forty years later, with one adored son and his marvelous wife, two wild grandchildren, an unimaginable inheritance and death cheated, Genevieve felt she was living a life straight out of a novel.

"Okay, G." Striding into the room, Philip startled her from her thoughts. Admiring his classic, handsome features, she couldn't help but smile. She never tired of the crinkles at the corners of his bright green eyes, of his lean, muscular frame, or his thick graying hair she still thought of as blond. Soon to be sixty-five, Philip could fill a room with his easy charm, and she still adored him.

"Sorry, I didn't wait." She grinned and handed him his glass. "You've been on the phone?"

"I have. I was talking to Captain Bruni." Two furrows etched Philip's brow.

"From your frown, I'd say whatever he told you was not good."

Philip sat next to Genevieve on a camel-and-black-striped loveseat. He clinked her glass before taking a long swig from the flute. "Bruni said the BEA, Bureau of Enquiry and Analysis, the group responsible for investigating incidents in French airspace, has a preliminary report. One of their inspectors is coming in the morning to speak to us."

Genevieve put her glass on the coffee table in front of them. "He didn't tell you what their findings were?"

"He did not. He said Inspector Boucher, the BEA agent, will brief us when he comes."

"What do you think that means?" Genevieve twisted her wedding ring round and round on her finger and searched Philip's eyes for answers.

Philip picked up Genevieve's hand from her lap. "I have no idea," he said. We'll find out tomorrow." He turned her hand over and ran his thumb back and forth over her palm. "You know, since we inherited this fortune, we've been talking about how we can use the wealth to make an impact on as many lives as possible."

Genevieve nodded.

"I'd say our little brush with mortality today was the universe telling us to stop fiddling around and decide how we're going to do that."

A smile bloomed on Genevieve's lips. "Trust you to think of a way to turn today's fright into a motivating experience." She laced her fingers through Philip's. "Have you come up with the grand plan?"

Philip was animated as he spoke. "Not yet, but I was thinking. Since we have museums and an art foundation, we need to use those as the basis. Why can't we break out of the cloistered walls of the museums and reach kids whose lives might be changed or even saved by the power of art?"

Usually the one bubbling over with schemes, Genevieve loved when Philip took an idea and ran with it. "I think when we meet with Lillie, that should be at the top of our agenda," she said, then leaned forward and planted a kiss on the tip of his nose. "If we can stay alive until then."

TWO

GENEVIEVE GUIDED THE tip of her belt through the gold lion's head buckle. As she slipped her feet into cordovan ankle boots and tugged up the zippers, she heard a firm knock on her bedroom door.

"Come in," she said, massaging her forehead. She and Philip had talked long into the night, then finished their eventful day with some post-trauma lovemaking, leaving her groggy this morning from lack of sleep.

The door opened a few feet and there stood Madame Morier, looking expensive. She was dressed in black from her turtleneck sweater to her body-hugging jeans to the tips of her Chanel ballerinas. The only relief was a vivid yellow and red scarf wrapped nonchalantly around her neck. Genevieve caught the glitter of huge gold studs in Madame Morier's ears, almost covered by her shiny bob. "I wonder what we're paying her," she mused and mustered a shallow smile. "Madame Morier, good morning."

"Countess, Monsieur Boucher from the BEA is here." She walked several steps into the luxurious bedroom and placed a business card on a round table next to a mass of coral roses. "The earl is with him and asked me to summon you. And so, I have."

Genevieve's left eyebrow shot up. "Summon?" She tried her best to look down her nose at Madame Morier but, as Genevieve was several inches shorter than the housekeeper, it didn't quite work.

Standing even taller, Madame Morier said, "Perhaps 'request' is a better word." She turned and, just before she pulled the door closed, said, "They are in the grand salon, countess."

"Merde!" Genevieve loved swearing in French. "This woman's going to be a problem," she thought. "I wonder what the French is for 'pain in the butt'."

Genevieve trotted down the curved staircase at a fast clip, one hand on the wrought iron banister, her camel skirt swishing around her ankles with each step.

As she neared the bottom of the staircase, she could hear two men talking. Philip's voice she knew. The other, a rich and elegant accent, conjured an image of a well-built, sensuous man with a Gauloise hanging from the corner of his mouth, eyes narrowed against the wafting smoke. Her step quickened across the foyer to the grand salon. Standing in the doorway, she blinked. She searched the room from one end to the other and saw no one but her husband. Philip was seated on the biscuit-colored sofa. Across the coffee table from him were two massive, overstuffed chairs facing away from her.

"Philip, are you alone?" Confused, Genevieve's eyes swept the room again, but there was no sign of another man.

The sexy voice from nowhere said, "Non, countess. Je suis ici!

I am here!" Like a jack-in-the-box, a short, stout man popped out of one of the chairs, huge cushions hiding him from Genevieve. The petit Frenchman scurried around the chair and over to where Genevieve still stood in the doorway. He bowed from the waist. "Enchantée, countess, simply enchanted. I am Charles Boucher, Investigator with the BEA." He grabbed her hand and brought it to his lips. "Bienvenue à Paris. I promise we shall do better to make you feel at home than we did welcoming you into the country. Quelle entrée, oui?"

He still cradled Genevieve's hand. She could feel the sweat building between them and slid her hand from his gentle grasp. Looking over the top of his head, which was, at most, three inches over five feet, she saw Philip struggling to keep his laughter at bay. She scanned Boucher's round face and smiled at him. "I'm sorry we're meeting under such circumstances, Monsieur Boucher. Thank you for coming so promptly." Genevieve turned to Philip. "Is Captain Bruni joining us?"

Boucher answered for Philip. "Non, countess. I wanted to interview you and the earl without him present."

"Really?" Genevieve's eyes widened. She looked at Philip, then back at Boucher.

Boucher shoved his lower lip into a pout. "Baahh, oui. This is normal. We like to have each party involved in such an event give us their impressions." Boucher gave a sweep of his arm, ushering Genevieve into her own living room. "Please, sit down."

Genevieve ambled to Philip, skirting the coffee table until she stood in front of him. Before sitting, she held out her hand. "Good morning, darling boy." Remembering their early-morning dalliance, Genevieve offered a sultry smile.

Philip took her hand and held her smokey gaze before pulling her down beside him.

The intimate exchange did not go unnoticed by Monsieur Boucher, who tucked it into his mental file. The investigator sat, scooching back into the deep chair. "Allons. Shall we begin?" He dug in one sagging pocket of his jacket and pulled out his leather-covered notepad, scuffed from use. In the other, he discovered the nub of a pencil, the erasure well-gnawed. He licked the pencil lead and was ready to go. "D'accord. So, tell me. Who would very much like you dead?" His voice was so cheerful, both the Warwicks thought they had misheard the question.

"Pardon, Monsieur. Did you just ask who would like us dead?"

"Oui, my lord. There is nothing but to be direct." His eyes sparkled and his face shone with enthusiasm. Then he slapped his forehead as if remembering something. "Ah, but of course, no one has told you." He reached into his battered briefcase and pulled out a few sheets of paper and handed them to Philip. "Significant water was found in your gas tank. Someone put the water there intending to cause the plane to crash."

A little choking noise rose from Genevieve's throat. "What do you mean?" Her head swiveled to Philip then back at Boucher. "Are you saying it was intentional? Maybe the gas cap was loose, and water seeped in from condensation, or...?" She threw out explanations that seemed plausible, anything other than someone wanting them dead.

Boucher's eyes filled with concern. "I understand this is upsetting, my lady, but I assure you, our people are excellent analysts and have ruled out all but this possibility. They are checking security cameras to see if they can identify the auteur."

"Auteur?" Genevieve cocked her head.

"Uh, the perpetrator," Boucher clarified.

Philip held up his hand to stop the inspector. "You're saying there could be cameras that will tell us who did this?"

"Oui. Security cameras will no doubt show us who put water in the tank, but that person will not be the real criminal." Boucher shrugged. "He—or she—is the hired hand." Without missing a beat, he said, "As I asked before, who would very much like you dead? Perhaps someone would receive great wealth if you and Lady Crosswick perished in a plane crash. Is that possible?"

Philip leaned forward, elbows on his knees, the muscles in his neck taut. His eyebrows almost touched as his forehead furrowed. "Our son and his family are the beneficiaries of the Crosswick estate, and I assure you they are not suspects."

"Mais, non, certainement. But I understand you had some difficulty the last few months in Angleterre; is that not correct?"

Sensing Philip's anger building, Genevieve put a cautionary hand on her husband's arm as he said, "Monsieur Boucher, that entire business in England was resolved and the person responsible is no longer a threat. There is no possibility the two situations could be linked. You're sure the water in the fuel tank was done on purpose? Are you telling us it couldn't be a simple mistake?"

The investigator shrugged his shoulders. "There is always a possibility the refueler in Leeds made an error." He tented his hands. "But it is unlikely."

Genevieve examined her manicured nails and pushed the cuticles back with her thumb. "The incident in Yorkshire had nothing to do with our wealth. At this point, I can't imagine who would want to kill us, or why."

His pencil poised over a blank page in his small notebook, Monsieur Boucher asked, "What were the events at Wilmingrove Hall about?"

Philip eased back against the sofa cushion. "Monsieur, my guess is you already know what happened at the Hall. You strike me as a man who doesn't ask a question he hasn't already answered."

Boucher's grin squished his chubby cheeks up to his eyes. "My lord, you are très perspicace."

"Oh yes," Genevieve chimed in. "Philip is nothing if not perceptive. But I doubt if our combined intuition will discern who wants us dead."

Boucher scooted forward in his chair, so his feet touched the floor. He wrote some notes in his scruffy notebook, then squinted at Philip and Genevieve. "My lord, my lady, why are you here?"

Confused, Philip and Genevieve looked at each other then back at the investigator. "What do you mean, why are we here?" Philip asked, his head cocked to one side.

"I mean what caused you to leave the safety of Wilmingrove Hall and come to Paris?"

"That's an interesting interpretation of what we did." Philip's anger simmered just below the surface.

Genevieve glanced at his profile. His jaw tensed and his eyes narrowed.

"With the resolution of what happened at the Hall, it never occurred to me Paris would be a dangerous proposition. What about you, G?"

"I wouldn't have thought so."

"I'm assuming you know about my recent inheritance."

Boucher nodded, "Uh, oui."

"I'm sure you also know we've been at the Crosswick family seat in Yorkshire since September. We've come to France, first to spend time at this property." Philip offered a sweeping gesture around the salon. "While we're here in Paris, we'll get to know our art museum, the Laney Musée des Beaux-Arts. We'll be working with Lillie Langdon, the executive director of the Laney Museum of Fine Arts Foundation that supports our two museums. We'll determine if we need to make any changes in order to ensure the integrity of the collection and the foundation's work. In fact, we're meeting with her this afternoon at the musée. From here we'll go to our vineyard in Saint-Émilion. Though everything appears to be well-run on paper, it's easier to make those determinations in person."

Boucher scribbled in his notebook as Philip spoke. When the investigator said nothing, Philip continued.

"Though we've read all the files on the vineyard staff, we haven't met any of them. Most of the permanent employees have been with the vineyard for years. In fact, the managing director has been at Château Beaulieu for almost forty years. Is any of this helpful?"

Boucher tapped his stubby pencil on the half-full page, then chewed his eraser. The only sound in the room came from a painted clock hanging between the French doors to the garden. The tick-tock of the swinging pendulum gave way to chimes announcing eleven o'clock.

Genevieve slipped off her shoe and drew her leg up under her on the sofa. She looked at Philip, who was watching Boucher.

Boucher jotted a note. "Hmm… almost forty years," he said under his breath. At last, he flipped his notebook closed. "D'accord." He stood, clicked his heels, and bobbed his head. "Merci beaucoup. I believe I have what I need for the moment."

"You do?" Surprised by his abrupt announcement, Genevieve stood and struggled to get her foot back into her shoe. "I don't understand. What just happened? Do you think you know who put water in our fuel?"

Boucher's head bounced up and down like a bobblehead doll. "I may have une idée that perhaps will grow into something significant."

Still seated, Philip snorted, then asked, "Would you care to share your thoughts with us, Monsieur Boucher?"

Putting his notebook back in his left pocket and his gnawed pencil in his right, the investigator said, "When I am a bit more certain of my theory, I shall be delighted to share it with you. I trust I may return as questions arise?"

"Of course. We'll help any way we can." Still confused, Genevieve extended her hand. "Thank you, Monsieur Boucher."

"C'est mon plaisir, countess."

Philip was unwilling to let the investigator go without him offering at least a hint of what he was thinking. "Monsieur, s'il vous plaît. Do you have a specific idea who put water in the fuel, or do you just have a general hunch?"

"Hunch. I like this word. Let us say I have a hunch that, if it proves correct, will lead us to a specific person. I will tell you one thing. I believe this mystery is tied to the art or perhaps to your vineyard."

Hugging herself, Genevieve rubbed her hands up and down her arms. "Hmm. I, um... Monsieur Boucher. Are you suggesting someone wants to steal our art or our wine, so they decided to kill us to make it easier?"

"My lady, perhaps it is a bit more complicated. Maybe steal art, maybe take your vineyard, maybe protect their jobs." Boucher shrugged. "I think each one is possible—a good start."

"Wow," Philip said as he stood, towering over the investigator. "That sounds, as you French say, un peu fou; a little crazy."

Bucher flashed an impish grin. "I assure you, my lord, I am completely mad. But in this case, I am right. Now, if I may, I shall leave you. But I shall be in touch." He headed for the door, then turned around. "In the meantime, please be cautious. I would like to solve the mystery before it becomes a fatal crime." He nodded, scuttled down the gallery and out of the front door, leaving Philip and Genevieve gaping at each other.

THREE

PHILIP AND GENEVIEVE waited for Lillie Langdon in a small conference room overlooking one of the museum galleries. When the door opened, she blew in like a breath of fresh air. Ballerina slim, she floated rather than walked. Her blond curls were piled high on her head, held with a single sterling silver clip, stray tendrils bouncing around her sculpted face.

"Lillie, how wonderful to see you again." Genevieve rose from a leather and chrome chair, a dramatic contrast to the elaborate nineteenth-century surroundings. She extended her hand, her eyes crinkling with an affectionate smile. From the moment they met four months ago in England, she had fallen in love with Lillie.

"Lord and Lady Crosswick!" Lillie grabbed Genevieve's hand in both of hers. "I can't begin to tell you how happy I am you're here. Since we talked at your fabulous party at Wilmingrove Hall, I couldn't wait to get you to the Laney Musée des Beaux-Arts." Lillie squeezed Genevieve's hand. "And Lord Crosswick." Lillie turned her radiance to Philip. "I've been so excited about showing off the LMBA and sharing all our plans, I couldn't sleep last night."

"Genevieve and I want to hear everything." Philip gave Lillie la bise, the traditional two-cheek French greeting. "But I insist you call us Philip and Genevieve."

As they took their seats around a small, round table, Genevieve jumped in. "Lillie, we have two things on our agenda. First, we want to hear all about your ideas for the future of the foundation. We've heard the most marvelous things about what you've already done. I'm wondering how you'll top your past successes." Genevieve scooted her chair closer and leaned forward, her elbows on the table. "We've heard about the exhibition two years ago where you combined paintings and sculptures of Degas' dancers with the London Contemporary Dance Theatre and the Experimental Strings Ensemble."

"We read the reviews in *The Times*." Philip smiled. "Brilliant, Lillie. Just brilliant."

"And what about the opening gala for 'The Circus Through the Eyes of an Artist', when you brought in performers from Cirque du Soleil to entertain the guests? Didn't the gala sell out the first day?" Genevieve heard herself gushing but didn't care.

"As I recall, the event netted over two million pounds for the foundation." Philip was impressed. "Do you think we can be that successful here in Paris?"

"I do." Her cheeks glowing from the praise, Lillie put up her hands. "But please, please," she said. "This is too much. I want to leave room to dazzle you. If you're overawed by my past accomplishments, it will be difficult to impress you in the future!" Her smile was irresistible.

"Not to worry, Lillie." Charmed by this sprite, Philip couldn't help but gush a bit himself. "As you know, art is one of our great loves. Inheriting responsibility for the Laney Museum of Fine Arts in London, Laney Musée des Beaux-Arts de Paris, and the foundation is thrilling for us. I hope it doesn't scare you when I tell you we want to become hands-on with the foundation and help any way we can."

"Which brings us to our second agenda item. Philip, tell Lillie what we want to accomplish."

"I can't wait to hear." Lillie straightened in her chair as Philip explained they didn't know what the project should be, but they knew they wanted to reach and enrich as many lives as possible. And they wanted to get started immediately. "We're thinking about something connecting art and children—art changing children's lives or something like that."

"That's smashing news," Lillie beamed. "And a challenge. I love a challenge. We do have a remarkable program called the Children's Art Forum already in place but let me gather my thoughts and I'll give you some ideas of projects as soon as I think of something brilliant."

Lillie looked up and saw someone struggling through the glass door with a tray. "Aha." She dashed across the room and pulled open the door for a young man bringing refreshments. "Lord and Lady Crosswick, this is Émile de Laudre, one of our interns. Émile is in his last year of the art history program at the Sorbonne." Lillie motioned to a carved chest sitting along one wall of the conference room. "Émile, you can put the tray over there."

Close to six feet tall and rail thin, Émile could have just walked off a Paris runway. His luxurious mane was parted in the middle and waved to his chin. In contrast to his dark good looks, his heavy-lidded eyes were pale blue. A waist-cinching olive-green jacket topped narrow black trousers tucked into polished black ankle boots. His demeanor was not subtle. Everything about him shouted wealth, privilege, and ennui.

"Bonjour," Émile threw in Philip and Genevieve's direction. He plunked the tray on the sideboard with a clatter that rattled the cups and French press. With a dramatic sigh, he looked at Lillie and said in French, "You asked for coffee; here it is," and he sashayed out.

"Oh my." Genevieve was unsure what else to say.

Philip's brows arched. "Um, Lillie. That, um… that young man is a Musée des Beaux Arts intern?"

"He is, Philip." Lillie blew out a puff of air. "I assure you there is a good explanation." She let silence fill the room.

Genevieve leaned forward, her elbows on the table and her eyes on Lillie while Philip tipped his chair onto the back legs, folding his hands in his lap. He waited several beats before he said, "Well, are you going to share this explanation with us, or do you want us to guess?"

"I thought I'd let the suspense build just a bit before sharing why this arrogant little tosser is filling a coveted spot at the museum when there are so many more deserving students. You see, his father is the Baron de Sézanne, one of the foundation's biggest donors."

"Enough said." Philip put his chair back on the floor, dropped his head back and studied the ceiling before turning his attention back to Lillie. "As I recall, the baron's name has been at the top of our donor's list for the last few years. Didn't he become one of our patrons with a huge initial gift?"

Lillie cocked her head. "If you call twenty-five million euros a huge gift, then I would have to say yes. As part of his patronage, he committed to an additional five million euros a year for ten years. This year marks the halfway point in his commitment. And he rather likes that Émile is an intern at the museum."

Her elbows still on the table and her hands pressed together, Genevieve tapped her fingertips on one another while she thought. "So, at this point, the baron has supported us to the tune of fifty million euros with another twenty-five on the horizon. Is that what you calculated, Philip?"

"Yup," Philip said, smiling at his wife. "And after hearing Émile's sterling credentials, I'd say he's our favorite intern, wouldn't you, G?"

Genevieve nodded. "I love everything about him, especially his winning attitude. Excellent job finding such an outstanding young man, Lillie."

"I live but to serve," she said, rolling her violet eyes.

With the question of the errant intern asked and answered, the three moved to the topic of future plans. Lillie's vision for the museums and the foundation was aggressive and creative. Some of her ideas were provocative. All were fresh and exciting. Throughout the meeting, Genevieve sat on the edge of her seat. Lillie answered every question with a quick response, demonstrating her deep knowledge of the foundation and describing future plans with enthusiasm.

After two hours of rapid-fire conversation, Philip asked, "Lillie, how can we use our properties to benefit the foundation? Could we create an event in conjunction with an exhibition, a gourmet and art weekend, maybe 'Palette and Palate' for the art gourmet at our Saint-Émilion vineyard? I'm sure we could raise a few euros with an event there, don't you think?"

"Lord Crosswick, that's the spirit! I'd love to do an event at Château Beaulieu. That would be smashing! And, since you've opened the door, I'm going to walk right through it." Lillie vibrated with enthusiasm. "We have a new show of Abstract Expressionists at the musée opening in three weeks. Would you consider hosting a cocktail party the evening before? You can't imagine how thrilled our patrons would be to meet you and be in your beautiful home."

"That's a fantastic idea. Let's do it. Philip and I need to meet the people who support our museum, and that sounds like a perfect opportunity to get to know a lot of them at once."

Lillie clapped her hands and smiled at her two bosses. "Thank you, Philip and Genevieve, for your enthusiasm, your support, and most of all the commitment to your personal involvement. We're going to have the most marvelous alliance, we three."

The glass door opened, and a studious-looking young man popped his head in. "Pardon, Lillie. "

"Ah, Bernard! I was just about to text you to join us. Come in, come in." Lillie bounced out of her chair and threw the door wide. "Lord and Lady Crosswick, may I introduce Bernard Reines, director of the Laney Musée des Beaux Arts."

Bernard smacked his forehead with his palm. "Merde, j'ai

complètement oublié," he swore, rolling his eyes. "Excusez-moi, I completely forgot." As he nodded an apology, his chestnut hair flopped over his brow. "Enchanté, my lord, my lady," he said, his chocolate eyes, sparkling at them through his horn-rimmed glasses. He raked his hand through his thick bangs, sweeping them back in place. "We have been anticipating your visit. Have you had a tour yet of your musée?"

"Not yet, Bernard." Lillie grinned. "I thought we could do that together. I was hoping you'd be back from your meeting in time, and so you are. But, you need me?"

"Oui, juste pour un instant, s'il te plaît. Rohh la la." Bernard growled and threw up his hands. "Nous avons un problème de livraison."

"A delivery problem? Is it serious?" Philip piped up.

Not expecting Philip to understand French, Bernard grinned. "It is just a little bit serious," he said. "Last month, La Cité du Vin in Bordeaux bought two paintings we had in storage. They were supposed to be picked up this morning and delivered before the end of the day, but our trucking service still hasn't collected them." He turned back to Lillie." Would you mind double checking the transfer documents? Émile did them and," Bernard rolled his eyes, "I need for you to make sure they are properly executed.

Lillie stood. "If you'll excuse me, I'll go down to the loading dock with Bernard."

"Of course, Lillie, go. Please don't mind us. Genevieve and I can wander on our own until it's convenient for you two to join us."

"Good plan," Lillie said as she headed for the door. "Never fear; we'll find you wherever you are. This first gallery is a perfect place to start. I'll text you as soon as we've sorted this out." She flashed a dazzling smile at Philip and Genevieve and dashed out the door with Bernard hot on her heels.

When Lillie and Bernard had disappeared, Genevieve turned to Philip. "Bernard seemed pleased when he realized you speak French."

"He did, didn't he? I'm sure my excellent command of French would shock most people."

"I'm glad you have such a healthy self-image." Genevieve patted him on his bottom, and they began to wander through their museum. "Well, well. Look at this, G." Philip grinned at the dynamic canvas of Lee Krasner, one of his favorite abstract expressionists and the wife of Jackson Pollock, another artist he revered. "In your wildest imagination, did you ever think we would own such great works of art?"

"It's not terrible to be outrageously wealthy, is it, my darling?" Genevieve slid her hand through the crook of Philip's arm, and they moved to the next canvas, a colorful painting full of movement and drama by Mary Abbott.

For an hour, Philip and Genevieve strolled from canvas to canvas moving from the Abstract Expressionists gallery to a salon filled with strange, avant-garde works by French artists.

Arms crossed and squinting, Genevieve stared at a white porcelain commode with a red and purple striped seat. The installation was tucked into the corner of the room. She turned to find Philip across the gallery, studying a thick rope hanging from the ceiling, with about six feet puddled on the floor.

"Am I to assume the significance of this toilet is that the artist feels the world is shit?" Genevieve said, adopting an intellectual tone. "Or, perhaps, it's just a convenient place to go to the bathroom, albeit not very private."

Unable to tear himself from the hemp cable in front of him, Philip said, "I'm fairly sure this installation is entitled 'When You Learn How Much You Paid For Me, You'll Hang Yourself.'"

At that, Genevieve exploded, her laughter bouncing off the soaring ceilings and marble columns.

"I've missed a great joke!" Lillie said, gliding into the room. "Tell me, what's so hilarious?"

Shaking his head, Philip smiled. "We're laughing at these two installations. I thought we had moved beyond this sort of thing in the late eighties, early nineties, but these are recent works. I can't wait to learn about our acquisition process."

"Please, Lillie, don't tell us you're on the acquisition committee," Genevieve begged.

Lillie wiped her hand across her forehead in mock relief. "Whew!" she said. "I am not, but it's something I want to discuss with you. I hope you've enjoyed wandering on your own. I'm so sorry our delivery issue took so much time and Bernard won't be able to join us."

"That's a shame," Philip said. "I was looking forward to getting to know him. I read his resume and wanted to ask him about his time at the China Academy of Art in Hangzhou. I'm hoping he's considering expanding our collection in contemporary Chinese art. I suppose I can get together with him later."

"We'll make certain that you do. You won't believe this, but the family who owns the château near you, Château Pitique, is the family with whom Bernard lived when he studied in China. They bought it three or four years ago. How's that for a small world?"

Philip's eyes rounded. "That's extraordinary. Do they live at the château?"

Lillie's curls bounced as she shook her head. "The parents live in China. They're huge in import-export. Their son, Hank—his name is Han Shou, but he goes by Hank—lives in Saint-Émilion at the château. He and Bernard are close, and Hank is a museum donor. Bernard makes sure of that."

"We'll take it any way we can get it," Philip said.

"I think his father bought the vineyard so Hank would have something to do." Lillie leaned in. "He's pretty much mucked up everything he's tried since he graduated. His father hopes he can make a success of the vineyard." She raised her brows. "The wine business is difficult enough if you have generations of winemaking behind you. I can't imagine how he's going to succeed with no experience, but so far, according to Bernard, he's doing a decent job exporting to China."

Philip scratched the back of his neck. "Jeeze, I can't imagine running a vineyard without any background in the industry. I can tell you, Genevieve and I are nervous about jumping into the world of fine wine and we have a spectacular team in place. It's one thing to be proficient at drinking great vintages—we're good at that—but it's a different challenge to ensure the continuity of winemaking at the level Château Beaulieu has maintained for over two hundred years. The idea that we could be the first generation to allow the quality to diminish is terrifying."

"Philip, Lillie has many other things to worry about besides us driving Château Beaulieu into the," she smiled, "terroir. Getting back to the subject, is everything all right with the delivery issue?" Genevieve asked. "Anything we need to worry about?"

"It's all taken care of. Shall we?" She led them into the center of the museum, a circular three-story hall, glorious to the eye with ornate plaster moldings, light pouring in from soaring windows.

Philip strained to look up at the domed ceiling. "As I recall, Philip Laney, the 9TH Earl, bought the building just after Haussmann built it."

Seeming delighted that the Warwicks were so well informed, Lillie's eyes sparkled at Philip and Genevieve. "You have done your homework. I'm impressed."

"And the collection we've seen is exceptional, with a few questionable choices," Genevieve chuckled.

"We're impressed with the quality of the works," Philip added. "The Laneys have done a wonderful job over 150 years and four generations, haven't they?"

"Indeed they have, and we want to continue that impressive record. The three of us are going to do exciting things." Lillie threw her coat over her shoulders. "Now, it's time for Champagne and gateau. How does that sound?"

From behind a column on the second floor, he watched the three leave the building, laughing, and talking as they went. He swiped tiny beads of perspiration from his upper lip with the back of his hand, then raked his fingers through his wavy hair. Now that everything was in place, the game could begin. And if the earl wouldn't play, there would be a high price to pay. Either way, this was going to be fun.

FOUR

Two weeks later, as RSVPs poured in for the Abstract Expressionist pre-opening gala at the Earl and Countess of Crosswick's home, Philip stood in the doorway of the study. He brought treats to the two women organizing the invitation responses, most of which were "oui": he carried a tray with coffee, cups, and a plate of hot pink, blue, mint green, and yellow macarons. Winter sun slanted through the French doors, filling the charming room with warmth, belying the chilly temperature outside. On opposite sides of an antique writing desk, Genevieve's straight chestnut hair huddled just inches from Lillie's mass of blonde curls. Philip smiled, watching the two chatter, make notes, laugh, erase one name, and add two more.

Philip crossed the room with his tray of goodies. "Ta da!" he said. "Your cookie daddy has arrived."

Rubbing her hands together, Lillie eyed the macarons and licked her lips. "Philip, you're a master at understanding what a woman craves."

"Only sometimes," Genevieve said, slicing open another envelope with her sterling paperknife.

As she reached for a cookie, Philip skirted her and held out the tray to Lillie. He looked at Genevieve with a sly grin. "Not so fast, my little ingrate. She who appreciates the giver gets the treats first."

"Men are so easy." Genevieve snatched a cookie from Philip's tray and popped the entire thing in her mouth. "Praise their egos and you own them for life."

"No wonder you and Philip have been married so long. You play him like a Stradivarius," Lillie said, two macarons safe in her possession.

"If you two aren't careful, I'll take my treats and go home."

"You are home." Genevieve licked crumbs from her lips.

"Ah, yes. So I am." Philip pulled up a chair and joined the two cheeky women. "I just got off the phone with David."

A smile glowed in Genevieve's eyes as she held up a cream-colored envelope. "We just got his RSVP and he's coming. I'm so pleased. Do you know when he'll be here? What did he say when you talked to him? We haven't heard from Becca yet. Does he know if she's coming?" One question tumbled over another.

"Whoa, there." Philip surrendered, holding both hands up in self-defense. "You're the one whose nose is buried in the responses. I should be hammering you with questions."

Enjoying the banter between the two, Lillie swiveled back and forth between Philip and Genevieve, like someone watching a tennis match.

Genevieve whipped her focus to Lillie. "You remember David, don't you, Lillie? You met him at our party at Wilmingrove Hall."

"Of course I do. He's your solicitor, isn't he? And very dishy, as I recall." As soon as the words were out of her mouth, Lillie grimaced. "Perhaps I shouldn't have said that." She scrunched her shoulders toward her ears and offered a sheepish grin.

"You're right. David is absolutely a hunk." Genevieve sat back in her desk chair. "But beware, Lillie, my girl. I'm pretty sure he and Rebecca Conway are an item." She gave Lillie a sympathetic look. "I don't think you've met Becca. You'll love her. I hope she's coming to the opening."

Her elbow on the desk, Lillie leaned forward, cradling her chin in her hand. "That's not the Rebecca Conway with the lifestyle channel, *The Most Interesting Woman in the Room,* is it?"

"One in the same." Philip took a bite out of a hot pink macaron. "And I have to say, she often is."

"Is what?" Genevieve and Lillie asked in unison.

"The most interesting woman in the room," he clarified.

"Aah." Both women nodded.

"You do, of course, mean when the two of us," Genevieve pointed to Lillie, then to herself, "aren't in the room."

"Mais oui." Philip threw up his hands. "That goes without saying. But, if I may, I'd like to turn the conversation from the two most interesting women in *this* room back to David. Lillie, will G and I have anything to show him on our world-changing project when he comes for the gala?"

"Voila! So glad you asked." Lillie reached into her tote on the floor beside her and pulled out a slim, spiral-bound booklet. She handed it to Philip. "I think you'll like the proposal."

As he leafed through the pages, Genevieve saw the cover. "La Cité du Vin. Interesting. Are we changing the world one glass of wine at a time?"

"Not a bad idea," Lillie said, "but there's a little more to it than that."

"While Philip's reading, give me the executive summary."

"The idea came to me the moment you mentioned creating something to change lives." Lillie grinned as she spoke. "The foundation, LMBA, and La Cité du Vin have been partners since 2016, when la Cité opened. We loan them artwork on a rotating basis, and, as you know, we recently sold them two paintings. In turn, they provide support for various programs at the museum."

Philip laid the proposal in his lap and listened to Lillie's overview.

"The gist of your new partnership is to create a work-study program we'll call "The Art of the Vine."

"I like the name," Genevieve said, anxious to hear more.

"The year-long program would accept students interested in learning about French viticulture. Their fees would be completely covered, but their obligation would be that, on completion of the program, they commit to work a minimum of two years at a vineyard in Bordeaux. As you know, there's a dire labor shortage in the wine industry in France. This would help both the wine growers and the students. There are a lot of kids who can't afford school fees, so they never learn a skill and eventually end up on the dole."

"It sounds like a good program, but it doesn't get my blood racing, Lillie." Philip picked up the prospectus. "Are all the details in here?"

"Yes, they are. I understand, Philip. It's not curing cancer, but I think it's exactly what you're looking for." Lillie still smiled, but her eyes no longer sparkled. "I promise, this program has the power to change the course of a young person's life. Spend some time with it and let me know what you think." She dug back in her bag, pulled out another copy, and handed it to Genevieve. "Ask me questions as they come up."

"Excusez-moi." Three heads turned to find Madame Morier standing in the doorway, holding a tray of envelopes. "Plus des réponses." She walked across the room and placed the tray on the desk.

"Just what we need." Genevieve rolled her eyes. "Merci, madame."

"How many are there so far?" Madame Morier asked. As she was responsible for the house looking its best and for the event running smoothly, she was anxious to assess how much trouble the cocktail party would cause her.

"Lillie?" Genevieve deferred to the foundation's director.

Lillie pointed to the stack in front of her. "Before this new batch, we have 122 'oui' and four 'non'. There's no question, people want to meet the Earl and Countess of Crosswick. What do you think, Madame Morier?"

Annoyance radiated from the statuesque woman. "Bernard told me when we spoke yesterday that everyone in Paris wants to come to this event." She arched a single brow, shrugged, and pouted, "Uuh bof."

Surprised that Madam Morier and Bernard had spoken, Genevieve asked, "Do you talk often to Bernard?"

"We have a little gossip from time to time." Before leaving the room, she handed Philip a large cream-colored envelope. "This was hand-delivered for you, my lord."

"Merci, madame." Philip dropped the mail into his lap.

"And, Lady Crosswick, Madame Beaufoy is here to see you," Madame said as an afterthought.

Genevieve looked blank. "Madame Beaufoy? Do I know her?" She frowned at Madame Morier, hoping the house manager would give her a clue who her visitor was.

Instead, Lillie spoke up. "I don't think you've met her yet."

Genevieve narrowed her eyes at Lillie, trying to decide if the fact they hadn't met was good or bad.

"She and her husband are big supporters of the foundation."

Genevieve brightened. "Wonderful."

"Hmm. We'll see what you think after you've met her. And another thing; she is the President of the Board of Cité du Vin." Lillie pointed to the study door. "Go on. Go charm our donor and potential partner. And remember, she has no idea what we are about to propose."

"She is in the salon," Madame Morier said as she walked out.

Genevieve followed her through the door then headed to the grand room.

"Madame Beaufoy, bonjour." Genevieve crossed the room to greet a woman who was fighting against time and losing the battle. Her eyes looked permanently surprised, her cheeks overfilled, and her lips too Brigitte Bardot for her advancing age.

Elise Beaufoy avoided Genevieve's outstretched hand and went straight for la bise. "Please call me Elise, Ah, ma chérie," she gushed. "I am so happy to meet you. Thank you for seeing me. I should have called, but I was just around the corner at my dressmaker and thought I would take a chance that you had a moment for me to say hello and welcome."

She spread her arms and turned a full circle. "This room," she said. "This manoir. C'est parfait. And the art. Mon Dieu!" She walked to the coffee table and picked up a box wrapped in heavy royal purple paper. Fresh gardenias tucked under its thick grosgrain ribbon, wafted scent through the room. "Happy crémaillère!"

"Elise, that's kind of you, but unnecessary." Genevieve was touched. "Crémaillère. Is that what we call a housewarming gift?"

Elise nodded, then leaned into Genevieve like a conspirator. "I could have waited until your gala, but it is important you know how much I want to be on the foundation board. I thought perhaps a very special bottle of Dom Perignon would help you decide I'm the best person to fill the next vacancy." She winked at Genevieve.

"Oh," was all Genevieve could say. "Um…" She searched for a few gracious words. "As you can imagine, I'm just getting my bearings with the foundation and—"

"Let's talk more later this week," Elise interrupted, then kissed Genevieve on both cheeks again. "I shall call you to make a plan, and we shall have a lovely lunch in a couple of days." She gathered her purse and her coat, which she had slung over the back of a chair, and was through the doorway, down the foyer, and out the front door before Genevieve realized she was gone.

When she returned to the study, Genevieve dropped into her

chair, bewildered. She plunked the gift box on the desk, and all she could say was, "That was a lot."

Lillie's laugh started with a giggle and grew into a full-blown guffaw. "She's a handful, isn't she? Did she press you for a seat on the board?"

"You knew she was going to do that, and you sent me out there anyway?" Genevieve wadded a piece of paper and threw it across the desk at Lillie.

Grinning as he watched the back and forth, Philip picked up the ivory packet Madame Morier had brought in earlier and looked at the front. His name was written in calligraphy. "Hand me the letter opener, G." He held out his hand and Genevieve slapped the silver knife into his palm. He caught the corner of the flap with the tip, sliced the envelope open, and pulled out two pieces of cardboard. As he held them up by one corner, four photos slid from between them and drifted to the floor, one facing up and three facing down. The color glossy facing Philip was of the Jackson Pollock that filled the wall on the landing at the top of their staircase.

Genevieve stood up and stretched across the desk. "What in the world are those?"

Philip gathered the four photos from the floor. "They seem to be pictures of our Pollock." A handwritten note was clipped to the cardboard. Philip cleared his throat and read aloud.

> Lord Crosswick,
>
> We regret the inconvenience we are about to cause you. The Jackson Pollock hanging in your home is not an original, but

rather an excellent forgery. If you alert the gendarmes, you shall never see the original painting again.

We would accept a small donation of €5,000,000 for the return of your painting. If we do not receive the money, we would be sorry to destroy such a magnificent work, but one must do what one must do.

We shall be in touch within twenty-four hours to provide the terms of exchange.

With best regards,

M. Gideur

He dropped the photo as if it had singed his fingers. "G, call Monsieur Boucher. We're either the targets of a bad joke or the victims of a robbery. Let's not touch any of this." He pointed to the envelope, cardboard, and glossies.

Lillie clutched each arm of her chair, her knuckles turning whte. For a moment she sat frozen, then shot out of her chair. "Bloody hell!" she shrieked, tearing out of the study, her blond curls dancing.

Genevieve's hand flew to her mouth as she watched Lillie streak from the room. She dug her fingers into her temples, trying to massage away the fierce throbbing already starting, then she pulled Boucher's business card from a small onyx box on her desk. She tapped a number into her cell and waited for a connection. After two rings a voice croaked, "Oui?", followed by a sneeze and a sniff.

"Monsieur Boucher?" Genevieve said.

"Oui," he said again.

"C'est Genevieve Warwick, La Countess de Crosswick. Hallo. Monsieur Boucher, we have another problem. It could be a joke, or it could be a spectacular robbery."

Genevieve told the BEA investigator what had just happened. "Oui...Oui," she said. "Of course, we will. Bon. À bientôt." She ended the call and laid her cell phone on the desk. "He'll be here within the hour. He's alerting the Paris police detectives as well. If it doesn't have anything to do with our fuel tank issue, it's not in his purview. Oh, and he said not to touch anything." She nodded at Philip, acknowledging his earlier advice.

Just as Genevieve asked, "Where did Lillie go?" she burst back into the room swearing like a sailor.

"That bloody bastard! The painting hanging on the landing is a goddamn giclee!" She spat out the word, fire in her eyes. "That's why he signed the note M. Gicleur. Giclee comes from the French word gicleur," she snarled.

"A giclee is made on an inkjet printer, isn't it?" Philip asked. His eyes closed as he pinched the bridge of his nose, trying to relieve the pressure building there.

Lillie rubbed her glazed eyes, thinking. "But once they had the print, swapping it had to be next to impossible. How did they take a five-by-eight-foot painting off the wall, replace it, and get the painting out of the house without being detected?" she said. "I bet Madame Morier keeps firm reins on who comes in and out of this house. It shouldn't be difficult to figure out who had the opportunity to swap the canvases."

"She keeps a close rein on us," Philip nodded, "so I wouldn't be surprised if she has a log of everyone's comings and goings."

Genevieve tapped her chin with a pen. "And, of course, we have security cameras. I don't know for sure, but I would imagine there's one focused on the stairs and landing." She stood up. "I have to agree with you, Lillie, this seems like an easy theft to solve. I want to see this giclee we've been walking by every day for who-knows-how-long."

Lillie grabbed Genevieve's hand and said, "I've got to get to the museum." Her voice was frantic. She turned and dashed for the door, then stopped. "Go look at the painting. I bet you won't be able to tell it's a fake until you run your hand over the canvas. And have the police call me if they need me. I'll be back as soon as I check on things at le Musée." Then she was gone.

Philip shoved himself out of his chair and put his arm around Genevieve. He could feel the tension in his wife's shoulders. "What was that all about?"

"I'm assuming Lillie wants to make certain nothing similar has happened at the museum."

Philip and Genevieve stood in the foyer at the bottom of the staircase, gazing up to the landing at the rectangular canvas hanging there. Philip pulled Genevieve into his side and kissed the top of her head. As if on cue, they each put a foot on the first tread and began ascending the stairs, unable to take their eyes off the forged Pollock. They trudged closer and closer, trying to detect the artifice with each step.

At the top of the stairs, Philip said, "I can't tell a thing, can you?"

Genevieve shook her head, then tiptoed forward. When she

was within a foot of the painting, she pulled her glasses from her trouser pocket, put them on, and leaned in until her nose was just inches from the riot of sweeping, swirling strings of paint. She squinted, walking back and forth in front of the long canvas. She stopped and turned to Philip. "What am I supposed to see? It looks good to me."

"Lillie said to close your eyes. Run your hand over the surface of the painting and tell me what you feel."

Genevieve's eyes squeezed tight as she concentrated on what she felt, her hand skimming over the canvas. "I'm stunned." She opened her eyes to look again at the drips. "There's no texture. One of the wonderful things about a Pollock is the texture of the drip layer."

Standing at the edge of the landing, Philip had been watching Genevieve's experiment. "You mean to tell me the canvas is flat?" He shook his head, disbelieving.

Genevieve turned from the wall. "Come feel for yourself."

Rather than close his eyes, Philip watched his hand brush over the painted surface before him. Even feeling the flatness of the canvas, it was hard for him to believe the texture didn't exist when his eyes insisted that it did.

"I had no idea a giclee could be so convincing."

Philip jumped at the "dring" of the doorbell. When he turned to look down the length of the grand foyer, Madame Morier was already opening the front door. From their perch on the landing, Philip and Genevieve could hear a rapid exchange in French before Madame Morier stepped aside and allowed three men to enter. Just inside the door, all three men pulled white booties over their shoes.

"Restez ici," Madame Morier demanded, with a gesture even a puppy would understand meant "stay right here!"

The house manager stormed toward the landing, her expensive pumps clacking on the marble floor. "My lord! The police..." but before she could finish her sentence, the bell sounded again. Without missing a step, she turned and charged back to the front door. She threw it open and there stood Monsieur Boucher, blowing his nose into a white handkerchief. He took two huge sniffs, winding up for an enormous sneeze.

Madame Morier stepped back to avoid his spray. "Mais bien sûr." Her words dripped with sarcasm. "Inspector, but of course, you're here as well. And you have un rhume," she said, disgusted by his cold. "Vous restez ici, aussi."

Embarrassed by his Rudolph-red nose, Boucher blinked his watery eyes. "Mais oui, madame." Not wanting to incur her wrath, Boucher stood frozen to his spot. He bobbed his head at the three men from the Paris police, who were also standing firm. They nodded back.

Boucher started to speak to them, then thought better of it. He'd wait for Madame Morier to tell them what to do next.

By the time Madame Morier reached the other end of the foyer, Philip and Genevieve had descended the stairs and were bracing for her fury. Madame Morier's posture was even more rigid than usual. Before she spoke, she took a shallow breath and looked at her employers with narrowed eyes. "My lord, que se passe-t-il? What's happening? With the Paris police here, this is not about the jet fuel."

Philip mustered his courage. "Madame, you are correct. This may not be related to the airplane incident. The envelope you gave me a few minutes ago was filled with pictures of the Pollock painting." He pointed back up to the landing. "There was a note from someone who says he has the original and replaced it with a forgery."

"Mais, non." Her voice was barely audible. "Ce n'est pas possible."

Philip leaned toward the stunned woman until their faces were just inches from each other. "It's not only possible," he said, "but it happened. The painting you're looking at is a giclee."

"Non, non, non." The blood drained from Madame Morier's face. "Ce n'est pas possible," she repeated. "How could this happen? There is always someone here."

"Madame," Genevieve moved closer to the distraught woman. "If that's true, it should be easy to find out who did this."

She took Madame Morier by the elbow. "Let's go sit down for a moment," she said, guiding her into Philip's study. They sat on the loveseat, their knees almost touching.

"Madame Morier." Genevieve started to put her hand on the house manager's knee but thought better of it and put her hand back in her lap. The comforting overture would not be welcome, she decided. "Madame," she started again, "this is not your fault."

"Of course, it is not my fault," Madame Morier snapped. "But it is my responsibility to keep Maison de Laney secure."

"Fair enough," Genevieve agreed.

"I need to consider when the criminals had time to commit this crime."

Much to Genevieve's surprise, she felt a pang of pity for the distressed house manager. "Madame, I know you said the house is never vacant, but if you think hard, maybe you can remember a time recently when no one was in the house for a few hours?"

Madame Morier stared at the engagement portrait, above the fireplace, of the 9TH Earl and Charlotte, as if she were looking for the answer in the thick brushstrokes.

For a long time, the two sat in silence—Madam Morier as still as a statue, legs together, crossed at the ankles, Genevieve with her legs crossed, foot bouncing.

"Les fumigateurs," Madam Morier mumbled at last. "Bien sûr. C'est les fumigateurs."

"Are you saying fumigators?"

"Oui. Fumigators came just before you and the earl arrived last week. The renovations on the house next door have disturbed some of les rats. We found evidence they had come into the manoir, so the fumigateurs came just before you arrived. No one could stay in the house for twenty-four hours, so the house was unattended for that long. That must be when they exchanged the painting. Mon Dieu!" Madame Morier ran her hands through her hair. Her bangs stuck out as if she had a cowlick. It was the first time since they arrived that Genevieve had seen her in any state except perfection.

Genevieve decided a hand on Madame Morier's shoulder wouldn't kill either of them. When she touched her, she felt madame flinch, but didn't care. A kind gesture was never wrong.

"Come on, Madame Morier." Genevieve stood. "We need to tell someone about your fumigator theory."

As they emerged from Philip's study, the four inspectors were making their way down the hall and Philip was coming down the stairs.

The alpha male from the Paris police spoke first. "My lord." He clicked his heels and gave Philip a brisk nod. "I am Capitaine Fabré. I head the task force for art theft and forgery." His erect posture relaxed as he turned to Genevieve, snared her in a heavy-lidded gaze, and said, "Countess, it is a pleasure to meet the magnificent Lady Crosswick at last. My wife showed me your profile in the holiday issue of *Vogue France*. Magnifique! She will be thrilled to know I met you, though not under the best of circumstances."

Much to Genevieve's surprise, Fabré took her hand from where it rested at her throat and brought it to his lips. Surprised by the gesture, she pressed her mouth into a tight smile. His velvety brown eyes caressed her lovely face, and then he winked. Genevieve coughed, trying to stifle a laugh. She cleared her throat, sniffed, and looked at Fabré with as much innocence as she could muster. "Excuse me, please, Capitaine Fabré," Genevieve said. "Perhaps I'm catching Inspector Boucher's cold." She cleared her throat again and turned to Fabré's sidekicks. "Now, who are these two gentlemen?"

Fabré's eyes lingered on Genevieve for a moment, then he turned to his underlings and introduced them. "My lord, countess, may I present Lieutenants Delique and Laurent."

Nodding at the BEA investigator, Philip said, "Gentlemen,

I assume you met Inspector Boucher. Lillie Langdon, our Foundation Director who confirmed the Pollock is a giclee, went to the museum to make certain everything is all right there. She'll return as soon as she can. The ransom note is still in the study. As Inspector Boucher instructed, we left everything untouched after I opened the envelope."

Not quite sure who should take charge, the police stood together in an awkward cluster. The cop quartet was a mismatched set: Boucher with his Danny DeVito looks and sexy Charles Aznavour voice; Fabré, swoon-worthy but smarmy; and the two lieutenants: a tall, thin man in his early twenties with remnants of acne near his thin-lipped mouth, and a middle-aged man so bland it would be difficult to pick him out of a lineup.

"Would you like to see the photographs and the note?" asked Philip, anxious for the investigation to get going.

Genevieve held up a hand. "Before you go to the study, I have a question. Are there any forensic people coming?" She wondered why the house wasn't already swarming with a team peering through magnifying glasses, combing through hours of security video and dusting anything that could be dusted for fingerprints. "No doubt this crime is a couple of weeks old. How in the world can you gather any evidence?"

Fabré regarded Boucher. Boucher nodded his deference and Fabré took over. "First, let me say, Inspector Boucher and I are quite certain what happened with your Jackson Pollock is not associated with what Inspector Boucher is investigating for the BEA. If that is confirmed, my team and I will take over all aspects of the investigation of this crime. The forensic squad is on its way and will be here soon. As for the delay in discovering the robbery, that should not be a problem. There are many things that will make it quite easy to track the perpetrators. Number one is, if this is a giclee, there are few printers in this country who can print on such a large scale. It will not be difficult to find who created the forgery."

The doorbell sounded again, and Madame Morier opened the door for the third time in less than ten minutes, this time ushering in a crew of six men and women, each carrying a bulging satchel. Fabré strode the length of the foyer to the front door and spoke to the group, gesturing at the forged Pollock still hanging on the landing. Even while he was issuing orders, the team dug in their bags, pulled out white hooded jumpsuits and booties, and suited up. Within minutes, the sleuths had dispersed, with their forensic tools, ready to gather any clues remaining from days ago.

"Inspector Boucher, Capitaine Fabré." Genevieve tilted her head as she spoke. "Shall we go into the study?" She smiled at the two policemen, turned, and led them toward the door. "Philip, could you please ask Madame Morier to bring coffee?" Genevieve caught the flash of terror in his eyes. "You'll be fine." Genevieve patted him on his back, happy he was the one imposing on the housekeeper.

Motioning for one of the forensic experts to follow them, Fabré, Boucher, and Genevieve made their way to the study. Still lying on the floor were the photos, envelope, and letter. Fabré pulled latex gloves from his suit pocket, tugging them on with a flourish and a snap. He squatted, his elbows on his knees. He stared for several seconds, then gestured toward the strewn paper and pictures and spoke to his crime scene technician in rapid

French. The specialist began to photograph the room, starting with the evidence on the floor.

"Shall we leave our forensic team to do what they do best?" Fabré ushered the others toward the door. "Is there someplace we can talk?" Fabré asked.

"Of course." Genevieve led the way to the petit salon.

The forensic team was in full action. Some members dusted for fingerprints. Others bagged bits of thread they discovered near the painting. For two hours, they examined every inch around the painting but didn't touch the canvas itself. Before they removed the painting from the wall, they wanted to make certain they had captured every fiber, print, morsel, and microscopic clue left behind.

When all their painstaking work had been photographed and videoed, they were ready. An officer gripped the thick stretchers at either end of the gallery-wrapped, eight-foot-long canvas. In the middle, a third investigator squatted to stabilize the structure by holding on to the bottom. On the count of "un, deux, trois," they lifted the painting off its cleats. Easing it onto the floor, the two men at the end angled the large piece away from the wall to inspect the back.

"Qu'est-ce que c'est? What's this?" One analyst thumbed the edge of the giclee that had been wrapped around the top rim of the stretchers and stapled on the back. Just below the straight edge of the forged painting, a frayed canvas showed itself, teasing the investigators like the flash of a lacy slip beneath a maiden's frock. The technician tugged gingerly on the loose piece of giclee, trying to release it from a staple.

"Don't pull on that," his colleague warned. "I think we had better get the capitaine."

"We need to see what's under the fake." The technician persisted, pulling a small screwdriver from his pocket and wedging it under the staple.

Rising from his haunches, the senior specialist settled the question. "Put that back in your pocket," he ordered. "I'm calling the capitaine."

Far away, in another part of the house, they could hear a phone ring twice.

"Fabré."

"Capitaine, please come to the landing. I am not certain what we have here, but I believe we may have another canvas under the giclee."

They heard Capitaine Fabré's footsteps hammering toward them. He burst into the foyer, bounded up the stairs two at a time, then took two deep breaths before he said, "Tell me. What have you found?"

Still holding each end of the painting, the forensic investigators again angled it away from the wall.

"Capitaine, if you look here," the head of the team tugged the border of the forged painting so Fabré could better see what was under it, "it appears the giclee has been stretched over another canvas, a canvas with a frayed edge. A much older canvas." Though he tried to keep his voice even, his excitement was hard to hide.

Fabré stared, confused. "Qu'est-ce que je regarde? What am I seeing?" he murmured to himself. Taking the edge, Fabré pulled hard enough to dislodge one staple, then another. The three analysts gasped. Fabré glared at his subordinates, daring them to challenge him. He wrenched the canvas away from three more staples. With six inches of the underpainting exposed, Fabré's hand fell to his side. He stepped back, keeping his eyes on his work. "Get the rest of the staples off," he said. "Let's see what we have here."

The investigators laid the canvas face down on the thick oriental carpet running the length of the landing and went to work. While Capitaine Fabré loomed over them watching their every move, they slipped their small screwdrivers under the staples, wedged them up, and plucked them out with tweezers. Within minutes of starting their work, the giclee had been released from the stretchers and the edge of the aged undercanvas was visible.

Fabré stood, hands on hips, a scowl creasing his brow. "Lift it back up and lean it against the wall," he said, holding his breath as the men raised the picture until it was upright. Not believing what he saw, Fabré squeezed his eyes shut, rubbed his hand over his face, and opened his eyes again. "Mon Dieu," he whispered. Puckering his lips, he let out a long, low whistle. "Boys." He looked at the three police standing with him. "I think we've just recovered our original Jackson Pollock."

FIVE

THE FOUR POLICE officers stared at a wall of squiggles, drips, swirls, rhythm and energy. This time there was no question. The texture was not just texture to the eye, but texture to the touch as well.

Philip puffed out a short breath that vibrated his lips. "Tell me again what happened."

A gentle smile played on Fabré's full lips. "When this officer took the painting off the wall," he nodded at the young man in a white jumpsuit, "he noticed an old, frayed canvas peeking below the edge of the giclee. When they finished unstapling the forgery, the original Pollock was there, underneath. It's been here the entire time. Very clever, but not very productive for the thieves." Fabré scoffed. "This was not a well-thought-out crime, certainment not the work of professionals."

Genevieve's mind raced. "Whoever did this must have known the original would be discovered before the ransom was paid. This seems more like a prank than a crime. It seems like something kids would do for fun or a dare."

Inspector Boucher sneezed into the crook of his arm. "Whatever the motive, it doesn't appear it has anything to do with my investigation." He pulled a red handkerchief from his jacket pocket, blew his nose, then shoved the soiled rag back into his pants. "If no one objects, I shall take my leave."

"By all means." Philip looked down at the stumpy figure, offering a sympathetic grin. "Inspector, you should be at home in bed with a hot toddy."

"Mais non, my lord," Boucher wheezed. "Ma mère swore by semolina." He wiped a knuckle under his damp nose. "First semolina, then a hot toddy." He returned Philip's grin, then winked a rheumy eye at him.

The inspector extended his hand to Fabré. "Capitaine, if I can be of any future service, please call me." He gave Fabré his business card then turned to Genevieve. "Countess, I shall be working avec diligence to discover who tampered with your avion, your airplane. Bien sûr, it will take longer to find the perpetrator of that mischief than the buffoon who committed this joke." He swept his arm around the landing, stopping at the painting. "This mystery should be solved by tomorrow. Any detective worth his salt will make short work of it."

Though he didn't disagree with the inspector, Fabré bristled at Boucher's dismissal of how complicated his job would be. Fixing the stubby, disheveled inspector with dagger eyes, he said through clenched teeth, "Inspector, please feel free to scurry home to your sickbed. I'm sure we'll manage very well without you."

Swooping in to avert further unpleasantries between the rival police officers, Genevieve took Boucher's arm. "I'll walk you out, Inspector," she said, pressing him toward the staircase.

Flattered by the countess's personal attention, Boucher didn't resist and gloated at Fabré, as he waddled—and Genevieve floated—down the stairs. They stood at the front door talking for several minutes before Genevieve extended her hand. Boucher cradled it in both of his, then bowed at the waist. Genevieve opened the door, and the BEA Inspector was gone.

Where just an hour ago there had been three forensic specialists assessing the Pollock and a few officers milling around, the house was now pulsing with people. On the landing officers rolled the giclee into a long cylinder. The original painting was hanging back on the wall. Fingerprint experts dusted everything that wasn't moving. Downstairs, detectives had taken over the study and were interviewing the entire staff one by one, and Madame Morier hovered and scolded and spat out orders to the police, over whom she had no authority.

At the base of his skull, Philip felt a pinch of tension he knew would soon bloom into a throbbing headache. A lesser man would have slipped off to a quiet corner of the house and pretended none of this was happening; instead, he closed his eyes and inhaled. As he exhaled, the trilling of someone's cell phone brought his attention back to the organized chaos whirling around him.

Fabré answered his phone with a terse, "Fabré." He held the phone so tight, the veins popped out on the back of his hand. "Oui. Déjà? Qu'avez-vous découvert? Vraiment? Bon. Appelez-moi dès que vous y êtes."

Philip's breath quickened as he listened to Fabré's side of the conversation.

As soon as the capitaine was off the phone, he turned to Philip.

"We have found the printer of the giclee. Two of my officers are on their way to speak to him."

"Already? That's amazing." Philip slapped Fabré on the back, much to the policeman's surprise. "Well done, Capitaine!"

"It was, wasn't it?" Well pleased with Philip's praise, Fabré worked to keep his smug smile in check. "They will call as soon as they have spoken with the owner of the shop. In the meantime, I must check on the progress of the interviews."

As Philip and Fabré descended the stairs together, Genevieve stepped into the foyer from the grand salon. She looked at the hive of activity on the landing and heard herself sigh. Then, her eyes lit on Philip standing with Fabré. Though Fabré was film-star handsome and at least twenty-five years Philip's junior, Genevieve would choose Philip's classic good looks and easy elegance every time.

"Is there any news?" she asked the pair as they approached.

Philip opened his mouth, but Fabré jumped in before he had a chance to speak: "My officers are on their way to the shop responsible for printing the giclee."

"My, that was fast," she said, echoing Philip. "It's going to be interesting to see what the printer can tell us." Genevieve slipped her arm through Philip's and the three strolled into the grand salon. She looked at Fabré, then her husband. "I don't imagine whoever did this would use their own name or pay with their own credit card, do you?"

Fabré walked to the sideboard where the kitchen staff had laid out coffee service. "May I?" Not waiting for permission, he filled a cup. He perused a tray of sweets, put a sablé Breton on his saucer and sat in a chair facing the garden. "What a charming view, even in the middle of winter."

Genevieve watched as Fabré took a bite of his cookie. A quiet "mmmm" vibrated at the back of his throat as the buttery confection melted in his mouth. His gaze panned from one end of the elegant room to the other, his eyes lingering on a four-foot-tall figure. "Is that a Giacometti bronze?" He put his cup and saucer on the table and pulled a small notebook from his inside jacket pocket. He uncapped his expensive Mont Blanc fountain pen, made a note, and said, "You live very well, don't you, my lord? Very well indeed."

Philip stopped in the midst of pouring Genevieve a cup of coffee and turned to look at the detective. "What an arrogant son of a bitch," he thought. He glanced at Genevieve, but she was focused on Fabré. Philip finished pouring her coffee and walked to where she was sitting on the sofa opposite the detective. He set the cup and saucer on the table in front of her and sat down close to his wife.

Philip fixed Fabré with an icy stare. "We have always worked hard and been smart about our money. As a result, we've lived well, but never so well as we are living now, since I inherited the estate from my cousin, the 12TH Earl of Crosswick," Philip said, his voice frosty. "Is there something you're implying, Capitaine? If there is, you're barking up the wrong tree."

Unphased by Philip's remark, Fabré continued, "My lord, I'm not implying anything, I am stating the obvious. You live very well. Very well, indeed. I imagine it costs a great deal to maintain all your properties and keep your private jet and helicopter flying." Fabré lifted one leg, intending to put his foot on the coffee table, thought better of it and crossed his ankle on his knee. "I was just wondering what the insured value of the Pollock is." His foot began to bounce on his knee.

"What are you suggesting?" Genevieve leaned forward on the sofa, her green eyes narrowing. She felt Philip's hand squeezing her bicep, pulling her back until she eased against the sofa pillows.

Philip watched as Fabré dropped his Mont Blanc between the upholstered chair arm and the seat cushion. As he dug the fountain pen from the crevasse, Philip could see a blue ink stain blooming on the expensive silk fabric. Fabré eased the edge of his suit jacket from under his right hip, and draped it over the blotch, saying nothing.

"I am sure you understand. We must look at every possibility." He resumed his explanation as if he hadn't just defiled a chair that no doubt cost more than a month of his wages. "Insurance fraud is always considered in cases such as this. You would be surprised how often it is the culprit. A hundred million euros would buy a lot of jet fuel."

Philip shot Genevieve a look that warned her to say nothing, then waited a moment before speaking. He relaxed deeper into the sofa and crossed his long legs. He draped an arm behind Genevieve's shoulders along the top of the couch. Before speaking, he cleared his throat.

"Capitaine," he began, his tone razor sharp. "I appreciate your need to turn over every stone, but it seems to me you are following this line of interrogation for your own amusement, or because you're curious about us and our lifestyle. Either way, I don't blame you, but I can't imagine you believe I'm behind this amateur crime." Philip was not a man to flaunt his talents or use his connections, but at the moment he was relishing this little drama in which he played the all-powerful lord of the manor and Fabré was at his mercy. "You can believe two things: first, if I had done this, it would have been flawlessly executed. I do nothing half-assed and I'm very clever."

Amused by what she was hearing, Genevieve turned her head to look at Philip.

"Second, with well over a billion pounds in our accounts, the chance is infinitesimal that I would put our fortune and our lives in jeopardy, period. So, shall we move on to something more productive or do I need to reach out to the Minister of the Interior? He'll be here at our cocktail party Saturday night before the opening at our museum, so I can speak to him then."

Realizing he had overstepped the mark and put himself in jeopardy, Fabré shot to his feet. "My lord, my lady," he said, his voice quivering. "I apologize for any implication that you attempted to deceive la compagnie d'assurance. Of course, the idea is preposterous! I shall take my leave and return to you as soon as I have plus d'information."

Philip remained lounging on the sofa. "By all means, let us know when you have additional information." Philip dismissed Fabré with an arch of his eyebrow. "I assume you can find your way out."

Chastened, the police officer turned and almost ran from the grand salon.

SIX

THERE WAS NO reason to believe he was not the architect of this ridiculous attempt at extortion.

Lillie's lacquer-red Porsche raced out of Avenue Foch. She darted in and out of the maze of traffic around the Arc de Triomphe, worked her way to the far-right lane, then streaked up the Champs Élysées. Sixteen minutes later she arrived at the LMBA, and slid into her reserved parking place behind the imposing building. She threw the car door open and pushed herself from her bucket seat in one explosive motion. Swiping her pass card over the electronic pad, she yanked open the employee door and raced up the back stairs until she hit the landing three flights up.

"Bugger," she swore, trying the door handle and finding it locked. Glancing at her mobile screen, she saw there was no service in the stairwell. Back down the three flights she flew, taking two steps at a time until she burst out of the building.

Without breaking her stride, Lillie loped to the front and tugged on the heavy entrance door, which, pushed from the other side by two exiting museum visitors, opened easily. She nodded at the aging, well-dressed couple and held the door for them. They stood in the doorway and blinked at the afternoon sun before sauntering onto the sidewalk.

Tapping her manicured nails on the edge of the door, anxious to dash inside, Lillie let the pair clear the entrance before she dashed into the building and bolted to the sweeping staircase. She put one foot on the first step, then stopped. Her chest rose and fell with each gasp of breath and her rapid pulse boomed in her ears. With a mighty inhale, she forged up the marble stairs, tripped once, recovered, and raced on.

One more flight and she burst into his office. "Bernard! What the hell have you…" She stopped mid-sentence, seeing Émile de Laudre, their intern, sitting across from the museum director.

Bernard's head jerked up from the brochure he was holding.

"Émile, get out," Lillie barked.

Eyes wide, the intern shot from his chair and ran from the room.

Bernard sat in shocked silence, his mouth hanging open. He watched as Lillie stormed across the room, slammed both hands down on his desk and loomed over him.

Her voice was low and dangerously calm. "Tell me. Tell me right now."

Bernard held Lillie's glare. "I have no idea what you're talking about. Qu'est-ce qui te prend?"

"I'll tell you what's gotten into me." Lillie's eyes were slits. "Someone did what you wrote in your novel. Someone—and I assume it was you—attempted to extort five million euros from the Earl and Countess of Crosswick by stretching a giclee over the original painting. They executed the plan to perfection, except that I discovered the giclee and the earl called the police. Tell me it wasn't you! Tell me, Bernard!"

A thunderous silence hung in the room for several seconds until Bernard leaned forward and the squeak of his chair split the air. "Mon Dieu," he said under his breath. "Impossible! There are three people who have read my manuscript: you, my brother, and Alain. You know Alain, my friend from uni." Lines etched his forehead. "Lillie, you couldn't possibly think I did this." His eyes clouded as he looked into Lillie's stormy face.

She looked away and took several deep breaths. When she turned back to him, her eyes had softened. "It's such a clever crime, such an original idea. You have to admit it's a bit too coincidental for there not to be some connection." Lillie sat down, settling into the chair facing Bernard on the other side of the desk.

He nodded. "It's hard to argue that point. But you know how I guard my writing until I send it to my publisher. In fact, this is the first time I've ever let Alain read anything before it's been published."

"Why did you let him read your book this time?"

"Remember he came to stay with me for a few days last month?"

Lillie nodded.

"He was not a happy man. His wife found out he was having an affair and threw him out, so he came knocking on my door. I let him read my manuscript to cheer him up. There's nothing better than a good novel about an art heist to raise a person's spirits." He chuckled and started to relax.

"My darling Bernard," Lillie pressed, "is there any chance Alain could have taken a page from your book, quite literally, and attempted to extort money from the earl and countess?"

"Absolument pas!" Bernard assured her. "Absolutely not," he said again, but with less conviction. "Non, non, non."

He stared at his fisted hands and shook his head. "He wouldn't." He looked up at Lillie. "I don't think he would. I've known him for twenty years."

Lillie moved around the desk to stand in front of Bernard. She squeezed his shoulder. "We should call Lord Crosswick and tell him about your book and who had access to the story."

"Bien sûr." His shoulders slumped and his head hung so low that his chin rested on his chest. "Je suis désolé," he mumbled. "I can't believe he would do such a thing, but I know he was terrified of losing everything in a divorce. Perhaps he saw it as a way out of financial ruin. It was an easy crime in my novel." Bernard looked up at Lillie.

With a reassuring smile, Lillie cupped his chin. "Let's call Lord Crosswick."

Philip answered at the first ring. "Lillie, where are you?"

"I'm at the museum. I have an idea who may have tried to extort money for the Pollock." Lillie told him about Alain and why she thought he would be worth questioning.

When she finished, silence filled the line for several seconds until Philip said at last, "Lillie, you can tell Bernard his friend is not the culprit. The police found the shop that printed the giclee and the idiot who had it done, used his own credit card. They're on their way to the museum."

SEVEN

TINY BEADS OF perspiration sparkled on his forehead, but the Baron de Sézanne's cool, arrogant voice gave no hint that he was trying, yet again, to snatch his son from the jaws of ruin.

The baron had pulled Émile out of trouble on many occasions throughout Émile's twenty-two years, but the stakes had never been this high. Breaking and entering, art theft, fraud, and intention to extort: each was a serious crime, but the four together could put Émile in prison for years. Having a child behind bars would blacken the family name and his wife wouldn't stand for it.

He looked around the Warwicks' sophisticated salon and knew he was dealing with a man of substance. "Do you have children, my lord?"

Philip nodded. "One son."

The baron looked down at his folded hands, then back at Philip. "I'm sure your son has caused you plenty of anxious moments."

"Not many." The corners of Philip's mouth pulled up and he chuckled under his breath. "My son's greatest transgression was when he and a friend drove his father's Porsche without permission. They got away with it and Duncan told us the story just last year, twenty-five years later." Philip shook his head. "Hardly Émile's situation, is it?"

The baron ran his hand over his face then shifted in his chair, uncrossing his legs. He leaned forward. "You see, my friend, my son—"

"Let's be clear, Baron. I am not your friend." Philip's voice was cool, and he could feel the slow burn of anger begin. All his life he had believed the best about people, but with his newly inherited title and wealth, he was discovering that people often didn't deserve that trust. Because of the pressure of his new responsibilities, his temper was closer to the surface than ever before. Much to his dismay, he was beginning to wonder if their inheritance was becoming more of a curse than a blessing.

"Of course, of course." For the first time, the Baron de Sézanne was flustered. He fumbled with the tip of his tie, picked imaginary lint off his sleeve, then looked out the window.

Philip crossed his arms and waited for the baron to go on.

"My lord, I am appealing to you as a father. Émile has always been a challenge to his mother and me. He was a beautiful little boy, and clever." The baron smiled at the thought of his son as a child. "He was a little cherub and he could always make me laugh, so it was easy to spoil him. And now, the spoiled child has become a spoiled man. It is my fault, and his mother's. If Émile is prosecuted for this," he paused, searching for the right word, "this serious prank, it will ruin his life and his mother will not survive the humiliation."

Philip rose and walked to the French doors overlooking the manicured garden. He stood for several minutes, staring at nothing. The room was quiet, each man deep in his own thoughts. After a few minutes, they heard the front door open and the clack of high heels approaching.

"Here come reinforcements," Philip said under his breath, just before Genevieve burst into the room.

Her cheeks pink from the cold and hair tousled by the winter gusts, she filled the salon with energy. "Bonjour, mon amour!" she said and blew a kiss to Philip before noticing the baron. "Ah, pardon. I'm so sorry. I didn't know you had company. I didn't mean to interrupt."

The baron sprang to his feet and smiled, encouraged by Genevieve's lively spirit.

Philip stood and accepted the kiss Genevieve planted on his cheek. "Darling, this is the Baron de Sézanne, Émile's father."

"Oh!" Genevieve made no attempt to hide her surprise.

"He's here to talk about his son and appeal to our better angels."

Genevieve walked to the baron, who shifted from one foot to the other. "Baron de Sézanne, I'm Genevieve Warwick."

The baron accepted her extended hand, shook it once, and gave her a curt nod. "Please, my lady. Call me Émile, just like my son. It is an honor to meet you."

"When you say the baron is here to appeal to our better angels, what do you mean, Philip?"

"He was just getting to that. Baron, proceed."

"Lord and Lady Crosswick." He stopped, cleared his

throat, and went on. "I assure you, my son will be grateful for any consideration you may give him and will execute any consequence you feel is just. S'il vous plaît, my lord. S'il vous plaît." Émile stretched forward in his chair, his hands folded and pleading. For a moment Philip thought he was going to drop to his knees, but he didn't.

"Baron, if you were in our shoes, what would you do?" Philip relaxed, interested to hear Émile's solution.

Feeling he had just been offered a sliver of hope, the baron sat back and unclenched his hands. "My lord, I've given this a lot of thought since the call from the gendarmerie. I believe my son would benefit from hard work and simple living. Perhaps he could work at Château Beaulieu, in the fields, and live with the workers."

To the baron's surprise, a scoff stuck in Philip's throat. "That's rich." A disbelieving smile crimped the corners of his green eyes. "Let me see if I have this right. Your son tries to rob us of a multi-million-dollar painting, and you want us to save his ass by employing him and offering him accommodation at our vineyard? Have I left anything out?"

Émile shook his head. "Oh, la la. When you say it like that, I am embarrassed to be asking such a thing." He turned to Genevieve. "Countess. Vous avez un fils." Émile's pleading eyes begged Genevieve to hear him out. "You have a son. Lord Crosswick told me he is spectaculaire! Intelligent, aiment, un fils merveilleux."

Philip looked at Genevieve, his shoulders next to his ears, his palms turned up. "I didn't say any of those things."

"But I'm sure they're all true," The baron said, his eyes wide, imploring. "Your son has two wise, loving parents who challenged him to be the best person he could be." Genevieve rolled her eyes. "My wife and I gave our son more money than he could spend, bailed him out of endless, uh, how do you say, um, scrapes, and never made him accountable for his actions." Émile plopped back into his chair, his elbows on his knees and his head in his hands.

Philip and Genevieve looked at each other, clueless about what to do next. Genevieve thought she heard the baron whimper but wasn't sure. She gave Philip a nod in the direction of the sofa, and they sat.

"Baron," Genevieve said, her voice soothing. "I can imagine how frightened you must be."

When the baron looked up, his eyes brimmed with tears and his hands trembled. "Countess, I will do anything to save mon enfant. I think he could learn a great deal from hard work and deprivation. It would be an opportunity for him to make something of himself rather than spend his life as a self-indulgent morveux—how do you say," he looked at the ceiling then back at Genevieve, "brat."

"Philip, what do you think?"

"I think it's too much to ask us to be responsible for changing the life of this twenty-two-year-old criminal."

Émile pulled a linen handkerchief from his pocket, wiped his eyes, blew his nose, and tried his best to stifle a sob.

Sensing Genevieve was about to go to the distraught father, Philip put his hand on hers. He shook his head and gave her a warning look. He knew his wife well and was sure she yearned to comfort the tortured man, but he was not going to make it easy for the baron. Genevieve's eyes pleaded. Philip shook his head again. Genevieve stiffened at his side, pulled her hand away and set her lips in a tight line.

"Émile." Philip crossed his legs and sighed.

"Oui?" Dark rings encircled the baron's eyes. His hair sprang out in random spikes where he had stroked his head in distress. He looked up with such hope that Philip couldn't help but smile.

"Émile," Philip started again. "If Genevieve and I were to agree to your proposal, your son would have to come to us himself. He must convince us that he wants to do this, that he wants to change his life. We need to believe that he will work hard and do everything our vigneron asks of him. He'll work long hours, have little time for himself and will live with the workers. It will be an enormous change in his lifestyle."

Genevieve turned toward Philip, tucked her legs under her and smiled at her husband. He rarely disappointed her. She looked at the baron. "What do you think, Émile? Do you think your son can do this?" She reached for Philip's hand and squeezed it. "Thanks to Lord Crosswick, Émile has two options. Whichever one he chooses, his life will change forever."

EIGHT

Genevieve leaned against the molding of the wide doorway to the grand salon, her arms folded. She watched as the young, elegant Émile wandered from painting to painting, his fingers laced behind his back, drifting around the room until he saw Genevieve.

"Ah, countess, bonjour." He swanned over to Genevieve, his right hand outstretched. With his other, he tucked a lock of hair behind his ear.

She was slow to shake his hand, but at last gripped his palm in hers, giving it a firm squeeze. "Émile, sit down," she said, motioning to a chair that faced the French doors. "Would you like coffee?"

"Oui. Café noire." He draped the overstuffed chair with his lanky body.

"I'm sure you meant to say café noire, s'il vous plaît," Genevieve chided.

"Hein?" Émile shrugged and took the cup and saucer, but Genevieve didn't let go.

"Do you have anything else to say, young man?" She had often used this tone with Duncan when he was growing up, to remind her son of his manners.

Émile's brow furrowed and he stared at the coffee, then it dawned on him. He threw a lopsided smile at Genevieve and said, "Merci."

"De rien." Genevieve relinquished the cup. She poured coffee for herself and returned to the sofa. She stared at Émile for several seconds and, before she sat down, she said, "Let me give you a little piece of advice, Émile. Lord Crosswick is on a phone call. When he comes in to speak to you, it would be in your best interest to convince him that you're grateful he's giving you an alternative to prison." She took a drink of her coffee. "I suggest you tell him not only will you do everything you are asked to do at Château Beaulieu, but you will strive to become a credit to your family and to everyone who helps you at the winery." Genevieve pointed her finger at Émile and continued, "I would also suggest that you assure him you will not betray his trust and you will never be able to repay his kindness. Can you do that?" She could feel the heat in her cheeks. "Émile, I'm rooting for you, but you don't make it easy."

Émile's eyes were wide, his mouth hung open, and he looked like a little boy. He blinked, then blinked again.

"Émile, I asked you a question." Genevieve was still pointing her finger at him, waiting for a reply.

"Merde, why did you speak to me that way?" His lower lip quivered, and Genevieve thought he was going to cry.

"Émile!" She dropped onto the sofa. "My goodness!" She shook her head in disbelief. "You are such a spoiled little baby, aren't you?"

He sat forward in his chair. He looked at his sleeve, picked an imaginary piece of lint from the tweed just as his father had done, then said, "That is not a very kind thing to say. Why are you being so mean to me?"

"Émile, you realize you tried to steal a priceless painting from us, don't you? You broke into our home, sent a letter demanding five million euros and cost the Parisian taxpayers a great deal of money. Don't you think you deserve a firm scolding, at the very least?" Genevieve felt her patience dwindling.

"But it was just a joke," he whined. "While I was copying Bernard's manuscript for him, I read about covering the canvas with a giclee and thought it was clever. I thought it would be fun to see if I could do it." He smoothed a wrinkle on his trousers. "If it hadn't been for Lillie, I think I would have gotten away with it." He looked at Genevieve, shrugged his shoulders and pouted his lips. "Je ne sais pas. It's really Lillie's fault."

At that, Genevieve leaned toward him. Her eyes turned flinty. Her voice hushed, but steel-edged, she said, "I don't think this is going to work. The only way you're going to understand who you are now, and who you need to become, is to spend some time in prison. You're not just a brat, you're a delinquent. You've been handed everything anyone could ever want in life, and you think you're owed even more, yet you've given nothing in return." Genevieve was on her feet and began to pace back and forth in front of Émile, who relaxed into his chair. "If you were my son," she said, her temper beginning to boil, "I'd send you to the most destitute country in the world to build hospitals and schools for children who have nothing, who yearn to be given a scrap, any kind of help. I'd make sure you slept on the dirt floor of a mud hut and ate bugs for your meals. I wouldn't expect your victims to send you to a beautiful vineyard surrounded by luxury, hoping you'd become a better person." She stopped in front of him and put her hands on her hips. "If that's what you expect us to do, you're delusional, Émile."

She glared at him and waited for a response. "Well?" she said.

He sat in silence, staring at the floor and twiddling his thumbs in his lap.

"You have nothing to say?"

When she saw Philip standing in the doorway, they locked eyes and she shook her head. Looking back at the young man, she said. "I was rooting for you, Émile. I thought you were a young man worth saving, but after our one-sided chat, I can't imagine there is anything inside of you to salvage. My friend, you're on your own." She gave him a final look of contempt and stalked out of the room.

"He's all yours," she said as she stormed past Philip, his eyes wide and his lips curled in amusement. He was looking forward to playing good cop to Genevieve's bad.

He ambled to the sideboard, poured a coffee, and turned to Émile. "Well, I don't know what you said or did, but it seems you have rather pissed off the countess."

Émile rolled his eyes. "Women," he huffed. "All I did was tell her that my little prank would have been successful if it hadn't been for Lillie, and, of course, you called the gendarmes even though I told you not to in my note." He sighed. "It would have been such a funny joke, but I don't believe the countess saw the humor in it."

Philip let out a long, low whistle. "Imagine that." He stared at the young man before him and tried to peel away the layers of bravado. The boy couldn't be as unconcerned about his situation as he appeared unless he was confident the Warwicks were going to bail him out.

Philip sat down, drank his coffee, and tried to bore into Émile's soul. From what he saw when they met at the museum, the kid's hubris was as thick as his hair. Philip had never witnessed such arrogance.

Émile pushed the sleeves of his khaki-green jacket up his forearms and fixed his eyes on the ornate ceiling. His ankle rested on his knee and his foot bounced, the only indication he might be anxious.

"All right, my friend," Philip said at last. "I think we've spent more than enough time on this." He put his cup on the coffee table and sat back, his arms spread on the sofa back. "I'm inclined to let you spend time as a guest of the Paris police."

"Pardon?" Émile shot forward in his chair. "Vous ne pouvez pas être sérieux!" The blood drained from his face.

"Oh, but I am. I'm deadly serious." Philip sat still as a stone and glowered at Émile. "You've given me—given us," he corrected himself, "no reason to help you. You have no respect for us, for your family, for anyone, as far as I can tell. Am I wrong?" he said, giving the kid an opportunity to help himself.

"Mais, mais…" Émile stuttered, panicked, realizing for the first time that he might be heading to jail. "S'il vous plaît, Lord Crosswick. Please give me a chance to plead my case. I cannot go to prison." His eyes were wide, moistened with tears. "Imagine what they would do to me!"

"Yes, Émile." Philip leaned forward, elbows on his knees and his hands tented. He smiled and said, "Just imagine what they would do to a beautiful boy like you in a place like that." He shook his head. "Tsk, tsk, tsk, not a happy thought." He stood. "Well, if we have nothing else to talk about, I should call the police and tell them how our conversation went. They may want to send a car and take you directly to the magistrate." Philip had no idea what he was talking about, but by now was having fun terrifying this little plonker. At least the brat was showing some signs of fear, some inkling that he might be in real trouble.

Émile's forehead glistened with a layer of sweat. He clutched his hands, walked around the coffee table and leaned within inches of Philip. "My lord, s'il vous plaît," his voice cracked. "S'il vous plaît. You have frightened me."

Delighted at Émile's confession, Philip nodded for the boy to continue. "Go on."

"I don't know what you want me to say. I don't know what you want to hear. I don't know where to begin. It doesn't seem to me that I did anything so bad. I never intended to take your money. My family is very wealthy. I did not mean to frighten anyone. When I read Bernard's idea, I just thought it would be a clever prank. It never occurred to me it would be considered a crime."

Philip poked Émile in the chest as he spoke. "And that's why I think you need a much harsher experience than you would have at Château Beaulieu, working in the fields and living in a very nice cottage. You don't understand how serious this is.

To his surprise, Émile grabbed Philip's hands and clutched

them in his. "Please, please, my lord." Tears oozed over the rims of his eyes. He whimpered as he said, "I promise I will go to the vineyard and work hard. I swear you will be proud of me."

"Why in the world should I believe you, Émile?"

"You should believe me because I am telling you the truth." He dropped to his knees, sobbing now and still clutching Philip's hands as if they were his last lifeline, which, indeed, they were.

Reaching down, Philip pulled the lad up by his elbows and handed him a napkin from under his coffee cup. He didn't know if this sobbing kid was being genuine or genuinely playing him.

Émile stopped to wipe his nose, "There's a very good psychiatrist on YouTube." His brow furrowed, and his lips puckered. "Hmm. Maybe she's not a real psychiatrist," he waved his hand. "Anyway, she said, I have never had to take responsibility for anything naughty I've ever done. According to her, my parents were afraid I wouldn't love them if they disciplined me. You're the first person who has ever threatened me with consequences for my actions and I'm terrified."

"That's quite a self-analysis. Who knew you could be analyzed on YouTube?"

Émile dried his eyes with Philip's hankie and hiccupped. "I thought she was really good." He smiled at Philip. "She was very pretty."

Philip threw back his head and laughed. He slapped the spoiled, young Frenchman on the back. "Okay, Émile. We'll give this a try, but if you screw up even once, you'll be in the Bastille so fast, you won't have time to say *Les Misérables*. Is that clear?"

"Mon Dieu! Mon Dieu!" Émile threw his arms around Philip,

wrapping him in a grateful hug. Philip staggered back onto the sofa with Émile falling on top of him just as Genevieve walked into the salon.

"My goodness," she said, looking at the two of them lying on the couch in a tight embrace. "It appears as if you've come to some kind of an agreement!"

NINE

WINTER RAIN PELTED the château windows and lights flickered throughout the house as the sound of thunder rumbled through Maison de Laney. Tucked into a cozy room just off the kitchen, Philip, Genevieve, and Château Beaulieu's Managing Director Daniel LaGrande enjoyed a hearty winter lunch of white sausage with truffled pasta.

"I know a grape who spends all his time in the sun. It's his raisin d'etre," said Philip, lifting his glass in Daniel's direction.

Daniel groaned at Philip's joke.

"I promise, Daniel, my business acumen is better than my jokes."

"Mon Dieu. I hope so." LaGrande's throaty chuckle filled the pretty salon. He had arrived a day before the Laney Museum party to spend time with the château's new owners. It hadn't taken long before Philip and Genevieve were Daniel's captives. His warmth, his passion for the grape, and his lust for the world of wine made him irresistible.

Anxious to know more about his personal life, Genevieve asked, "Daniel, do you have a family? We haven't heard if there is a Madame LaGrande at the château." She hoped she wasn't being too forward.

"Alas, no. I have no wife or children. I am married to the vineyard and the grapes are my babies."

Genevieve smiled at his poetic description of his life.

He turned the conversation back to Château Beaulieu. "Though we are one of the smaller vineyards, we were one of the original First Great Classification Growths when the designations were established in 1955 and we continue to deserve our fine reputation." Daniel swirled his glass of cabernet sauvignon before bringing it to his lips. "The Château Beaulieu name conjures images of life's most special occasions: an important birthday, a milestone anniversaire. We are too expensive to drink every day, but, then, we are not a vin de table. Our pricing reflects quality, and we sell everything we produce."

"So," Genevieve said, "if we wanted to grow the business, we would need to bring in cheaper grapes from another vineyard and add a mass-market wine to our offering or raise our prices. Is that right?" Noticing Daniel stiffen, she raised both hands. "Don't panic. I'm not suggesting we do either of those things. I'm just asking an academic question."

He relaxed back into his chair.

"That must sound very American to you," Philip said. "We know Château Beaulieu was founded before the US was born. I promise you we respect the history of the vineyard and what has been accomplished over the centuries. We're in awe of how you and your team have kept the château on an ever-upward course, and we have no intention of interfering with success."

Philip lifted a linen napkin from three small baguettes, still warm from the oven. He offered the Quimper breadbasket to Daniel, who plucked a piece from the ceramic platter and ripped a bit from the end of his loaf. With his elbows on the table, he popped the yeasty morsel into his mouth. A few crumbs fell on the sky-blue scarf around his neck.

The rain had stopped, and clouds were breaking into whimsical shapes before blowing off to the east. The sun slanted into the small dining room, splashing Daniel's shock of white hair with a golden light. "Are you familiar with Clos Peyra?" he asked.

Philip and Genevieve looked at each other. "No," they said in unison, both shaking their heads.

"What is Clos Peyra?" Philip asked.

Daniel sat back and took a drink, savoring the wine before answering. "It's the vineyard next door to Château Beaulieu. It is maybe four hundred years older than we are. They say their history dates back to the eleventh century." He shrugged. "It may. It may not, but it is an old vineyard."

"Why is it called a clos rather than a château?" Genevieve was curious.

Daniel smiled. "Ah, une bonne question. A clos is a walled vineyard. It was used to protect the grapes from theft. Some clos were monasteries, and some vineyards still use the term even though they are no longer walled."

"You said Clos Peyra is our next-door neighbor?"

"Oui. After hundreds of years of ownership by the same French family, a Chinese family bought the vineyard ten years ago. Since then, they have tried to buy Château Beaulieu several times, twice while your cousin was still alive, and most recently just after he died."

"Really?" Philip's eyebrows arched. "That's very interesting. Lillie Langdon, the director of our foundation, told us the château across the road from us is owned by a Chinese family, too. Is that possible?"

Daniel's ice-blue eyes saddened. "It is. And that winery, Château Pitique is, well…" Daniel couldn't find words for what he wanted to say, so he left the sentence unfinished and went on to explain. "In the last decade, the Chinese began an intense love affair with French wine, particularly those of Bordeaux. Twenty percent of our wines are now exported to China. Those with means came to Bordeaux, began buying our vineyards and shipping home eighty percent of the wine they produced. By 2010, Chinese individuals and businesses owned more than a hundred seventy-five vineyards. It sounds like a lot, but with almost six thousand vineyards in Bordeaux, it's only about three percent of our wineries." He paused, filled his fork with the last bite of pasta, and popped it into his mouth.

Genevieve sat back. "I had no idea there had been a Chinese invasion in Bordeaux. Are they still buying?"

Daniel swallowed his food, wiped his mouth then draped his linen napkin back in his lap. He drained the last of his cabernet sauvignon, then said, "The pace has slowed to a trickle, in great part due to China's tighter control on overseas investments. Also, they have made it more difficult to get a visa to France. Those who made the investment early were lucky." He turned up his palms. "And then, there are some who are wishing to expand, like the Wangs wanting to buy Château Beaulieu."

"Do you know who handled the request on our behalf?"

"I don't, but I suppose it was someone at Holmes Fitch Smythson Morrow, the trustees who managed all the properties until you were found."

"Do you know David Weatherington?"

Daniel grinned and nodded his head. "He is fantastique, is he not? He has been to the château several times in the last few years. He is supérieur to work with. I do know it was not David who spoke to the agent from Clos Peyra." He knitted his brow and hummed for a moment. "Perhaps it was someone named Michael Holmes?"

"Sir Mark Holmes?" Genevieve said.

"Peut être."

"That makes sense. He was the principal trustee."

"Obviously, each overture was rejected," Philip said.

"Mais oui. There was never a question. The earl would never sell. He loved the château."

"Daniel, do you know why they want to buy Château Beaulieu?" Genevieve said.

"Ah, oui. It is a matter of growth and quality. It is impossible to grow a vineyard if it is run at maximum efficiency and you sell all your bottles at the highest price possible. It is very different than most luxury products. If Louis Vuitton wants to expand, they can buy more leather, make more bags, sell more product." He pouted his lips. "We cannot make more grapes, hein?" Daniel took Genevieve's hand. "And always remember, Genevieve, we do not grow grapes. We grow soil. If we grow the right soil, everything else will be fine. For Clos Peyra, acquiring Château Beaulieu gives them two things they need."

"What are those?" Genevieve asked.

"Terroir et Prestige."

TEN

GUARD LE RIO

The Earl and Countess of Crosswick
request the honor of your presence
at their home,

MAISON DE LANEY,
22 AVENUE FOCH,
75116 PARIS

SATURDAY, 28 JANUARY 2023
AT 5:30 P.M.

to celebrate the opening of
Le Musée des Beaux-Arts exhibition,
"The Women of Abstract Expressionism"

PARIS IN FULL designer regalia was a sight to behold. Through the Warwicks' front door, one dazzling couple after another made their entrance. A statuesque woman draped in a silver sheath with plunging neckline paused to pose for the *Vogue France* photographer and anyone else who might be looking. She accepted a faceted flute of Champagne from a tuxedoed server, greeted Philip and Genevieve, then disappeared into the growing throng of France's elite.

Jazz wafted from the landing at the top of the stairs where a quartet played in front of the Pollock. The music wove its way throughout Maison de Laney, sophisticated and cool.

Watching Philip and Genevieve greet their guests, no one would have ever known they were newcomers to the world of aristocracy. Philip was the picture of elegance in his Givenchy tuxedo. Not wanting to offend the French supporters of the musée and foundation, he had agreed with Genevieve that he should wear a French designer. He had, however, drawn the line when the House of Givenchy's personal shopper suggested an avant garde, star-patterned tuxedo that Philip thought would look perfect on a circus ringmaster.

Echoing the Helen Frankenthaler painting hanging in the grand salon, Genevieve carried out the theme of the evening, "The Women of Abstract Expressionism". Her long-sleeved gown, belted at the waist, was a showstopper with yellow, periwinkle blue and red splashes of color spilling across a billowing floor-length skirt. Diamonds flashing at her ears, a Crosswick heirloom diamond on her right ring finger, and her wedding band were just enough sparkle. She and Philip greeted each guest with the perfect mix of hauteur that the French love and elegant informality, making each person feel special to be in attendance.

Lillie Langdon had created the initial list, which Genevieve supplemented with a few friends and several English philanthropists she and Philip hoped would become donors. Few had declined the prized invitation.

Just as Philip and Genevieve finished greeting the Mayor of Paris, Genevieve looked back at the entrance and squealed. Through the doorway breezed a dazzling blonde, looking like an F. Scott Fitzgerald heroine. She held the arm of a dashing man, his warm good looks a perfect foil for her cool elegance.

"Becca! David!" Genevieve grabbed a fist-full of skirt in each hand, hiking it to mid-calf, and sprinted to the couple. She threw herself into Becca, squeezing hard. The pale beauty returned her lusty hug.

Genevieve released her friend into Philip's embrace and moved into David's outstretched arms. "You can't imagine how thrilled we are that you're here."

"I knew we'd be welcome, but I had no idea you'd be this overjoyed to see us." David Weatherington held Genevieve at arm's length, giving her a critical look. "What's going on that Becca and I don't know about?"

Philip pumped David's hand and slapped him on the back. "There's plenty of time to bring you up to date, but right now come in and meet some of Paris's posh people. Your job tonight is to schmooze them and convince everyone to donate lavishly to the foundation and the musée."

Genevieve looked around for someone to take Becca's coat,

but there was no one to be seen so she laid it on a bench. She slid her hand through the crook of Becca's arm and the two chatted their way into the music and laughter of the party. "After the masses have gone, we'll tell you all about what's been happening in the last few weeks."

There was mischief in Becca's eyes when she said, "David and I have something to tell you, too."

"What is it? From your smile, I bet it's something wonderful." Genevieve badgered Becca as she plucked two flutes off the tray of a passing server. "Tell me, tell me."

"I'll tell you after the party; after we hear all your news."

"You go ahead and start enjoying yourself." She put her hand on Becca's arm. "I've got to go tell Madame Morier no one's manning the door. Brace yourself for a small explosion when she hears the staff is falling down on the job."

She strode toward the kitchen, pushed through the swinging door, and squinted. The bright white lights were a stark contrast to the soft warm glow of lamps and the candlelight flickering throughout the party salons. Looking around the bustling room, Genevieve saw no trace of the woman in charge of Maison de Laney.

A chef was fussing with an hors d'oeuvre of potato slices, crème fraiche and caviar. Genevieve was about to ask him where Madame Morier might be, when the woman in question emerged from the dark kitchen office, smoothing her hair, and buttoning the front of her black silk blouse.

The moment she saw Genevieve, her eyes popped wide, and scarlet flooded her cheeks. "My lady," she said, rushing to

Genevieve. "Please excuse me." She plucked at her skirt to make certain it was in place. "I was just, um," she ran her tongue over her lips then wiped the edges of her mouth with her finger, "um, checking the wine. What may I do for you?"

Over madame's shoulder, Genevieve caught a glimpse of a man slipping from the shadow of the office and out the back door.

Genevieve was so surprised she couldn't speak for several seconds. At last, she said, "I, I… uh, came to tell you that no one is at the front door to greet people or take coats."

Thunder flashed across Madame Morier's face. "My lady. I shall remedy that at once." She spun on her heels and marched toward an unsuspecting underling. There was nothing for Genevieve to do but go back to the party.

Slipping his arm around Becca's waist and gripping David's shoulder, Philip ushered his two close friends into the midst of diving necklines, haute couture tuxedos, and flashing jewels.

At the far end of the room, Lillie Langdon stood in front of the glowing fireplace chatting with a group of men twice her age, all of whom were hanging on her every word. She dazzled, draped in midnight blue velvet, neckline high in the front and sweeping low in the back. Her long arms and elegant hands fluttered through the air emphasizing a point, teasing her admirers, touching a shoulder or patting a back as her laugh filled the air. Philip could feel her energy even from across the room.

"Brace yourself," he said. "We're going to make our way over to Lillie." The three of them wove through the salon, stopped every few feet by someone who wanted to meet Philip or tell him what a smashing party it was.

A breathtaking young twenty-something brunette grabbed his shoulders, kissed him on one cheek then the other, then planted her ruby lips on his mouth.

"Je suis Bernadette Lavigne, Émile's girlfriend. Thank you, my lord, for saving my darling boy from prison. He is so grateful, as am I." She held Philip's gaze and pressed her body against his. "I would do anything to repay you," she said. "Anything."

Her plea was melodramatic and filled with clumsy sensuality, and Philip couldn't help but smile. He took her hands from around his neck and let them fall to her side. "Lady Crosswick and I are glad we could help. I hope you enjoy the evening." As he moved back into the crowd he felt her eyes following him.

"What was that all about?" Becca snickered. "That young lady looked as if she wanted to take a bite out of you." She laughed. "Not that I blame her." She gave Philip a loud smack on the cheek. "You could get into quite a bit of trouble around here, couldn't you?"

"You have no idea, my friend." Philip rolled his eyes at Becca, then pressed forward until they got to Lillie.

"So, what's happening in this little corner of the world?" Philip leaned in and kissed Lillie on each cheek.

"Philip! Sir David!" Pleasure lit Lillie's face. She put a hand on Becca's arm. "Ms. Conway, I'm delighted to meet you and so pleased you were able to come. Genevieve hoped both of you would make it, and voila! Here you are."

She turned to the four men who were waiting to be introduced to Philip and his entourage and made the presentations. Then with a flourish, Lillie said, "Lord Crosswick, I'm happy to tell you that this evening, these four gentlemen have told me they have formed an alliance. Each of them will match the other's donation to the foundation's education fund starting this year, with a spectacular contribution of one million euros each."

"Indeed?" Philip said, eyes twinkling. He raised his Champagne glass and nodded. "Lady Crosswick and I will not forget your generosity. Thank you, gentlemen."

"What a smashing way to kick off Lord and Lady Crosswick heading up the musée and foundation," David chimed in. "Bully for you, chaps," he added, in his poshest English accent.

"Lillie, I'm sure you already have plans to make a big splash of this news, don't you?" Philip smiled at the four new donors.

"Oh, yes. We were just talking about grand ways to make the announcement. Monsieur Beaufoy has several clever ideas." She nodded at the president-directeur general of Credit Alliance. "We'll have a big reveal at the donors' party next month." Lillie beamed at her four conquests. "How does that sound, gentlemen?"

Though these men were top players in the world of finance, they were no match for Lillie's charm. Each was putty in her hands.

Philip leaned to whisper in her ear. "Well done, Lillie. It's obvious they never knew what hit them. You're pretty good at this."

Lillie felt a rush of pleasure at Philip's compliment and moved on to her next conquest.

Philip turned and, without taking a step, found himself in another small group comprised of David, Daniel LaGrande, and Émile de Laudre.

"Look who we have here." David slapped Philip on the back.

"David, you and Daniel are old friends, right? And it looks like you've met Émile. Daniel, have you two had a chance to talk?"

Daniel put his arm around Émile's shoulder and gave it a firm squeeze. "We have indeed, and I'm quite certain we understand each other perfectly. Don't you agree, Émile?"

Émile stood straight as a soldier. "Oui, Monsieur. Absolument." He gave Daniel a sharp nod and Philip a nervous smile.

Yesterday, within the first few minutes of the meeting, Philip and Genevieve were smitten by their charming managing director. They were lucky to have LaGrande heading Château Beaulieu and didn't want Émile upsetting the status quo. From all appearances, Daniel had the newest member of his staff well in hand.

Philip stopped a passing server, said something, then let him go about his business. "As you know, Daniel, after we spoke yesterday, I was anxious for you two to meet." Philip put his hand on Émile's shoulder. It was important for you to approve of this grand experiment before thrusting this bad boy on you and the vineyard."

"It's going to be my pleasure to torture this jeune coquin."

Everyone laughed but the young rascal Émile.

The server was back. "You requested whiskey shots, my lord?"

"I did, indeed. Perfect timing." Philip took small, faceted glasses from the server's tray and gave one to each person in their circle. "I think we need a toast. Here's to Émile's miraculous and hopefully speedy reformation, with special gratitude to everyone who is about to help him on his way."

"Santé," the group cheered, before tossing back their shots.

Hearing the shout, Genevieve searched the room for the uproar. Everywhere she looked, she saw beautiful people. There was no denying, the French were attractive. She grabbed a Champagne flute off the tray of a passing waiter and began to snake her way toward Philip.

"Geneviève! Geneviève, darling!" Genevieve stiffened hearing the French pronunciation of her name. She recognized the nasal accent of Elise Beaufoy. Though Elise was high on the Parisian social pecking order, it was clear that she wanted to add Lady Crosswick's title to her close circle. Genevieve wasn't having it.

She planted a smile on her lips and turned to greet the social climber.

"Ah, ma cherie. Quelle belle soirée." With her hair pulled back into a tight bun at the nape of her long neck, it was impossible to miss the stunning chandelier diamond earrings dangling from Elise's lobes. Genevieve felt them flap against her cheeks as Elise came in for la bise. "You have all the best people here, don't you? Have you heard? My husband is donating one million euro to the foundation."

"No, I hadn't heard, but that's wonderful." Genevieve was sure surprise shone in her eyes. "How marvelous! When did he decide to do that?"

"He decided last week when I told him what wonderful work the education fund is doing. I went to the Children's Art Forum you recommended and was very impressed avec les enfant."

"Elise." Delighted Elise would spread the word about their children's program, Genevieve offered a genuine smile. "I'm so pleased you attended the event. And I'm not surprised you were excited by what you saw. What the foundation team has accomplished on a shoestring is quite remarkable." She clinked the rim of her glass to Elise's flute. "Your contribution will give the program a real boost."

"C'est notre plaisir. Now, perhaps you will find a place for me on the foundation board." Her eyes had turned from warm to glacial and her over-plumped lips drew into a tight, frosty smile.

"There's no free lunch," Genevieve thought. "Well, Elise, I'll be happy to have that discussion with the board members." She had a sick feeling in the pit of her stomach. "Now if you'll excuse me, I need to circulate." She was already edging backward, trying to escape into the crowd.

Craning her neck, she again searched the room for Philip, who was nowhere to be seen. She drained her Champagne glass just as arms encircled her waist and hot breath teased her ear. "What's up, Lady Crosswick?"

She twirled in Philip's arms and planted a kiss on his lips. "Well, well, well. If it isn't my favorite husband." She kissed him again then leaned back in his arms. "I'll tell you what's up. Did you know Michel Beaufoy donated a million euros to the foundation's education fund?" She felt smug with her insider information.

"I did know that." Philip grinned. "He and three of his buddies each tossed in a million euros a year for the foreseeable future."

"How did you find out?"

"When I took Becca and David to see Lillie, she was with Beaufoy and his boys, and they shared the news." He loosened his arms from around Genevieve's waist. "According to Lillie, they just decided to do this last week."

Genevieve straightened his bowtie. "I know all about that." She went on to tell Philip about her conversation with Elise Beaufoy, ending with, "I can't believe we're going to have to work with her as the Presidente of the Cité du Vin Board and now she's trying to extort a position on our foundation board."

"Is there a seat open?"

"There is."

"Would it be so bad to have her on the board?"

"It would." Genevieve was emphatic.

"Really?" Philip looked surprised. "Why?"

Genevieve stuck three fingers in Philip's face. "She's a social climber, she's overbearing and I couldn't get the votes to put her on the board even if I wanted to, which I do not." She lowered a finger as she recited each reason. "Since just after we arrived in France, she's been trying to insinuate her way into my life and I don't want her there

Philip threw up both hands in defense. "Okay, okay. This is your territory, G. Yours and Lillie's. But you two might have to find a way to offer her a seat at the table."

"I guarantee Lillie will echo my sentiments when she hears what Elise is demanding. You should have seen how she turned from warm and saccharine sweet to frosty and frightening in the blink of an eye. It was clear she was daring me to cross her."

Genevieve felt a push in the back. When she turned, she was nose to nose with Bernard.

"I am so sorry, Lady Crosswick. I did not mean to shove you."

"That's quite all right, Bernard. There are a lot of people in this room, aren't there?"

"It is a beautiful party," he said, smiled, then turned back to his group of friends.

For a moment, Genevieve had forgotten they were surrounded by ears that shouldn't be hearing their conversation. She leaned into Philip and whispered, "Do you think anyone heard what we just said?"

"I hope not, but there's not much we can do about it now." He took her hand and led her into the foyer. "Where've you been? The last time I saw you, you were headed to the kitchen to find someone to greet guests and take coats."

Genevieve took a deep breath then blew it out. "You're not going to believe this." She proceeded to tell Philip about what she had witnessed in the kitchen.

Philip's laugh boomed through the hall. "Wow, who knew? I thought she was too frosty to…" he wiggled his eyebrows, "you know."

"God, Philip. Don't be such a twelve-year-old." Genevieve gave him a light shove on the shoulder.

"Did you recognize the guy?"

"No, thank goodness. I don't want to know who it is."

Philip's laugh ebbed to a chuckle.

"When she saw me I thought she was going to faint, she was so embarrassed. She couldn't get away from me fast enough." Genevieve bit her lower lip. "I guess I'm not so surprised that she has a lover, but I am surprised that they were in the kitchen doing whatever they were doing during the party. That seems out of character, doesn't it? I know she's used to having the run of the house, but do you think by having a tryst in the middle of our party she's flipping us the bird? I wonder if she's thinking about resigning as our chef de menage."

Philip smirked. "How would you feel about that if she did?"

"I don't know." She looked at the ceiling and thought for a moment. "She's terrifying, opinionated, inflexible, and has a rather nasty streak, but she knows everything about this property. She knows the history of the house. She runs it to perfection. And, as we know, having looked at the books, she's almost miserly with the household budget and won't spend anything that's not absolutely necessary." She shook her head before saying, "You're going to be surprised to hear me say I think she's exactly what we need at this property."

Taking her face in his hands, Philip stared into Genevieve's eyes before brushing a kiss on the tip of her nose. "Actually, G, I'm not the least bit surprised. One of the many things you do well is recognize quality and Madame Morier is quality from the top of her well-coiffed head to the tip of her Louboutin-shod tootsies."

"Whoa, you know Christian Louboutin shoes?" Genevieve's eyebrows shot up.

"Embarrassing, isn't it? I must have overheard you talking about them to someone." Philip spun her around and swatted her on her bottom. "We need to get back to our guests, cute girl."

Genevieve looked at her watch. "Seven thirty. People should start leaving soon, don't you think?"

Philip shook his head. "I don't think so. Not while there's still plenty to drink and a morsel left to eat."

Genevieve groaned, and as she and Philip moved back into the fray, they heard angry voices bellowing from the salon, followed by glass breaking. The crowd silenced, then resumed almost immediately.

"What the hell?" Philip craned his neck in the direction of the ruckus but could see nothing but people eating, drinking, and enjoying themselves.

"What in the world was that?" Genevieve tugged Philip's arm, pulling him into the crowd. "I think it came from over by the fireplace. I hope no one's hurt."

They snaked their way to the far end of the room. When they edged out of the crowd, they found Daniel and Bernard hissing at each other, hushed, angry words flying back and forth in rapid French. Hank Shou, Bernard's long-time friend from China, watched the heated exchange, fear in his eyes and beads of sweat glistening on his upper lip. At their feet, one server picked shards of glass off the plush rug while another sopped up Champagne from the precious Savonnerie replica carpet.

Philip saw Daniel's hand clench into a fist and grasped his wrist before he could draw back and punch Bernard. Philip's face froze in a smile meant for the few guests near enough to see the confrontation. Most of the partygoers were so consumed by their own conversations and merrymaking that they hadn't noticed the brouhaha.

"What the hell?" Philip hissed, drawing the two into a tight circle. "What's going on here?" He looked from Daniel, red faced and wild eyed, to Bernard, who had already composed himself.

"Lord Crosswick, please accept my deepest apologies for our outburst. Daniel and I simply had un malentendu, a misunderstanding, and allowed it to get a bit out of hand." He put his arm around Daniel, who stiffened at his touch. "I assure you it was nothing. N'est-pas vrai, Daniel?"

Daniel pushed out of Bernard's grasp. "Lord Crosswick." He stood in front of Philip, head bowed. "There is nothing I can say."

Watching the events unfold, Genevieve had no idea what had just happened between the two men, but her heart wrenched when Daniel raised his head and she saw the tortured look on his face. She grabbed his hand. He patted hers, squeezed her shoulder and walked into the crowd. She searched the guests for Bernard, but he was nowhere to be seen, nor was Hank.

"Well, that was a strange scene," Philip muttered into her ear. "I don't think those two like each other very much."

"To say the least. I thought Daniel was going to punch Bernard. Thank goodness you stepped in to save the day." She stretched on tiptoe to kiss Philip on the cheek.

Just as Philip started to reply, Lillie appeared with an elegant, aging couple, donors who were anxious to meet Lord and Lady Crosswick. Philip and Genevieve plastered their benefactor smiles on their faces and went back to work.

ELEVEN

The clock in the foyer chimed eleven o'clock. The last party guests had just been ushered out the door and five exhausted people were draped across the overstuffed sofas and chairs of the grand salon. An army of catering staff rolled through the room like a Zamboni, leaving everything pristine in their wake, glasses, napkins, and plates gone as if they had never littered the salon. Surfaces were polished and the floor had been vacuumed without disturbing the weary bunch.

"Who's hungry?" Philip dragged his feet off the coffee table, put them on the floor and pushed himself to a more upright position.

Perking up at the idea of food, Becca said, "I bet none of us had much to eat during the party, which was smashing, by the way. Let's go to the kitchen before the caterers take away all the food."

"Great idea," David agreed, getting a second wind at the prospect of eating.

They dragged themselves through the house and into the kitchen, still bustling with end-of-party activity.

Madame Morier stood in the center of the room watching

every person, particularly those returning wine bottles to storage. She trusted no one and thought everyone suspect. When she saw the group push through the swinging door, she moved to intercept them.

"What are you all doing in here? What do you need?" she snapped, her tone sharp enough to cause the group to take a step back.

David nudged Philip forward. He scowled back at his friend, then looked at madame with pleading eyes. "We've come begging for food. None of us ate during the party, too busy trying to pry money out of everyone's pockets. And that's made us very hungry. Is there anything left?"

She flashed an uncharacteristic smile, much to the relief of the beggars. "Mais oui. I'll have Chloé fix plates for you. She'll bring them to the study. You will be comfortable there, and out of the way," she added. "Allez, allez." She shooed them from the kitchen with a flick of her hand.

As directed, they ambled back across the foyer and through the double doors into the cozy study. Philip put a flame to the fire already set on the hearth and they settled in, each person flopping into a comfy chair.

"Crikey! She's no Mrs. MacIntosh," David said, referring to the motherly Scottish head housekeeper at Wilmingrove Hall.

"You have no idea how often Genevieve and I have lamented that in the last few weeks. At first, she scared the hell out of us. Now we're just grateful when she's civil."

David slapped Philip on the back. "I never thought it would suck to be you, old man, but in this case…"

Lillie leaned forward in her chair. "The last couple of weeks while I've been working with her on this event, I've gotten to know her and I quite like her," she said.

"Do you?" Genevieve scoffed. "What's your secret?"

"I think my secret is, I don't have any power over her. I don't hold her fate in my hands. She doesn't fear me."

Genevieve and Philip barked a laugh in unison. "You're not suggesting she's afraid of us?" Philip said.

"I don't think she's afraid of you, but maybe she fears what you could do to her. You know what I mean?"

"Maybe I do." Genevieve furrowed her brow, thinking. "You mean she's been running Maison de Laney for the last fifteen years without interference, and now we're here, and she's concerned we might want her gone. Is that what you're saying?"

"It is." Lillie crisscrossed her legs on the cushion of her chair. She pulled the full skirt of her gown over her knees, so she looked as if she were sitting on a blue cloud.

"You know, that had never occurred to me," Philip said as he sat down in a chair next to the fireplace. "You might have something there, Lillie."

"I guess the best thing would be for us to tell her we appreciate how well she runs the Maison, don't you think, Philip?"

"We'll do it tomorrow. Why don't we add a raise and an additional week of holiday to prove our point?"

David grimaced. "I think you'd better check to see what you're paying her and how much holiday time she gets now."

"Spoken more like our accountant than our attorney, David." Philip laughed then put his finger to his lips. "Shh," he said, as the sound of a trolley could be heard in the foyer.

Over a feast of leftover hors d'oeuvres and Champagne, Lillie reported what a success the night had been. Several people had committed to making sizable donations to the Foundation. Toasts were made and applause filled the room. Philip and Genevieve updated David and Becca on the past week's events, starting with their near-disastrous arrival in Paris, moving to the story of Émile's botched attempt to extort five million euros from them, and ending with the ultimate resolution of Émile going to Château Beaulieu to work as a laborer. Lillie interjected, telling David and Becca how Émile had gotten his idea from a book written by Bernard Reines, the LMBA's director.

"You're kidding me!" David choked, laughing. "That's unbelievable! You two caught up in another book-inspired crime. Wow."

Genevieve threw up her hands. "I know, David. We Warwicks are becoming a bit of a cliché, aren't we?" She turned to Becca. "Before we talk about anything else, how is Olivia?" Becca's daughter, who had caused havoc at Wilmingrove Hall last fall, was a patient at a private mental hospital near the Warwick's family seat. It could be years before she was released, if ever.

"We saw her just last week," Becca's eyes misted. "She's doing well, making excellent progress."

"I'm so pleased. Maybe there will be a happy ending to this story."

Becca's cool smile didn't reach her eyes. David squeezed her hand and warmth flowed back into her lovely face.

"On another subject, as you two know, Philip and I want to do something meaningful with the wealth that fell into our laps. We're working with Lillie on a project in Bordeaux that will impact both young people and wine growers. So, beware: we're going to be picking your creative minds."

"That sounds exciting. Can you tell us more?" Becca said.

"By all means." Genevieve directed everyone's attention to Lillie, who described the project with enthusiasm.

"So, there you have it," Philip said. "All it takes is lots of organization, creativity and euros."

"You know, Philip, you can count on us to spend your money!" David gave his friend a sly smile.

"We know we can," Genevieve said. "But enough about us. Becca, you said you and David had something to tell us." She rubbed her hands and curled her lips into a Cheshire cat smile. "I think I know what it is."

"There's no way you can know," David said.

Beaming, Becca looked at David. "I bet she does."

"I am very much an outsider in this group and I'm quite sure I know what your news is," Lillie chimed in.

Philip looked blank. "What are you all talking about?"

"Wait, wait, wait. Before you say anything, just in case I'm right." Genevieve grabbed the bottle of Veuve Clicquot and went around the room refilling glasses. She returned the bottle to the chiller and sat back in her chair. "Okay. Tell us. What's your news?"

David stood up, walked to Becca, and pulled her to stand. "Last week, Becca and I went to Gleneagles for a few days before coming here." He took Becca's hand and grinned at her. "While we were there, I asked her to marry me."

"I knew it, I knew it!" Genevieve shrieked. She shot from her chair and engulfed Becca in a hug. Then she moved to David. "You! You!" She kissed him on both cheeks. "You're smarter than you look, aren't you? I knew at Christmas something serious was going on."

Becca pulled a ring from her skirt pocket and slipped it on her finger.

"Stunning," Lillie said, examining the large square-cut diamond. On her other hand, Becca wore the Laney family heirloom given to her years ago by Philip's cousin, Jonathon.

David beamed. Philip shook his hand, then pulled him into a bearhug. "Good job, man. I can't wait to hear how you're going to manage living on two continents. Ha!"

"We're still working that out. It's all rather new," David said.

Genevieve squealed when she saw the ring. "That's a stunner," she said, her excitement bubbling over. "Now, Philip, will you please make a toast?"

"It would be my pleasure." Philip raised his glass. "To two of our favorite people. It's been a bumpy journey that's brought you to this very special place. Thank you for letting us be a part of the road you've traveled and thank you for letting us continue to walk down the path with you. We know it will be an exciting journey. Here's to your happiness." Glasses clinked, kisses were exchanged all around, and the promise of a bright future filled the room.

TWELVE

"I LOVE THIS." GENEVIEVE looked out of the window at the fields racing by. "I've always wanted to take the TGV. Look, Philip." She pointed to the electronic board on the wall at the end of the aisle. The digital readout announced 297 kilometers per hour. "That's almost 185 miles an hour, isn't it?"

"It is. Not as fast as a Formula One race car, but pretty fast."

"And a heck of a lot safer." Genevieve put her hand on top of Philip's, lying on the armrest. "Yet another adventure," she said, turning back to the window.

Philip's phone vibrated on his tray table. Though he didn't recognize the number, he hit accept anyway. "Oui," he said. "Daniel, bonjour." A smile curled his lips. Let me put you on speaker so Genevieve can hear."

"Bonjour, Lady Crosswick." Daniel's sober voice crackled through the weak connection. "I am just calling to see if you are still coming to Château Beaulieu."

"Of course, Daniel. We're on our way. Did you think our plans had changed?"

There was silence on the line. "Daniel, did we lose you? Can you hear me?" Philip asked.

"Non, non. I am here. I just want to tell you how wonderful it was to spend time with you in Paris. I loved meeting you." Again there was silence.

"We so enjoyed meeting you, Daniel. We're looking forward to working with you." Genevieve smiled at Philip.

"Is there anything else?" Philip looked at his screen that was announcing a call from Duncan. "I have a call from our son that I should take. I can call you back."

"No, Lord Crosswick. That is not necessary. I shall just say goodbye. Goodbye, Lady Crosswick, goodbye."

"We'll see you soon, Daniel," Genevieve said, but he said nothing in return. "We're looking forward to having dinner with you this evening. Bye."

Philip hit 'accept' and put the phone to his ear. "Hi, buddy. We've been calling you." He was silent for a moment before he said, "Huh. Okay, Okay. Let me put you on speaker."

"Hi, darling. What's going on?"

"Hi, Mom. I was just telling Dad that Ella has bronchitis, so Julia is going to stay here with the kids. I'm taking a commercial flight tonight. When Ella's well the three of them can come on the Bombardier if you don't mind the plane being here for a week or so. What do you think of that?"

Genevieve looked at Philip. "Your dad and I think you shouldn't come until we find out for certain what happened to the plane."

Philip leaned closer to the phone and kept his voice quiet.

"We have no idea yet what's going on and until we do, nobody should use the plane."

Duncan hesitated. "That makes sense. I'm sure Julia will agree the smartest thing is to wait until Ella recovers and we know there isn't any danger flying the plane. But I'll be there tomorrow," he said firmly.

"All right, if you're not worried about coming. We're anxious to see you. We're disappointed Julia and the kids won't be with you, but we don't want them here until it's safe."

"Where are you two?"

"We're on the bullet train to Bordeaux."

Excitement buzzed in Duncan's voice. "How fast are you going?"

Philip looked back up at the monitor. "We're slogging along at 299 kilometers an hour. Wish they'd get this old crate moving." The three of them laughed.

"Text us your arrival time and we'll pick you up. It's going to be exciting to explore the vineyard together." Genevieve couldn't stop smiling at the prospect of her son coming to Château Beaulieu. "Bye, sweetheart. Give Julia and the kids a kiss and tell Ella to get better fast."

"Bye, buddy." Philip hung up and chuckled under his breath.

"What?" She gave him a playful shove on his shoulder. "Why are you laughing at me?"

"I'm not laughing at you." His gaze lingered on his annoyed wife. "I'm just enjoying your enthusiasm over Duncan coming. You're such fun to watch."

She shook her head and patted Philip's hand. "I know I'm cheap entertainment."

"I wouldn't say cheap." He gave her a full-throated laugh.

"In keeping with my spendthrift reputation, I think I'll go get something to drink." She reached into her handbag and pulled out her wallet. "What do you want?" She kissed his cheek.

"If they have an iced tea with lots of ice, that would be perfect."

"That's unlikely. Second choice?"

"A beer and a bottle of water, but not mixed, please."

"I'll see what I can do." She slid between Philip's knees and the seat in front of him, felt him pinch her bottom, and knew she would have been disappointed if he hadn't.

The line was long at the café-bar, but the service was efficient and within a few minutes Genevieve was headed back to the first-class car with drinks and plenty of things to nibble. Humming and smiling, she moved down the aisle, swaying with the movement of the train.

As she approached their seats, ice hit the pit of her stomach. Philip stared at a piece of stationery, his jaw clenched, lips drawn tight, and color flooding his cheeks. After loving this man for forty years, Genevieve knew when something was wrong. Three more steps and she was in front of her husband. "What is it? What's the matter, Philip?"

"Sit down," he said through clenched teeth.

Genevieve edged back into her seat, holding on to her goodies as best she could. "Philip, what the hell is going on? What is that?"

He took the drinks and she put the chips and peanuts on her tray. He handed her a sheet of paper.

"I opened my briefcase to get the report on this year's wine sales and this was on top." He waved a thick, cream-colored envelope. Philip's name was scrawled across the front in black ink. In the same strong handwriting, someone had written:

> *The water in your gas tank*
> *was only the beginning.*
> *Your lives are in danger at the vineyard.*
> *People will die.*
> *Stay away.*

THIRTEEN

THE BLOOD DRAINED from her face. Genevieve couldn't breathe. She had stood next to death at Wilmingrove Hall and she didn't want to do it again. She tried to reread the note, but the words swam on the page. She blinked. She blinked again and drops of water plopped onto the stationery. She looked at Philip. His face was stone, his eyes steel.

"This is a little late," he spat. He took the note from Genevieve, put it flat on the tray and snapped a photo with his phone. With his thumb, he scrolled through his contacts until Boucher's name appeared.

"I just opened my briefcase. This was sitting on top of my papers. Call me," he wrote, then sent the text. Before he could lay his phone back on the tray, it rang.

"Boucher, I..." Philip was immediately interrupted.

"Où êtes-vous? Are you on your way to Bordeaux? Mon Dieu, you are not flying in the Bombardier, are you?" Boucher's rapid-fire questions shot through the phone.

"No, we're on the TGV. The jet is in Washington, D.C. Captain Bruni flew there two days ago to bring our kids to Bordeaux tomorrow." Philip brought the BEA detective up to date with the family's change of plans. "And now, according to the note, Genevieve and I are headed into the eye of the storm." Beads of sweat lined Philip's upper lip.

"This is good that your children are not coming. Lord Crosswick, I am certain the note was written to frighten you. You survived an aeronautical event, what could possibly happen at a vineyard, you drink some bad wine?" Philip could hear Boucher chuckle at the other end of the phone. "Pardon. I made a petit blague, a little joke."

Philip put his head in his hand, not at all amused.

The inspector went on. "Put the envelope and note back in votre briefcase. Try not to touch them. Use a tissue, anything to keep your hands off the paper and the case."

"What should we do with it?"

"I shall send an officer to meet the train. When you arrive in Bordeaux, remain in your seats. The officer will board the train and come to you."

Philip massaged his left temple. "So, you need my briefcase as well as the note?"

"Absolument." Boucher was emphatic. "Disturb nothing. Now, if you will excuse me, I shall call our bureau in Bordeaux."

"Of course, Inspector. Merci."

Philip stared past Genevieve at the fields streaking by. For a long time, he didn't speak and, though she knew him better than anyone in the world, she couldn't read his expression. She put her hand on his cheek and studied his blank face before saying, "I can't tell what you're thinking. What's going on in this head?"

Philip twisted in his seat to look at Genevieve. He laced his fingers through hers but said nothing.

"Philip," Genevieve said, trying to control her annoyance.

"You're not going to like what I'm about to say." His expression gave away nothing and a seed of fear began to blossom in the pit of her stomach.

"I've had enough."

Confused, Genevieve waited for him to explain, but no explanation came. "What do you mean?"

Her vacant expression told Philip she didn't understand what he was saying. Though he didn't mean to, he raised his voice. "I'm telling you I don't want the money anymore. Since we received this inheritance, we've been plagued by one dangerous event after another. We had a wonderful, perfect life before all of this. We were prosperous, happy, and safe. This isn't worth it. I don't want the title and I want to give the money back."

Struggling to believe what she was hearing, Genevieve searched his eyes for any indication he was making a joke. There was none. "You're serious."

Philip attempted a smile but failed. "I told you that you wouldn't like what I had to say."

"That's the only thing you have right in this conversation." Her head swimming, Genevieve pulled her hand from Philip's, sat back in her seat, and stared out the window until they pulled into the Gare de Bordeaux-Saint-Jean.

⁂

Passengers struggled into coats, gathered newspapers and magazines, and made their way down the aisle to the exit.

Still reeling from Philip's announcement, Genevieve turned from the window to look at her husband. "Obviously, we need to talk more about the inheritance, but for now, shouldn't we keep this between the two of us?"

"Of course, we should." Philip reached for her hand and squeezed it. "I just wanted you to know what I've been thinking."

Genevieve rolled her eyes and said, "*Now* he wants to share his feelings. This is going to be quite a back and forth. And for the record, I think now that you've embraced your link to the past and the future, you're crazy to even consider giving back the inheritance." She tilted her head then went on. "Changing the subject dramatically, I wonder how long we'll have to wait for Boucher's people."

"I'd say not long. Look." Philip nodded toward a lean woman of about forty, wearing a limp trench coat, her short, brown hair fringed around her square face. She pushed toward them against the wave of departing travelers. "You think she might be the officer?"

"Hmm. Maybe." Genevieve chuckled under her breath.

"Bonjour. Lord and Lady Crosswick?" she said when she arrived at their seats.

"We are." Philip stood up and moved into the aisle, now clear of passengers. "And you are with the BEA?"

"Oui. I am Officiere Palmarie. You have the briefcase?"

Philip reached up to the narrow luggage shelf above his seat. Careful to only handle his valise where he had wrapped his

Burberry scarf around it, he handed it to the officer. "I'd like the scarf back and do you have a receipt for the briefcase?"

Palmarie looked surprised at the request. She shrugged her shoulders. "Rohh la la," she grunted. "Call the Paris bureau if you wish." She took the case and was gone before Philip could respond.

"Well, that was strange," Genevieve said as she slid across Philip's seat to the aisle. "I thought the officer would want to talk to you and find out the details of what happened." She tugged on her coat then plucked her purse from the hook.

"Maybe they'll call later to set up an interview. Don't forget your gloves." He pointed to where the fingers of her black kid gloves peeked out from between the seats.

As Genevieve reached back across the seats for her gloves, she looked through the window and saw Palmarie flanked by two burly men, all hustling toward the exit. "Look at that," she said to Philip. "She has a security escort. I'm glad to see they're taking this so seriously."

He leaned over her shoulder just in time to see the three agents retreat through the door to the street.

"Lord and Lady Crosswick."

Philip and Genevieve turned in unison to see a tall man with short salt-and-pepper hair standing in the aisle.

"Yes," Philip said.

"I am Detective Boulaine from the Bordeaux bureau of the BEA." He offered an official-looking badge, then put it back in the pocket of his topcoat.

"You're from the BEA?" Genevieve asked.

"Oui. Were you not expecting me? Inspector Boucher said he told you I would meet you on the train, did he not?"

"Shit," Philip said under his breath.

"Monsieur? Qu'est-ce que c'est?" Boulaine cocked his head. "What is the matter? Do you have the briefcase for me?"

"No." Philip and Genevieve looked at each other in disbelief. "I'm afraid we gave the case to someone else, perhaps the people who are trying to kill us."

FOURTEEN

AFTER TWO HOURS of intense conversation with officials at the BEA and Inspector Boucher on Zoom from Paris, Philip and Genevieve were now speeding through the countryside on their way to Château Beaulieu on the outskirts of Saint-Émilion, a picturesque medieval town whose fame far exceeded its size. Exhausted by the day's events, the pair had retreated into their own thoughts during the forty-five-minute ride to their château.

Henri navigated their Citroen C6 limousine through undulating fields lined with rows of bare winter vines. Though they were dormant above ground, below they were busy drawing energy from the soil into the roots in preparation for spring, when the plants would explode with new shoots.

Just as Genevieve was about to ask Henri how much farther it was to the château, the car turned left between two stone walls inset with large, bronze plaques that announced, "Château Beaulieu." They proceeded slowly down a lane flanked on both sides by linden trees, which touched each other's outstretched branches overhead. Now leafless, they stood at attention, greeting everyone who drove beneath their glory.

"Venus's very own trees," Genevieve said to herself.

"What was that?" Philip said.

She turned her head from the window to look at him. "I just said how wonderful it is to have the allée lined with linden trees. They're dedicated to Venus, you know, the goddess of love and fidelity."

"Interesting."

"Just wait until the spring. The smell is wonderful." She smiled at Philip. "I love linden trees. They're a very old species. You'll see. They have a mysterious, spiritual aura."

"If you say so." Philip took Genevieve's hand and squeezed it. "I'm so lucky to be married to someone so full of useless information."

"You're such a wise ass." She shook her head and smiled at Philip. "Trust me, there's more where that came from." She looked back at the road just as they came to the end of the lane and made a slight right onto a circular drive. "Philip, look!"

Before them stood a classic château, its limestone glowing in the winter sun. On either side of the four-panel burgundy door, arched French doors graced the length of the elegant façade, while white shutters stood at attention like soldiers guarding each window.

"What do you think, Lady Crosswick?" Henri asked as he pulled to a stop at the front door. "Is it what you expected?"

Genevieve admired the ornamental olive trees, planted in aging stone pots, dotting the front terrace. "It's perfection, Henri. Absolute perfection."

"But, given the House of Crosswick's taste for excellence,

I'm not the least bit surprised." Philip opened the car door. He stepped out and, mesmerized by the grandeur of their château, tried to channel the spirit of his ancestor, Philip George Winston Laney, 9TH Earl of Crosswick, the force behind the family's two acquisitions in France. He closed his eyes, waiting for his distant cousin's spirit to course through his veins. It did not. He opened his eyes and looked again at the château, feeling nothing but admiration for the stunning property.

"What are you doing?" Genevieve took his hand.

"I'm just trying to feel the 9TH Earl's presence."

"Are you?" She snorted and peered at Philip through dark glasses. She leaned into his side and whispered, "And you want to give all of this up?"

Ignoring her, he said, "Maybe you should try to get in touch with Charlotte. I bet she spent a lot of time here."

Genevieve snatched her sunglasses from her face and squinted at the top floor of the house. "Of course she did!" She gasped. "I hadn't thought about Charlotte's ghost since Madam Morier showed us the wedding portrait." She clapped her hands. "Won't it be wonderful if she's here? You can bet, I'll be sniffing for roses."

"I'm sure you will be." Philip blew into his fisted hands. "Let's go in. It's cold out here."

Henri pushed open the heavy front door and stood aside.

Genevieve held her breath as she crossed the threshold. This was the fifth property of Philip's inheritance they had visited in the last six months. Each residence was breathtaking, beyond anything the couple could have imagined owning, and each residence had been full of history and adventure. Genevieve hoped Château Beaulieu would treat them well and allow them to live the simple, beautiful life associated with a vineyard in Bordeaux.

"In this fantasy château, what could possibly go wrong?" she said under her breath and walked into the bright foyer.

"What did you say?" Philip asked as he leaned over her shoulder and took in the warm beauty of the entry hall.

"Oh, nothing," she said. "Isn't this perfect?" She turned where she stood, admiring the glowing limestone floors, boiserie paneling scrubbed to a dusty green patina, and light, graceful furnishings.

"Bonjour, bonjour!" Through a doorway under the sweeping stairs, a woman strode into the foyer. She was about forty, wearing a navy-blue apron and wiping her hands on a white linen towel. "Lord and Lady Crosswick, bienvenue. I am Delphine Dumont, house manager for Château Beaulieu." She glanced at her palms, grabbed a fist full of skirt in each hand, and bounced an awkward curtsy. She looked at the driver. "Henri, take the bags to Lord and Lady Crosswick's room. Do you know which one it is?"

"Mais oui." Henri was already on his way up the stairs, a bag in each hand.

Turning her attention back to Philip and Genevieve, she said, "You were quite delayed, weren't you?"

Unprepared for the question, Philip stuttered. "Uh, well, uh, yes. Yes, we were."

Genevieve jumped in. "Madame Dumont—"

"Please, call me Delphine."

"Of course, Delphine. We decided to spend a bit of time in Bordeaux before coming to the château. We went to Le Quatrieme Mur, the restaurant in the Opera House, drank some crémant and people watched. We had a wonderful time. I hope we didn't upset anyone's plans."

"Non, non, non. C'est bon." She shook her head and the banana clip wrangling her thick hair wobbled back and forth. "Come with me. I shall show you to your room." She dashed up the stairs, with Philip and Genevieve trying their best to keep up. "I am certain you want to rest," she said, looking back at them as she hit the top step. "Dinner will be served at seven thirty, unless you would prefer a different time? And Daniel is joining you, n'est ce pas?"

"Yes, he'll dine with us. But I want to see him before dinner. We have greetings from Madame Morier to deliver to him."

Delphine whipped around on the stairs to face Philip and Genevieve. "Oh la la!" She threw her hands up. "That woman has such a beguin on Daniel!"

Philip and Genevieve stopped just short of smashing into Delphine.

"A beguin?" Philip's mouth twisted as he said the word.

"I think you say crush. She fancies him. You know…" She pooched her lips together and made kissing sounds.

Genevieve's mouth dropped open. When she realized it was agape, she shut it with a loud snap of her teeth. "You think Madame Morier likes," she wiggled her eyebrows up and down, "you know, really likes Daniel LaGrande?"

"Absolument. They used to go back and forth from here to Paris, then back here again. But that was years ago. For quite a while now they have been just friends, but perhaps, how do you say…?" She pouted her lips and drew her brows together, then her face brightened. "Ah oui!" She raised her finger in the air and said, "Friends with benefits." She turned back around and ran the rest of the way up the stairs while Genevieve clamped her hand over her mouth to stifle a laugh.

"Daniel is in the wine office. I shall get you settled, then I must get back to the kitchen."

"If you can just show us where our room is, we'll take it from there," Philip said.

As soon as Delphine left, Genevieve collapsed onto the bed, laughing. "Can you imagine, Philip? Mean Madame Morier has a crush on darling Daniel? But that makes no sense. I'm pretty sure I witnessed her with another man the night of the party."

"I have to admit, I didn't see that coming. But who says she has to be a one-man woman?"

"Good point."

"I didn't know what to say when Delphine questioned us about being late. Since we aren't supposed to tell anyone about the note and the woman stealing my briefcase." Philip pulled his shirt out of the waistband of his jeans and began unbuttoning it. "You, however, were brilliant." He leaned over and kissed her on the nose. "Listen, cute girl, I'm going to stay here while you go see Daniel. I want to shower and unpack. I'll see him at dinner."

"Okie dokie." She returned his kiss, but hers was full on the mouth.

Genevieve skipped down the stairs, excited to see their new friend again, and perhaps learn more about his relationship with their Paris house manager. Thinking about the two of them together, she couldn't help smiling. As she crossed the back terrace, she stopped. The sun hung low in the sky, just above the hundreds of perfect rows of vines and she felt the sting of tears as she stared at the stunning panorama. Maybe Philip couldn't feel the 9TH Earl's presence yet, but Genevieve was sure Charlotte's spirit wafted beside her.

She shivered at the cold and continued to the small building, which had a sign that said "Bureau de Vin." Pulling open the door, she breathed in the warm air and found herself in a small lobby. Classical music wafted from an open door and soft light spilled out into the hall.

"Daniel," she called. "Daniel?" she called again as she walked to what she assumed was his office.

The room was classic, just like the man. Rugged brick floors complemented hand-buffed oak-paneled walls. On the corner of Daniel's massive desk, a vintage cut-glass bowl was filled with corks and an open bottle of Château Beaulieu cabernet sauvignon sat on a copper tray.

Genevieve cleared her throat. There was no answer. Daniel's tall-backed leather chair was turned toward the window so he couldn't be seen. Perhaps he's on the phone, she thought. She walked around his desk. He didn't look at her. She walked toward him until they were just feet apart. His elbow rested on the arm of the chair, but his fingers were splayed; they had not long ago held a glass of wine. The glass lay in his lap, ruby red wine spilled across his grey wool pants.

Genevieve didn't understand what she was seeing… until she looked into Daniel's intense blue eyes that had sparkled with life the last time she saw him. Now, all their exuberance and vitality was gone. And so was Daniel.

Daniel LaGrande was dead, and the note on the train was coming true.

FIFTEEN

Though it seldom snowed in Bordeaux, a few flakes wafted past the window in the study. Genevieve sat staring into the fire, a paisley pashmina snug around her shoulders. The pot of tea Delphine had left steaming on the table next to her an hour ago was untouched and cold. The sorrow of Daniel LaGrande's heart attack yesterday sat in her chest like a stone.

"This is irrational," she told herself. "We only knew him briefly and he was not a young man." She rose, took a poker from the fireplace and stirred the fire before adding another log.

"G, we're back. I brought you a present." She jumped at Philip's voice and turned to see two handsome Warwick men walk through the door.

"Hi, Mom." Duncan's broad smile washed over Genevieve like the sun coming from behind a cloud.

Her eyes brimming with tears, Genevieve rose on tiptoes and threw her arms around her son. His firm hug quelled her sadness and replaced it with strength and a calming energy.

"It seems I got here just in time." Duncan held his mother at arm's length to look at her. "I leave you for a month and everything falls apart! The jet, the painting, our managing director! What the hell, guys?" Duncan's grin crept into his eyes, and he wiped away a tear clinging to his mother's jaw, then he sobered. "I have to say, I'm pretty concerned about what's going on here."

Genevieve gave him a kiss and another squeeze before releasing him. "I can't say it's been smooth sailing since we got here. But before we get into the discussion of the perils of France, are you exhausted? Are you hungry? What do you want to drink?" Now in full mom-mode, Genevieve bombarded him with comfort questions.

"It's taken care of, G. We saw Delphine on the way in. She's bringing a tray." Philip slid his arm around her and stuck out his cheek. "Do you have a spare kiss for me?" He accepted the peck and ambled to an overstuffed chair opposite Genevieve, then motioned for Duncan to sit on the sofa facing the fire.

"Duncan, tell your mom what you and Julia talked about before you left."

Duncan unwound the burgundy scarf from around his neck and sat down. "Jeeze, Dad. You want to get right down to it, don't you?"

"Why not? This is going to make your mother very happy."

Genevieve looked back and forth between them, feeling a tickle of anticipation. "All right, you two. What is it? Do you want me to start guessing?"

Duncan studied the muffler and flipped the fringe with his fingers before looking at Genevieve. He took a deep breath and let it out.

Exasperated, Genevieve threw up both hands. "Duncan! Out with it."

"Okay, okay." He lay the scarf on the sofa beside him and rested his hands in his lap. "As you know, Julia and I have been talking about how we could help with the estate and all its moving parts. When you called yesterday morning with the news about LaGrande's death, it seemed pretty obvious what we should do."

Genevieve leaned forward in her chair, watching Duncan fold and unfold his hands. "And what do you and Julia think that is?"

For several seconds, the room was silent except for the crackling fire. Before Duncan could speak, Delphine came through the door carrying a large brass tray filled with tempting treats.

Duncan jumped up, took the heavy tray from Delphine, and put it on a small, ornate sideboard. She pulled a bottle of white Bordeaux from an apron pocket and handed it to Duncan with a wink and a quick smile.

Duncan tore a small baguette lengthwise, smeared the bottom with butter, piled it with thinly sliced ham and Gruyere, popped the top on and took a bite. "Hmmm." His eyes rolled as he inhaled the smell of the fresh bread and chewed. He picked up the bottle. "Shall I?" he asked, his voice muffled through the jambon beurre.

"By all means." Genevieve watched her son slice the foil, screw the worm into the cork and pull it out with a quiet thunk. He poured a glass and handed it to Genevieve.

"Thank you," she said. "Now, maybe you could tell me what your big revelation is."

Duncan handed a glass to his father then poured one for himself. "It's not a big revelation, Mom. It's an idea we think has merit."

"Go on."

He sat back down on the sofa and put his plate on the coffee table in front of him. "I realize you two have been blindsided by Daniel's heart attack." He looked at Philip, then Genevieve. "I'm assuming it was a heart attack."

Philip nodded. "That's what the doctor put on the death certificate."

"I'm sure you haven't had time to figure out who will take over the managing director position. True?"

Genevieve leaned forward and nodded, waiting for Duncan to continue.

"So here's the proposal. Julia and I think we should move here." Duncan watched his mother, looking for a reaction.

Genevieve pursed her lips. "And?" She waited.

"And I should take over as managing director and learn the wine business… post-haste."

Now on the edge of her seat, Genevieve squinted. "And Julia's on board with this?"

"She thought of it first. She thinks it would be good for Alex and Ella to live in France, be exposed to another culture, learn a second language." He paused and squinted at his mother before saying, "What are you thinking? I can't tell what you're thinking."

"Hmm," Genevieve said. "What about her practice? She wouldn't be able to practice medicine here, would she?"

"That's the best part. For several years, a colleague of Julia's at Georgetown Hospital has been after her to be a visiting professor or take a research fellowship at the University of Bordeaux. His father is on the executive board, which, I assume is like our board of trustees. He says they're always looking for skilled physicians, particularly from the US." Duncan's eyes flashed with pride as he talked about his smart, skilled wife. "Visiting professors and researchers from the States are prestigious for the university."

"Would she want to do research rather than be with patients?" Genevieve tried to temper her excitement at the prospect of her family being together at Château Beaulieu.

"She's ready for another challenge. Learning French and teaching the crème de la crème of medical students fills that bill. We've been talking about it off and on since you learned about your inheritance, Dad." Duncan nodded at Philip. "At first it was just a 'wouldn't it be fun' kind of conversation. But after the extraordinary Christmas at Wilmingrove Hall, we got serious."

He walked to the fireplace, gazed into the blaze, then turned to face his parents. "Just last week we decided we'd talk to you about it when we were here." He ran his hand through his cropped hair. "I had no idea how I could best help you here at the château, then Daniel died. It seems almost like a sign."

Genevieve blinked and tears plopped into her lap.

"Mom, are you crying?"

She went to her towering son, slipped her arms around him, and squeezed. "You know I believe there's always a glimmer of sun, no matter how dark the situation. Losing Daniel is devastating. But having you, Julia, and the kids here would be an incredible gift." She leaned back and smiled.

Then her mind began to work. "This is just perfect," she began. "All your hospitality experience is perfect for running the business side of the château." She began to pick up steam.

"We need a huge announcement. Then a big party introducing you and…"

Philip interrupted. "G, don't you think we should get Daniel's death, the cremation, his celebration of life, all the administrative things taken care of first?"

"Of course, of course." She leaned back in her chair, looking sheepish. "This is just so unexpected and I'm… well, I'm just overwhelmed." Tears streamed down her cheeks, and she made no attempt to stop them. "I'm just so happy," she said, grinning. "Have you talked to Alex and Ella?"

Duncan shook his head. "We didn't want to say anything until we talked to you two. Whenever they get here, we'll have a big jolly family dinner and tell them how their lives are about to change, drastically."

Her husband and son could see the wheels spinning in Genevieve's head and smiled at each other, knowing that the matriarch of the family was about to kick into high gear. They were aware she was already plotting and planning and knew that soon Château Beaulieu would be a bubbling caldron of activity, energy, and boundless creativity. The next few months would be challenging, but exciting, and the Warwicks were up to it all.

But first, Daniel LaGrande's work and memory had to be honored. In two days much of Bordeaux would come to the château, not just to pay tribute to an extraordinary man, but to see if the next generation of owners could carry the Château Beaulieu mantel. It was the Warwicks' task to show the gathering that they were ready to step up and take the helm.

SIXTEEN

Angry clouds hung over the rows of naked vines. There were two hours until Daniel's celebration of life, where people would say goodbye to the man whose name had been synonymous with Château Beaulieu for decades. The stage was set.

In jeans and a baggy sweater, Genevieve strode from room to room with Delphine at her side, making notes of things that were not perfect. When they arrived at the tasting room, the fragrance of lilies and roses was overwhelming. Sent from all over the country, sumptuous bouquets lined the limestone walls of the tasting room, two deep in some places.

Genevieve wrinkled her nose. "Delphine, should we take some of these arrangements out of here?"

Delphine sniffed. "They are a bit strong, non? Perhaps we should put a few of the larger ones in Daniel's office. No one will go in there."

"I think that's a good idea. This is just too much. Why don't you ask Émile to move them?"

"Mais oui, my lady."

"Do you think we have enough chairs?" Genevieve turned in a circle, trying to assess if they were prepared. "We have no way of knowing how many people will be here, do we?"

Delphine shook her head. "No, but there will be hundreds. The overflow will have to stand in the vat room."

They peered into the vast adjoining space where oak barrels lay side by side, aging their precious liquid to perfection. The two women shrugged their shoulders in unison.

"They may even have to flow onto the terrace," Delphine said.

"That would be perfect if it weren't February. I suppose if everyone has several glasses of wine, they'll be fine."

"A very good point. And what do you think of this? Do you like it here?" Delphine pointed to a heavy column carved with grapes and vines, which stood in front of the wall of French doors that overlooked the broad terrace and the vineyard beyond. On the pillar was a large photograph of Daniel smiling into the camera, his eyes crinkled at the corners and his lips curled into a relaxed grin.

Genevieve ran her hand over the picture of the man she had known for such a short time but liked so much. She returned his smile. Behind Daniel's photo was a massive bouquet of yellow roses tinged with orange, his favorite. They were the roses planted at the head of every row of vines; the rose that stood guard over his beloved grapes and served as an early warning system to announce any pest or disease that intended to harm the vines.

"Everything is perfect, Delphine. Just perfect." She squeezed the housekeeper's hand, then glanced at her watch and was surprised that an hour had flown by. "I'd better get going. I've got to shower and change. Is there anything else we need to check?"

'Non, madame. Tout est prêt. Daniel would be proud."

Genevieve felt a lump forming in her throat and forced herself to swallow it. "I'll be back in a minute."

With her head down and her mind a million miles away, she raced out the door straight into a wool-covered wall of muscle.

"Crap! Oh my goodness, I'm so sorry." When she jerked her head up, she was nose to nose with a stunning man, his perfect features just inches away.

She took a step back, realized her palms were still resting on his well-formed chest, and said again, "I'm so sorry."

Assuming he was a guest, she extended her hand. "Welcome. I'm Genevieve Warwick."

His brows shot up. "Ah, Lady Crosswick. C'est mon plaisir. Je suis Paul LaGrande. Daniel was my uncle."

Confused, she pulled her hand from his. "Your name is Paul?"

He nodded. "Oui."

"Paul, you've caught me by surprise. It was our understanding that Daniel had no relatives."

Understanding flashed in his eyes. "Ah, of course, you wouldn't know about me." He put his hand on her arm. "My father and Daniel were brothers. They hadn't spoken in many years. They had a... umm, I think you say falling down?"

Genevieve smiled. "A falling out?"

"Ah, oui. A falling out." Paul shrugged. "It is a long story, and it was a very long time ago."

"Perhaps you can tell us about it later. We're having a dinner tonight for everyone who was close to Daniel. I hope you'll join us." Knowing she was running out of time, she looked at her watch again. "Right now, I'm going to have to excuse myself." She gestured toward the tasting room. "Please go on in and make yourself at home," she said, and shot out the door.

As she loped across the courtyard, Philip and Duncan walked out of the château. She stopped just long enough to tell them about Paul.

"Daniel's nephew?" Philip said. "How odd."

"You didn't know about this guy?" Duncan tilted his head.

"No, we didn't. The time we spent with Daniel was brief, but I got the impression he had no family, didn't you, G?"

"I did. But right now, I have to shower and change. You two go make him feel welcome."

"We'll take care of him. You just hurry. Duncan and I don't want to be left with all these elegant French people. You know how shy we are." He slapped his son on the back.

"Yeah, Dad. We're a couple of shrinking violets," Duncan chuckled as they walked toward the tasting room.

Duncan heard a grand march playing faintly and rolled his eyes.

"Dad, your phone's ringing. *Les Marseilles*? Really?"

Philip dug in his pants pocket. "I think it's perfect, don't you?" he said, defending the French national anthem as his ringtone.

"Jeeze, Dad, just answer your phone."

When Philip saw his screen, his brows shot up. "Inspector Boucher, bonjour. Ça va?"

Listening to Boucher on the other end of the line, Philip looked at Duncan and nodded. "Yes, he arrived yesterday." He smiled at his son. "Yes. Yes, we were." His smile dissolved as he listened to the inspector.

Duncan motioned that he would go into the gathering, but Philip shook his head.

"Of course… of course." He held up his index finger indicating he wouldn't be long. "Just ring us with your schedule and we'll send a car to pick you up at the station." A brief silence, then, "We look forward to your arrival. It sounds as if you have a lot to tell us… Indeed, au revoir."

"So, what was that all about? Boucher. Isn't he the officer who's investigating the issue with the jet fuel?"

"He is. He's coming the day after tomorrow. He has a lot to tell us, and he thinks it's best if he comes here rather than discussing the new information over the phone."

Duncan put his hand on his dad's back. "This is getting interesting, wouldn't you say?"

Philip looked up several inches into his son's blue eyes. "Duncan, ol' buddy, I can honestly say, since this inheritance dropped into our family's lap, life has been one adventure after another."

When Philip and Duncan walked into the tasting room, there were already people milling around, each clutching a glass of Château Beaulieu's finest red. Almost immediately, a line had formed near Philip and was growing. People wanted to meet Lord and Lady Crosswick, but instead were greeted by Lord Crosswick the older and Lord Crosswick the younger. Genevieve had not yet returned.

The line moved at a snail's pace. French and English ebbed

and flowed and sometimes merged. Laughter came easily to most people as they shared charming memories of Daniel. Young, old, those who worked with him or for him, business associates, friends. Everyone was richer for having known him and everyone was sad to have lost him.

A classic, aged beauty stood next in line. "Je suis Madelaine Duveau," she said, her voice somber and her accent refined. Her fine, white hair was pulled into a chignon and her black wool crepe dress was perfectly tailored to her petit frame. She held Philip's hand in both of hers. "Daniel and I were close friends for forty years. We told each other everything. He telephoned me when he returned from your merveilleuse soirée à Paris." She dabbed at the corners of her mouth with a lace handkerchief then tucked it into her sleeve. "I could tell Daniel was very excited about working with you and your wife here at Château Beaulieu."

Philip couldn't look away from her piercing blue eyes, the deep crow's feet only making them more compelling.

She motioned for him to come closer. Philip leaned over until he was eye to eye with the petite woman. She brought her lips close to his ear and whispered, "Daniel told me something I must share with you, but not here. Come to 5 Avenue de Verdun tomorrow at four o'clock." She tucked a folded piece of paper into his hand. "I do not believe Daniel's death was from natural causes. I believe it was tricherie."

"Tricherie?" Philip had no idea what the word meant.

"Foul play," she said and moved into the crowd.

SEVENTEEN

Knowing she was late, Genevieve ran across the courtyard between the château and the tasting room, her low-heeled boots tapping on the smooth stones. As she dashed through the door, she remembered a beautiful medal she had seen lying on Daniel's desk. How perfect it would be draped across his photograph, that was standing on the column. Making a detour, she trotted down the hall to Daniel's office. Even this far away, she could smell the flower arrangements Émile had put there. When she was just outside the door, she heard rustling, then a drawer open and close. She stopped. She listened. Nothing. She held her breath, closed her eyes to listen more intently. And then, the crash of broken glass sent Genevieve's heart into her throat and before she realized it, she was through the door.

"Paul!" She looked down where Paul LaGrande squatted, picking up shards of glass that sparkled on the floor. A photograph of Daniel holding a prize-winning bottle of wine was still in its frame, but the glass was shattered.

He looked up, wide-eyed, open-mouthed. "Lady Crosswick, mon Dieu! Je suis d— d— désolé," he stammered.

"What are you doing in here?"

Paul's hands covered his face, and he said nothing.

"Paul, what's going on?"

With a grunt, he stood, pulled a tissue from his trouser pocket and blew his nose. "I must sit down," he said, and walked to a leather armchair in front of Daniel's desk. He plopped into the chair with a great sigh, and his head dropped forward.

Anxious to get to Daniel's memorial, Genevieve felt her annoyance rising. "Paul, I don't have time for this. I should have been in the tasting room half an hour ago. What's this all about? What are you doing here? Do I need to call the police?"

With that threat, his head shot up. "Non! Mais, non, madame," he wailed.

She crossed the room and loomed over the weeping man. "Stop it," she commanded through gritted teeth. "Tell me this instant. What are you doing in here? And what's that?" She pointed to the corner of a blue file folder he was trying to hide inside his jacket.

She stepped even closer. "I want to know why you're stealing a file folder, and I want to know what's in it. And, for god's sake, stop sniveling!"

He inhaled with three gasping breaths and sniffed, wiping his sleeve across his nose. Genevieve grimaced to see his nose had left a slug-trail up his arm.

Genevieve pulled up a chair, so she was almost knee to knee with him. "Well?"

Paul held up both palms in defense. "Bien sûr, of course. I know this looks suspect, uh, how you say, suspicious?"

"To say the least."

He gazed at his Italian loafers. "Daniel was a kind man."

"Yes, he was."

Paul blew his nose again with the crumpled tissue. "Even though he and my father hadn't spoken since they were in their twenties, he always sent me birthday cards and a small cadeau de Noel, you know, Christmas present. He was a good uncle. When I was at université, I would visit him here at the château and once I met him in Paris, where I met Clarisse." He tore his gaze from his shoes. His eyes met Genevieve's and the corners of his mouth lifted.

"Clarisse?" Genevieve said.

"Madame Morier."

"Ha! It never occurred to me that Madame Morier had a first name."

"Doesn't everyone?"

"Of course. I've just always thought of 'Madame' as her first name." Genevieve caught a glimpse of the time on a brass clock hanging on the wall, ticking the seconds away. Philip was going to be irritated with her absence from the celebration, which was about to start.

"Please, Paul, get to the point so I can decide whether or not to call the police." She tapped her wrist. "I have to get to Daniel's celebration of life."

"Please, Lady Crosswick, go. This is nothing. I was just looking for some business papers relating to an arrangement I had with my uncle."

"Don't take me for a fool, Paul. If, as you said, this is nothing, you've picked a very bad time to do it. With everything that's happened to us over the past month, Lord Crosswick and I are more suspicious every day of anything even slightly out of the ordinary, and you breaking into Daniel's study certainly qualifies." She made a show of looking at her watch once more. "Out with it, now."

He slid the folder from inside his jacket. "Here. Just take this and we shall be done with it." He thrust it into her hands then stood and walked toward the door. "Daniel is dead. There is nothing he can do to make difficulties for me now."

"What do you mean, 'we shall be done with it'?" Genevieve was so confused, she felt lightheaded. "We are not finished with this." She glanced at her watch one last time. "Jeeze," she said. "I have *got* to get to the tasting room. You, Philip and I will talk about this tomorrow."

She followed him, then remembering the medal, grabbed it from Daniel's desk. "In the meantime, stay out of Daniel's office. Is that clear?"

Paul didn't miss the razor edge in her voice. "Oui, countess. Je comprendre."

With a sweep of her hand, Genevieve indicated he should precede her out the door. She pulled it closed and walked behind Paul to make certain he made it to the tasting room without any more detours.

EIGHTEEN

After an hour of meeting and greeting, Philip took his place at the podium and surveyed the guests who filled every nook and cranny of the tasting and vat rooms. He was relieved to see Genevieve enter the room, Paul LaGrande at her side. Still carrying the folder Paul had given her, she brought the medal to the podium, draped it over the corner of Daniel's photograph, kissed Philip on the cheek and took her chair between Duncan and Paul.

As people noticed Philip standing at the front of the hall, conversations began to quiet. He switched on the handheld microphone and tapped the wire mesh head.

"Bienvenue. Welcome." He waited for the last voices to still, then began again. "Je suis Philip Warwick et," he swept his arm toward Genevieve in the front row, "c'est ma femme, Genevieve." He gave the crowd a sheepish grin. "Et maintenant, je vais passer à l'anglais." Polite laughter rippled through the crowd as Philip warned them he was switching to English. "We join you today to honor a man Genevieve and I met only recently, but who became an instant friend."

He told the rapt audience about the day the three of them spent together in Paris. He talked about the plans they had discussed for a radiant future and how he and his family would protect all that Château Beaulieu was now and would become in the future. "For almost forty years, Château Beaulieu enjoyed the energy, the excellence, the creativity and the joy of Daniel LaGrande."

Though Philip's words were eloquent, Genevieve couldn't focus on his tribute. What had just happened in Daniel's office? The scene was on a loop in her head, playing over and over. Fingering the edge of the folder, she wondered what she would find when she read it. She forced her attention back to Philip's final words.

"Genevieve and I experienced his extraordinary spirit for just one day, but we consider ourselves lucky, indeed." Philip's eyes swept the room. "Please raise your glass to un homme magnifique. To Daniel LaGrande."

Everyone stood, held their glasses high and said in unison, "À Daniel."

He handed the microphone to Edouard Comte, the next person to speak, and sat next to Genevieve, who grabbed his hand and squeezed it hard.

The twenty-seven-year-old vigneron gripped the podium, blinking hard, trying not to cry. Hired by Daniel just three years before, Edouard's sweet face was ruddy from long days among the vines. At first his voice was low and halting, but as he looked out at so many people he knew, his confidence grew. Soon he was sharing charming memories of his boss that brought many to tears.

Genevieve's foot bounced at the end of her crossed leg. The longer Edouard spoke, the more agitated she became. Longing for x-ray vision, she looked at the closed folder in her lap. What if it contained information that was so shocking, it had caused Daniel's heart attack? How much longer could she wait to see what the folder contained? She dragged her mind back to the tasting room. Edouard was still speaking. Would he never stop?

Edouard paused to survey the crowd and gather his final thoughts. "I am young and, some might say, arrogant. My responsibility at Château Beaulieu, as Daniel taught me, is to grow great dirt. If you grow outstanding soil, fine grapes and excellent wine will follow." His face clouded with emotion. "Before Daniel impressed that philosophy on me, I thought a great vintage was all about my skill as a vigneron, about how clever I am. Ah, the hubris of youth." He looked down at the podium and a sad smile played on his lips.

He paused and swallowed. The sadness passed. "Daniel was not a young man. He was a bit too cautious for my aggressive spirit, but I will always be grateful for that very special lesson, and I shall dedicate my life to growing extraordinary dirt as a steward of Château Beaulieu."

Throughout the room, guests sniffled, dabbed at their eyes, and wiped tears from their cheeks.

Edouard stepped from behind the podium and looked toward the heavens. He raised his glass and said, "Daniel, you will live in the soil of Château Beaulieu forever. À la vie!"

Together the people in the room repeated "À la vie," and drank.

With the tributes finished, everyone drifted toward the hors d'oeuvres table. Before he could move away, Genevieve slipped her arm through Paul's and pasted a dazzling smile on her face.

"Philip," Genevieve said through her artificial grin, "Paul and I have quite a story to tell you. Don't we, Paul?"

His face blank, Philip looked at the pair, connected by looped arms. "Am I supposed to know what you're talking about?"

"You are not, but tomorrow morning all will be revealed. Right, Paul?" She poked Paul in the chest with her finger. "We'll see you in the orangerie at nine thirty. Now go do your uncle proud. Have a glass of his favorite red."

Genevieve leaned into Philip. "I'll fill you in when this day finally ends." She gave him a kiss and walked toward the guests, looking for a safe place to stash the folder before delving back into the crowd.

Still confused, he watched her as she stopped at a massive sideboard. She opened the blue file she'd been carrying since her encounter with Paul and studied a sheet of paper. She closed the folder, slipped it between two thick books that sat on the chest and disappeared into the masses.

Three hours after Daniel LaGrande's celebration of life began, the hors d'oeuvre table was empty, the wine nearly gone, and the throng was at last thinning.

By the time the last guest was out the door, Genevieve was exhausted. But there was one more event before the day could end. In a little over an hour, a dinner in the château dining room would entertain Daniel's closest local friends, and out-of-town guests, many of whom had come from Paris.

Tonight the small group of Daniel's friends would feel his spirit in the food, the flowers, the wine, and the music. The dining room was a stunner and she smiled at the magic she and Delphine had created. It was the perfect backdrop to the quartet that would play his favorites during dinner, honoring his love of jazz. Genevieve was sure the evening would sparkle from start to finish and Daniel would enjoy it, wherever he was.

NINETEEN

HAND IN HAND, Philip and Genevieve descended the château's staircase. Looking like a fashion magazine photo, they were a perfectly matched pair. Philip was dashing in black trousers, a gray and black striped sweater, and a gray scarf looped once around his neck. With understated elegance, Genevieve dazzled in a black windowpane checked skirt that swished at her ankles and a black cashmere sweater, the generous cowlneck draping to the back, showing the curve of her neck.

Strains of Miles Davis's "So What" wafted from the dining room. Midway through the foyer, Philip stopped, pulled Genevieve into his arms, and swayed to the music. When their eyes met, his grin was full of mischief. In perfect time with the sultry jazz, he took four beats in place, twirled her away from him, her skirt lifting with the spin, then pulled her back into a dip. Her head dropped back, and he leaned forward to kiss her throat before folding her into his arms.

Much to their surprise, applause filled the foyer. Arriving guests who had wandered in just in time to witness Philip and Genevieve's spontaneous floorshow, clapped and whistled in appreciation.

Still holding her hand, Philip flung Genevieve to his right. She paused, bowed, swept her arm toward her partner and the hall erupted. "Bravo! Magnifique!" The guests engulfed their hosts, hugging, kissing cheeks and chattering their way into the dining room where glasses of crémant, Bordeaux's delicious version of Champagne, awaited.

Without any decoration, the dining room was a classic Bordeaux beauty. Centuries-old paneling lined the walls of the enormous room. A long table made of a single piece of white oak had pride of place in the center of the room, lustrous from years of oiling and rubbing. A coffered ceiling tamed the massive chamber, making it cozy and inviting, rather than cavernous. This evening, it had been turned into a magical vineyard wonderland, with vines, branches and curly willows lining the walls from floor to ceiling, hundreds of tiny white lights woven throughout, sparkling like stars.

For an hour, guests mingled, drank, nibbled exquisite morsels and introduced themselves to those they didn't know. By the time people were seated, everyone seemed like old friends.

Midway down the long table, Philip and Genevieve sat opposite each other. As soon as the servers poured each diner a glass of Château Beaulieu's grand cru, Philip stood and tapped his glass with a spoon, the pretty tinkle quieting everyone.

"Good evening to you all," he said, his smile lingering on each person around the table. "Genevieve and I love having Daniel's closest friends gather here for the final sendoff of a man who will leave an emptiness in all of our lives. For the second time today, I have the privilege of honoring Daniel LaGrande, Château

Beaulieu's North Star for almost four decades.

"I'm told that when he first arrived at the vineyard, Daniel was a young, brash vigneron, full of new ideas and ready to implement them at Château Beaulieu. One of his first challenges was our soil. There was dire concern our vineyard's excellent dirt was compacting, and if we wanted to maintain the quality of our wine, we needed to improve our methods of cultivation. Daniel didn't miss a beat. After consulting with some of the most forward-thinking minds in the industry, he gave them a nod and looked to the past when horses worked the fields." Laughter rippled through the room.

Around the table, those who had spent their lives nurturing their vines, nodded.

"Many have followed Daniel's example of bringing horses back to the vineyard. We at Château Beaulieu are lucky. That decision, like so many others Daniel made over the years, assured that ours is a château that will continue to produce fine wines well into the next century. Daniel was an extraordinary friend to the vines and a beloved friend to all who were privileged to know him. Please stand and raise your glass."

Chairs scraped on the stone floor as everyone stood.

"Merci, Daniel pour tout. We shall always be grateful for your dynamic thinking, your wisdom, and your love of Château Beaulieu. To Daniel."

"To Daniel," the crowd said in unison, and drained their glasses of the wine he loved.

"Everyone please sit down, enjoy the meal, and enjoy yourselves. It's the best way we can honor our dear friend." He pointed to the musicians. "Maestro," he said, and the music resumed.

Before he sat down, Philip surveyed the sumptuous scene, the men and women laughing and talking around the table. When he got to Genevieve, he smiled to himself, watching her in animated conversation with the mayor of Saint-Émilion. As his gaze lingered on his wife, he felt the uncomfortable sense of someone's eyes on him, and continued his sweep around the table until he came upon Edouard Comte, staring at him. He shivered with a chilling thought. What if one of the guests celebrating Daniel's life were responsible for the note warning them to stay away from the vineyard. He shook his head to clear the absurd thought and sat.

The meal was everything Daniel loved. The five-course menu began with foie gras, followed by Aquitaine caviar, oysters, pavé de boeuf de Bazas, and a finale of canelés and dunes blanches, and a perfect wine paired with each course.

The guests assembled in the dining room were an interesting mix of young, old, urban, rural, sophisticates, and the unsophisticated. The one thing they all had in common was they were old friends of Daniel LaGrande, and they loved him.

Across the table, Madame Morier and Paul LaGrande sat with their foreheads nearly touching. Genevieve couldn't help but watch the two of them. "Curious," she thought. She remembered putting the madame's place card between the chairman of their biggest exporter and the president of the Bordeaux Institute, but seated in that place was a well-dressed, youngish woman Genevieve hadn't met. Her head whipped back and forth between the two men as she chattered non-stop.

When Genevieve glanced back at Madame Morier, Paul's lips were at Clarisse's ear. He whispered something that made Clarisse raise her eyebrows and curl her lips into a coquettish smile. His arm was draped on the back of the chair, and he ran his thumb back and forth on her shoulder. Genevieve couldn't take her eyes off them. "I wonder what in the world is—"

"Lady Crosswick." Sitting on her right, Kim Wang jolted Genevieve from her musings. "This is a beautiful gathering. My wife and I appreciate you including us." His English sounded more Oxford than Hong Kong.

Genevieve smiled "We're so pleased to have you, Mr. Wang."

He took Genevieve's hand, held her gaze with his chocolate eyes. "I insist you call me Kim. And may I call you Genevieve?" His full lips curved upward.

She nodded. "Of course."

Genevieve was surprised at how young and good looking he was. When Daniel told Philip and her about Kim Wang owning Clos Peyra, the vineyard next door to Château Beaulieu, she had expected a middle-aged, solemn man. He was neither of those. She guessed he was in his mid-thirties at most. His fine features were chiseled just enough to make him handsome, not pretty, and his thick hair was stylish and spikey to match his whimsical personality.

Genevieve looked across the table at Kim's stunning wife, Jing, who sat next to Philip, smiling and laughing. Quite possibly the Warwicks were going to enjoy having the Wangs as château neighbors.

TWENTY

Philip's hand rested on Genevieve's hip as they waved the last of their guests goodbye.

Walking back into the foyer, Genevieve yawned, stretched her arms overhead and said, "Merde, I'm exhausted."

"Too exhausted for a nightcap with… 'the kids'?" Philip made air quotes.

"Yes, but I'd never tell." She tickled him in the ribs. "Come on ol' man. We have to keep up."

When she pulled him into the salon, a cheer went up from Duncan, David, Becca, and Lillie. The fire was crackling and the drinks were poured.

David jumped up from his cozy seat by the fire and handed Genevieve a glass of Veuve Clicquot. "Sit here." He ushered her to the chair where he had been sitting. "As wonderful as crémant is, I know you've been dying for a glass of The Widow all evening, haven't you?" He sat down close to Becca on the sofa, picked up her hand and smiled as he looked at her engagement ring.

"Get a room, you two," Genevieve teased. She brought the slender faceted glass to her mouth, closed her eyes, and took a long sip. "Yum," she said and smacked her lips. "Now that's more like it." She took another drink, then thought a moment. Her brow furrowed. "You don't think anybody could tell while I was drinking crémant I was longing for Veuve, do you?"

The group booed and laughed at her.

Duncan threw a wadded napkin at his mother. "I'm pretty sure most people were thinking about Daniel, Mom."

"Good point." Genevieve took another sip.

Duncan rolled his beer glass back and forth in his hands before savoring a swallow of Cool Jazz, a local craft beer. Holding up the glass, he assessed the color. "I'm surprised how delicious this is."

"May I have a sip?" Genevieve held out her hand.

"Sure, Mom, but you're not going to like it. It's too hoppy."

She whipped her hand back and wrinkled her nose. "Thanks for the warning." She held up her glass of Champagne. "I'll stick with this."

"Okay. Okay!" Lillie vibrated with excitement. "Enough about drinks! I have gossip! Well, not gossip, because I can confirm it's true."

Becca leaned forward on the sofa, eyes glistening. "What took you so long to tell us?" She licked her lips waiting to hear the scuttlebutt.

Lillie tossed back the rest of her drink. "Are you ready for this?" she asked and set her glass on the table beside her.

"Lillie!" Becca wailed. "Tell us."

She lowered her voice so everyone had to lean in to hear her.

"Well," Lillie began in a dramatic whisper, "during dinner between the entree and salad, I went to the loo and you'll never guess what I saw." She leaned back and paused for effect.

All eyes were wide with anticipation and glued to Lillie. Her lips drew into a smile.

"Well?" Genevieve pressed.

"Believe me, this is worth waiting for." She sat forward again. "When I came out of the toilette and walked back toward the foyer, I heard a sort of moaning as if someone were hurt." Lillie shook her head. "But when I crept around the corner to see if someone needed help, they did not." She stopped, enjoying the confusion on all five faces.

"I don't understand," Philip said.

Genevieve shrugged her shoulders, palms up. "I'm with Philip. I don't know what you're telling us, Lillie."

David took over. "I think what Lillie's saying is that there were two people… uh, where were they, Lillie?"

"In the little alcove under the main staircase."

"So, right there, under the staircase, Lillie saw two people in flagrante delicto." David rested his case.

"Wow," Genevieve said. "Trust the lawyer to use Latin! That's pretty dishy."

"So two people were shagging under the stairs? Were they staff or dinner guests?" Becca said.

"Ooooh, they were dinner guests, all right," Lillie said, relishing keeping her audience in suspense.

"Well?" Becca and Genevieve said in unison.

"Don't you want to guess?" Lillie teased.

Philip walked to the fire, gave it a poke, then tossed a fat log onto the glowing embers. A shower of sparks flew up the chimney and the wood burst into flames. With the poker still in his hand, he turned on Lillie. "If you value your life, you'll tell us who was under the stairs," he teased.

She raised her hands in defense, and a laugh rolled from her throat. "All right, all right. I'll tell you. It was Madame Morier and Philip LaGrande." She plopped back against the cushion, a self-satisfied grin on her lips.

"After what I saw at dinner this evening, I'm not at all surprised. Those two were very, very chummy. As the French would say, rohh la la." She shook her hand in French fashion. "And, Philip, remember I told you during our party in Paris I saw Madame Morier come out of her office, rather disheveled, with a man sneaking out behind her?"

"Of course, I do."

"I bet that was Paul LaGrande. What do you think?" She raised a questioning eyebrow.

"I suppose it could be. You didn't see his face, did you?"

"No, but given what Lillie saw, it seems logical."

"You saw madame in another compromising situation in Paris?" Becca said. "She gets around, doesn't she?"

"I don't care about how sexual she is," Genevieve said. "I'm just blown away that Paul and Clarisse are having an affair."

"Who's Clarisse?" the question rang out.

"Ha!" Genevieve laughed. "Who knew Madame Morier had a first name?"

"Clarisse, huh?" David said. "If you had asked me what her first name was, I would have said Cruella."

Snickers rippled through the room.

"Back to business, please," Genevieve said. "I'm assuming

Paul is Madame Morier's Parisian mystery lover." Genevieve watched her hands fold and unfold in her lap. "But, in addition to being a boy toy," she lifted her gaze, "he's a snoop, if not a thief. I caught him nosing around Daniel's office just before the celebration of life."

"What are you talking about?" Philip set his goblet on the table beside him. "When you said you two had a story to tell me, I had no idea you meant he was trying to rob us!"

Genevieve raised her hand to Philip. "Calm down and I'll tell you about it," she said, and told the group about finding Paul in Daniel's office. "The infamous file," she said, holding up the blue folder. "When I opened this, there was a single sheet." She waved the page.

"And what does it say?" Duncan asked.

Genevieve held the paper so everyone could see.

"That's it?" David said. "Just this hand-written IOU for a hundred thousand euros?"

"Did he explain what this is all about?" Becca asked.

Genevieve shook her head. "He just shoved the folder at me, hoping that would be the end of it. I had to get to Daniel's memorial, so I didn't see the IOU until after the celebration of life." She turned to Philip. "I told him we'd discuss it with him tomorrow. We'll meet him at nine thirty in the orangerie and get to the bottom of this."

Genevieve rolled her shoulders. "I've got to go to bed. Philip, are you coming?" She stood, holding out her hand.

"There's one other thing," Philip pulled a crumpled piece of paper from his pants pocket. "An old friend of Daniel's,

Madelaine Duveau, wants me to come to her home tomorrow at four o'clock. She cornered me at the memorial. She said Daniel told her something just before he died, that she needs to share with me."

"Is that all she said?" Genevieve's body sagged from exhaustion. "You don't have any idea what she wants to tell you?"

"That wasn't quite all. She also said she thinks Daniel didn't die of natural causes. She thinks it was foul play. I'll find out more tomorrow at four o'clock."

TWENTY-ONE

Philip extended his leg, feeling for Genevieve, but instead of her warm body, he was greeted with the chill of unoccupied sheets. He opened one eye and saw the imprint in Genevieve's pillow where she had been not long ago. He listened and heard nothing. The only thing to tickle his senses was the faint aroma of baking bread, no doubt wafting from the kitchen.

As he pondered getting up, his phone pinged, announcing a text:

> *Were meeting with Pall at 9:30. Get your burt out of bef.*

Chuckling, Philip wondered if Genevieve would ever learn to proofread her texts before sending them.

He threw off the covers, grabbed his heavy terrycloth robe and headed to the shower to start what he was sure would be an interesting day.

"Delphine, would you please ask Émile to bring the flower arrangements from Daniel's office here to the orangerie?"

"Mais oui, madame. I'll text him."

"Let's make sure they're all still pretty, then take them to the hospital where patients can enjoy them. What do you think about that?"

Delphine tapped a message to Émile on her phone and hit the send arrow. "That's a very good idea, my lady. Even though these flowers are for a sad occasion, they will brighten many spirits at l'hôpital."

Genevieve had been up since seven thirty and operating at full speed. She and Delphine were a good team. The housekeeper executed Genevieve's ideas almost before she came up with them. "Did you ask…"

Delphine answered Genevieve's question before she could finish asking it. "Breakfast has been laid out in the orangerie. Lizette and Chloé have outdone themselves. You will be pleased when you see the petit dejeuner they have prepared."

Genevieve was in awe of Lizette. Since they arrived less than a week ago, she had been devouring the cook's croissants and baguettes nonstop. Just this morning she had sworn off pastries, but her resolve dissolved when she walked into the orangerie. She couldn't resist a warm pain au chocolat with her rich, black coffee.

She was alone in the orangerie, a pretty building connected to the château by a stone and glass corridor. Even as late as the last century, it had served as a greenhouse, preserving delicate flora incapable of wintering outside. Today, orange and lemon trees lived in ornate pots around the room. They thrived, bathed by the sun streaming through a wall of French doors. During balmy weather, the doors were thrown wide to the broad terrace and vineyard beyond.

Sitting at a small table, Genevieve stared out at the naked grapevines while she sipped her coffee. She smiled as her mind replayed yesterday's send off, pleased with everything they had done for Daniel. But now, she was ready to move on. There was no shortage of things to be done. The sooner she understood the basics of how the château was run, the sooner she could move on to more complicated issues.

"My lady, plus de café?" Chloé pulled Genevieve from her thoughts.

"Ah, Chloé, oui s'il vous plaît. Merci."

Lizette's kitchen helper was petite, tidy and an Audrey Hepburn clone, and Genevieve had liked her from the moment they met, just days ago. She refilled Genevieve's cup and dusted a few crumbs from the yellow linen tablecloth. "Is there anything else I might do for you?"

Genevieve flashed a smile. "I think I'm fine, thank you."

She turned back to her notebook and ticked off several chores she had already completed, then began to add more to the bottom of the list.

"Madame." Paul LaGrande's voice cut through her concentration.

"Paul!" Genevieve said, startled. "Are you early?" She looked at her watch.

"No, my lady. I believe I am punctual."

Paul's fresh-from-the-shower fragrance wafted to Genevieve.

His dark hair was still damp, and he was dressed in wool camel pants and a navy hooded sweater, a classic French look. "It's not hard to see how Clarisse is smitten," Genevieve thought. Her eyes lingered on Paul's elegant features, until over his shoulder she saw Philip walking across the room toward them.

Distracted, Philip nodded. "Bonjour, Paul."

"Bonjour, my lord. I am appreciative that you and Lady Crosswick will speak with me today and allow me to explain what happened yesterday."

"You need to give me a moment, Paul," Philip said with a quick nod. "G, could I borrow you?" He offered his hand and pulled her out of her chair. When they were in the corridor, he showed her his phone. "Read this," he said.

"Who is this?" She didn't recognize the name on the "From" line, which said, "DREETS."

Philip took a deep breath and said, "It stands for the regional directorates for the economy, employment, labor and solidarity."

As Genevieve opened her mouth to ask what all that meant, he held up his hand.

"It's the French regulatory agency that investigates cases of fraud, you know like counterfeit wine. It looks like someone named Jules Lambert is paying us a visit this Friday."

Scowling, Genevieve asked, "Why? Are we counterfeiting wine? Should we be worried?"

"I have no idea." Philip shook his head. "Duncan and I will sit down with Edouard and find out what this is all about. Find out why they might be coming." He sighed. "But right now, we need to deal with Paul."

Resigned to a lengthy session with Paul LaGrande, they went back to the orangerie. Philip sat across from Paul and noticed little beads of perspiration glistening on his forehead. "All right, Paul, where do we start?" he said and leaned back in his chair, settling in for a long haul.

"Let me begin by saying I meant no disrespect to my uncle, to you or to Lady Crosswick." Paul fiddled with the string of his hoodie like a nervous twelve-year-old. "Three years ago I got into a sticky financial situation. I discovered my partner in an import-export business was a man avec sans scrupules; unscrupulous I believe you say. He borrowed money from some very bad people to cover a…" He thought for a moment. "A shortfall in our company, then he ran away." Paul ran his hand over his face, then went on. "My father and I have an impossible relationship. I could not ask him for help. So, I asked my uncle to lend me the money."

"And that's what the IOU is?" Philip said.

"Exactly."

Genevieve began to understand. "So when you learned Daniel died, it was the perfect opportunity to retrieve the IOU. Is that about it?"

"Oui." His shoulders slumped and he hung his head.

Genevieve rolled her eyes and Philip stood.

"It seems to me this was between you and your uncle," Philip said. "I don't see any reason to be further involved, do you, G?"

"No, I don't," Genevieve said, anxious to bring this to a close and move on to more important things.

Genevieve handed Paul the file folder containing the IOU and the three agreed the matter was concluded.

They walked Paul to the front door, shook hands, then watched him get into his red Jaguar. The throaty engine hummed to life and as Paul backed out, Philip saw Clarisse Morier sitting in the passenger seat. It appeared they were quite the item.

TWENTY-TWO

Pleased to have the issue of Paul LaGrande behind them, Genevieve poured a second cup of coffee into a toile-patterned china mug and wondered where Émile was with the flowers. Annoyed that he hadn't done the job, she stabbed at her phone, texting Delphine.

Did you ask Émile to bring the bouquets to the orangerie?

Within seconds, her phone rang. "Oui, madame, I told him to do it an hour ago. Did he not do as I asked?"

"He did not."

Delphine could feel Genevieve's exasperation through the phone. "I am helping in the kitchen, but I shall go find him."

"Never mind, Delphine. I'll take care of it." She shoved her phone into the pocket of her grey flannel pants and, disappointed in Émile, charged out the French doors toward the vineyard office. As she stepped onto the terrace, an icy drizzle pricked her cheeks. She snuggled the collar of her grey sweater up to her ears and quickened her pace, more irritated by Émile with every step. They had given him an opportunity to save himself from prison, and all he had to do was what was asked of him. Moving a few vases of flowers was not a difficult task.

Opening the door to the building, Genevieve was hit with a welcome blast of warm air. She leaned over, shook her head like a puppy and a fine mist sprayed from her hair. She swept her hands over her hair, straightened her shoulders, and marched down the hall ready to give Émile a verbal spanking. She bolted through the office door expecting to see him lounging on the leather sofa, absorbed in his phone. But, except for the pungent aroma from the fifteen or twenty vases of flowers in the exact same spot they were yesterday, Genevieve saw nothing.

She felt an ache in her jaw and realized she was clenching her teeth. She released her bite, rolled her head to ease the tension and her neck crackled.

She heard a groan and stepped further into the room. She heard it again but, turning in a slow circle, saw nothing. She cocked her head and listened. This time the groan rolled into a low moan. She took another step forward and saw a foot sticking from behind the desk. As the memory of discovering Daniel's dead body just days ago splashed through mind, the blood drained from her head. Two long strides and she was there.

Émile lay on his stomach, his face smooshed against his outstretched arm, vomit oozing from his slack mouth onto the floor. On the desk was an empty bottle of Château Beaulieu's Bordeaux blend and a glass with a splash left in the bottom.

"Drunk," Genevieve spat out. "You little shit. You're drunk."

His moan was guttural.

Genevieve squatted next to him and pulled his eyelid up so she could see his pupil. She wasn't sure what she was looking for, so she released his lid. She slapped his cheek. "Émile." She slapped him again, harder this time. "Émile, are you drunk?"

A squeeze on her knee startled her. She clasped Émile's clammy hand and leaned over so her lips were close to his ear. "Émile, are you sick?" The longer she watched him, the more she thought he was ailing rather than intoxicated.

He whimpered and mumbled something. She leaned in to hear what he was saying, but the words were garbled and confused.

Genevieve pulled her phone from her pocket and pressed Philip's number. She counted the rings, tapping her fingernails on the brick floor.

At last, he answered.

"Philip, where are you?"

"I'm with Duncan in the study. Where are you?"

"I'm in Daniel's office and Émile is lying on the floor in a puddle of vomit. At first I thought he was drunk, but I've changed my diagnosis." Concern creased her brow. "I think he's sick; really sick. We should call an ambulance." Still holding Émile's hand, she plopped from her haunches to her butt, so she was sitting on the floor. "I don't know if it's an emergency, but he seems to be in pretty bad shape. He's clutching his stomach so maybe it's appendicitis. Whatever it is, we need help."

"Leave it with me. I'll ask Delphine to call an ambulance. Duncan and I will be right there."

There was little she could do but cradle Émile's hand in hers. She had nothing with which to clean his face or the floor around him, so he continued to drool into his vomit.

Within minutes, she heard footsteps racing toward her in the hall. She tried to stand, but Émile's grip on her hand was strong.

"Genevieve?"

"Mom, where are you?"

From where they stood in the middle of the room, Philip and Duncan couldn't see behind the desk.

Still clutching Émile's hand, Genevieve leaned on her elbow and stretched as far as she could to peek around the bureau. "We're here." She was surprised to hear her voice croak.

Philip and Duncan were stunned when they saw the pair, Genevieve sitting with her knees up to her chin and Émile sprawled on the floor, pink-tinged vomit everywhere.

"Mom, is he alive?" Duncan said, concerned by Émile's deathlike pallor.

"He is," she confirmed. "He's gripping my hand and moaning, both good signs under the circumstances."

They heard the door open down the hall and voices approaching.

"My lord. Ce qui s'est passé? Est-ce qu' Émile va bien? Les ambulanciers sont là. Que puis-je faire d'autre?" Delphine asked in rapid-fire succession.

Duncan slipped his arm around Delphine's shoulder and gave it a comforting squeeze. "Delphine, you've done a terrific job getting the paramedics here so fast. We're not sure what happened to Émile, but the medics will figure that out. The faster we get him to the hospital, the better."

Working efficiently, the medical team lifted Émile onto a gurney. One EMT listened to his heart, then took his blood pressure, which was dangerously low. Another collected a sample of the vomit from his blue-tinged lips and popped it into a vial. She cleared his airway, wiped his mouth, and eased the elastic over his head to hold an oxygen mask in place. The third medic bagged the empty wine bottle, poured the wine from the glass into a sterile jar, and put the glass into a separate bag. Within five minutes they were wheeling the sick young man across the terrace, through the house and lifting him into the ambulance.

Keeping pace with the EMT as he rushed to the driver's seat, Philip asked, "Do you know what's wrong with him? Will he be all right?"

The medic heaved himself up and behind the wheel. "It appears he has been poisoned. From his extremely low blood pressure, his abdominal pain and his ataxia, we believe we are dealing with methanol poisoning."

"What's ataxia?" Philip yelled as the medic pulled his door closed.

"His coordination is impaired. If we are correct about the methanol, he will be fine after we give him the antidote. As long as we don't waste time." He gunned the engine and gravel sprayed from under the wide tires. When they came to the D122, the siren began to scream, the ambulance squealed onto the main road, and was gone.

TWENTY-THREE

"Well, that was a hell of a deal." Shivering in the icy wind, Duncan blew into his fists. "I'd suggest we go in. It's cold out here." The wind was building, and clouds scurried across the sky. "Dad, what did you say to the EMT?"

Philip's hand rested on Genevieve's shoulder as they walked toward the house. "They said they believe Émile was poisoned."

"What?" Genevieve stopped in the middle of the driveway. "What do you mean he was poisoned? Why would they think that? Who would want to poison a kid who's just working in the vineyards and doing chores around the house?"

Philip slipped his hand into hers and pulled her toward the house.

"He hasn't been here long enough to make enemies, has he?" Genevieve frowned, bewildered. "Could it have been an accident?" A hopeful note hung in her voice.

"I'm sure it could have been. We'll just wait to see what the doctors say. I'll call in an hour or so and find out how he's doing. I suppose I should phone his father, but I'd like to wait until we have some positive news about his condition. Did Becca and David go into Saint-Émilion?"

"They did."

Philip pulled her limp body into a hug. "You look like you need a nap."

"I do. I'd like to go back to bed, pull the duvet over my head, and stay there until Émile is hale, hardy, and back at the château being his annoying self."

Tilting her chin up, Philip kissed her forehead. "I think this is all too much," he said. Not wanting Duncan to hear, he leaned down and whispered in her ear, "It would be a lot easier if we gave the money away."

Genevieve pushed out of his arms. "I'm not having this conversation out here in the cold."

"What conversation aren't you having?" Duncan asked.

"Never mind," Genevieve said. "Your dad is just being ridiculous." She looked up at the grey Bordeaux sky, searching for a sign that things were going to get better. Just then, a sliver of sun sliced between two black clouds. Taking it as a sign, she said, "I'll make you a promise. Things will be much better tomorrow."

"I'll hold you to that," Philip said, opening the front door for her.

For a moment, they stood together as if they were guests in Château Beaulieu, a house filled with the history of generations and the heritage of the great wine the family had nurtured. They admired the foyer in front of them: the graceful stairs to the first floor; the well-buffed limestone tiles; the view at the end of the hall through the French doors, onto the terrace and out to the vineyard. For a moment they stood in awe of the lineage that, until recently, they had not known was theirs.

"You know Julia loves Wilmingrove Hall," Duncan said, breaking the silence. "We still talk about the exciting time we had over Christmas. But I think she's going to be thrilled to live here. And Alex and Ella." Duncan glowed as he spoke of his family. "They're going to be crazy about every nook and cranny of Château Beaulieu."

Genevieve's eyes stung. She blinked and a lone tear trickled down her cheek. It hung on her chin for a moment then plopped to the floor.

Duncan put his arm around his mother and pulled her to his side. "You're pretty happy about this, aren't you, Mom?"

Their eyes met. Their smiles were identical, mother and son.

"It's a dream. What could be better than having my family all under one roof, working, playing, growing together?" She slipped her arm around Duncan's waist, holding him tight.

"It's going to be a wild ride." Philip chuckled then kissed the top of Genevieve's head. "Alex and Ella are going to keep us on our toes."

His phone vibrated. He looked at the screen and, not recognizing the number, tapped reject. Almost immediately, it rang again. "Given all that's happened this morning, I guess I should answer this," he said, and walked across the hall to his study.

As the creaking hinges of the front door echoed through the foyer, Duncan and Genevieve turned as Becca and David shivered into the hall, pushed by an icy wind, their scarves snapping at their faces.

"You're back." Genevieve strode across the foyer and gave them each a kiss on the cheek.

They peeled off their gloves, struggled out of their coats, unwound their mufflers and piled everything on an upholstered bench.

"Crickey, it got cold." David rubbed his hands then tucked them into his armpits.

Tucking her arm through Becca's, Genevieve ushered her shivering friend into the salon and to the fireplace where logs simmered, waiting to be brought back to life.

"I can't wait to hear how you liked Saint-Émilion." Genevieve tossed wood on the fire and it sparked to flames, then she walked to the corner of the room to an ornate pull and gave it a single tug, calling for coffee. "Did you enjoy your poke around our charming village?"

Stretching his legs in front of him, David leaned back in an overstuffed chair and crossed his ankles. "We did. We went to Chai Pascal, the café Philip recommended. It was wonderful, but we had the strangest experience with the wine."

"Let me tell," Becca interrupted, her cheeks flushed from the cold. "We ordered a bottle of the Château Beaulieu grand cru and had to send it back."

"How strange. Had it turned?" asked Duncan.

David shook his head. "No. It just wasn't good. It tasted like a cheap corner shop wine. They gave us a new bottle, which was superb. It was just odd how the first bottle was a completely different, certainly inferior, wine."

Philip walked in just at the end of the story. Looking at his sagging shoulders and weary eyes, there was no question he was about to tell them something serious.

"What's the matter?" Genevieve asked, instantly on high alert. "Did you hear something from the hospital? Is it Émile?"

"What about Émile?" David asked. Having been gone all morning, he and Becca knew nothing about what had happened.

"In a minute, David." Genevieve narrowed her eyes at Philip. "Something's wrong. What is it?"

Philip eased himself into a chair and leaned his head back against the cushion. "The call I got as you two walked through the door," he nodded toward David and Becca, "was from the hospital."

They could hear a cart rattling down the hall, and in a moment, Chloé wheeled through the salon doorway with trolley piled with pastries, coffee cups and an urn. "Excusez moi, madame. Would you like me to serve?"

"No thank you, Chloé, we'll be fine." Genevieve picked up a small linen napkin and a cup and saucer. The pretty gamine bobbed a curtsy and was gone.

Philip pushed himself to stand and trudged to the cart. He poured a cup of coffee and, spying a bottle of Irish whiskey on the cart's lower shelf, added a generous shot to his steaming java.

"Will you please finish telling us about the call from the hospital?" Genevieve's tone was sharper than she intended.

Returning to his chair, he set his cup on a small side table and plopped down. Every move seemed to be an effort. "So, I have the proverbial good news and bad news." He crossed his legs and sank deeper into the cushions. "The good news is Émile is going to be fine. The bad news is he was definitely poisoned."

As he scanned his friends and family, he looked from one blank face to another and another. His words had not registered.

"Dad, I don't understand. How was he poisoned? Did he eat something that was contaminated?"

"Wait a minute." Genevieve's voice was almost inaudible. "Wait a damn minute, Philip. I saw the EMS guys bag the wine bottle and glass. Those were still in Daniel's study from the day he died. That's where Émile got the wine, isn't it?" She could hear her heart pounding in her ears.

"And if Émile was poisoned from that bottle of wine, does that mean…?" Duncan couldn't finish the sentence.

"Yeah," Philip said. "That's what it means, Duncan." He drained his coffee cup. "Daniel didn't die of a heart attack. He was poisoned."

"But why wouldn't the police have discovered that?" David said. "Why would a bottle of poisoned wine be sitting there days after a man died in that room?"

"Very simple," Philip said. "Because Daniel was seventy-four and had a few minor heart issues, the police automatically ruled his passing a death by natural causes."

Genevieve jumped in. "Because everyone was busy organizing his celebration of life, no one has been in there to clean, so the bottle was still there."

"I'm assuming he was cremated," Becca said.

"He was, so at this point, there's no way to confirm if he was poisoned or not." Genevieve was on her feet and pacing. "Philip, did the hospital tell you what the poison was?"

"The chemical analysis says it's methanol, a very clever poison to use in wine. It's odorless and tasteless so it's difficult to detect, until someone goes blind or dies, of course."

"Yeah, that's kind of a dead giveaway," Duncan said. "Pun intended."

Becca had been silent, thinking. "I'm assuming the police will get involved now."

Philip nodded. "I expect to hear from them anytime. We've been in France less than a month and already we've dealt with dozens of cops. Now we're about to add another gendarme to our list of acquaintances." He cradled his head in his hands for a moment. He took a deep breath, then another "No one can say that our lives are dull, can they?"

"A little less excitement might not be a bad thing," Genevieve said.

As the sound of *Les Marseilles* announced a call on Philip's phone, everyone jumped and nervous laughter rippled through the room.

"This is probably the police now." He stood up and headed for his study as he accepted the call. "Hello. Oui. Oui, this is Lord Crosswick."

"My lord. This is Frederick Picard, Chef de la Police in Saint-Émilion. I am calling about Madelaine Duveau. She has written your name on her calendar for four o'clock today. Were you coming to see her, Lord Crosswick?"

"Yes, I was. Is there a problem?"

"Do you know Madame Duveau well?"

Philip sat in his desk chair. "Not at all. I met her yesterday."

"If I may ask, why are you coming to see her?"

He swiveled his chair back and forth, trying to imagine what Picard looked like, but the policeman's monotone voice conjured nothing. "She told me to come to her home today because she has information about our deceased general manager, Daniel LaGrande." He stopped moving and leaned on his desk. "Look, chef, you need to tell me what's going on here."

Without changing his tone, Picard said, "I'm sorry to inform you, Lord Crosswick, your appointment has been canceled. Madame Duveau died earlier today."

Silence filled the line for several seconds. "Lord Crosswick, did you hear me?" Picard finally asked.

"I did, chef. How did she die?"

"She was sitting in a sunny window overlooking the garden, drinking a glass of wine and reading a book."

Philip heard a smile in Picard's voice, his first emotion during their conversation. "Not a bad way to go at eighty-six," he said.

Philip imagined the elegant octogenarian enjoying a glass of wine and a favorite book as she sailed out of this world into the next. Then, the words "drinking a glass of wine" screamed in his head. "You said she was drinking wine?"

"Oui."

"What kind of wine?" Philip held his breath.

"Un moment," Picard said and yelled to someone, waited, then came back to Philip. "My lord, it was a bottle of your Château Beaulieu blend. Why do you ask?"

Philip ran his hands over his face as if he were trying to wipe an image away, then he repeated the words. "She was drinking a glass of wine… and then she was dead. You need to check the bottle for poison. Chef Picard, I don't know what the hell's going on here in Saint-Émilion, but whatever it is, it's not good."

TWENTY-FOUR

David poked the embers of the spent logs, tossed a chunk of wood on the pile and within seconds the fire was crackling, hungry flames lapping at the wood.

When Philip returned to the salon, he was as pale as snow and his brow wrinkled in a ferocious frown.

"My god, Philip," Genevieve said, looking at her husband. "Every time you take a call, you return looking like death warmed over. Who was on the phone?"

"Just as I thought, it was the police. But they didn't call about Daniel or Émile. It's Madelaine Duveau. The woman I was going to see this afternoon." His eyes clouded. "She died earlier today. Her daughter stopped by to bring her a gateau and found her. The police saw my name and number on her calendar on today's date and called me to let me know."

"How old was she?" Duncan asked.

"She was eighty-six. But, the big news is she was drinking a bottle of Château Beaulieu wine." He paused to let his words sink in.

On the sofa, Becca covered her lap with a soft wool throw she had pulled from the basket next to her. "I don't understand," she said.

"I asked them to check the bottle to confirm there wasn't anything suspicious about it."

"What did they say?" David asked.

"At first they weren't interested, but their attitude changed pretty fast when I told them about Daniel, Émile and the poisoned wine in our vineyard office. Given Madelaine's note and the timing of her death, I won't be at all surprised if she was poisoned."

TWENTY-FIVE

A RAP AT HIS study door caused Philip to look up from the stack of papers he and Duncan were reviewing.

"Ah, Edouard, come in." Philip shoved his glasses from the bridge of his nose to the top of his head.

"Bonjour, my lord. You asked to see me?"

"Oui, asseyez-vous." He motioned for Edouard to sit. "Duncan and I have several things to discuss with you."

Philip moved from behind his desk to a chair next to Edouard, who had flopped down on a loveseat.

Completing the cozy group, Duncan sat on the other side of their vigneron.

Philip looked down at his jeans and brushed away a crumb left from his lunch. "It's been a busy time since we arrived." He looked back at Edouard. He was in no hurry to fill the silence in the room.

Edouard cleared his throat and stared at the floor. He tapped his signet ring on the wood of his arm chair until he realized how annoying the sound was, and stopped.

At last Philip said, "I got a message yesterday that a representative from DREETS will be visiting us Friday. My understanding is that they are the agency that investigates fraud in the wine industry. Is that true?"

Surprise flashed across Edouard's young face. "Oui. That is the agency that looks into such matters. Why would they make a visit here?"

"That's what we're asking you, Edouard," Duncan said, his voice sharper than he had intended.

"Has there ever been an issue of counterfeiting wine at Château Beaulieu, that you know of?" Philip didn't hide his wariness.

Edouard stiffened in his chair. "No," he spat. "Absolument pas."

"All right." Philip reached out and put his hand on Edouard's knee. "We'll wait and see what they want. But we want you to meet with us when he comes."

Edouard laced and unlaced his fingers in his lap. "Friday morning, I must be at the Saint-Émilion growers' breakfast. But I can be back by eleven o'clock."

"That will be fine." Philip softened his tone and changed the subject. "Edouard, how are you doing? We know Daniel's death has been very hard on you and we want to do what we can to make the next few weeks as easy as possible for you; for everyone here at the vineyard." He paused, waiting for Edouard to say something.

The young man relaxed back into the cushions and said, "I don't think there's anything to be done. Nothing will ever be the same without Daniel. That may be a bad thing." He paused, looked down at his fidgeting fingers and quieted them. "Or it may be a good thing. We'll just have to wait and see, won't we?"

Duncan looked at his dad then back at Edouard. "Did you just say Daniel's death might be a good thing?" Furrows appeared between his eyebrows.

"What I mean is, Daniel had been here for a very long time. Perhaps it is the right time for new energy. We say un peu de sang neuf, some new blood." He tilted his head back and assessed Duncan with a critical eye. "My lord, you are not young, but you are not old."

"Thank you, I guess." Duncan shrugged.

"It is my understanding that though you have not worked in the wine industry, you are a businessman. Oui?"

"True." Duncan nodded and went on. "I'm going to rely on you to teach me about wine and this industry, Edouard."

Edouard shook his head. "No, no, no. I would suggest you manage the numbers, the cash flow, the paying of the bills, ordering of the supplies—all of that business." He fluttered his hands in the air. "And I shall manage the vineyard, the quality of the wine, everything that is the reputation of Château Beaulieu."

Stunned into silence, Duncan turned to catch his father's reaction. He wasn't surprised to see the color rising in Philip's face and his lips in a tight line.

"Edouard, I don't understand." Philip kept his voice even. "You realize we Laneys own Château Beaulieu, don't you?"

"You may own the vineyard, but you do not own the heart and soul of Château Beaulieu. That will take generations. Until then, your family will have to rely on me to be the—I believe you say—steward of the land, and all that comes from it." He rose and headed toward the door. Before making his dramatic exit, he turned and said, "Now if you will excuse me, I must attend to *our* land."

Minutes ticked by. Philip and Duncan didn't speak. Each sat, replaying what they had just heard, wondering if they had misunderstood this twenty-seven-year-old's arrogant words.

Duncan was the one to break the silence. "Wow, Dad. I didn't understand. I thought Daniel was Edouard's mentor, his close friend," he said. "And he couldn't possibly think he's not going to have to answer to anybody."

"He's going to have to answer to you, Duncan. Good luck with that." Philip scoffed, walked behind his desk and sat down. He rifled through a few papers and pulled out a sheet. "I found this when I came in here after lunch." He handed the stationery to Duncan.

"What is it?" Duncan scanned it and handed it back to his dad. "Very funny. It's in French."

"Oh, is it?" Philip smirked. "Is that a problem?" he teased. "It's from our bottle purveyor. It says the order for the extra bottles for our shipments to China will be delayed by two weeks. This leads me to ask: what do they mean by extra bottles?"

"I guess it could either mean that we're sending more bottles to China than we normally do, or we don't usually send wine to China and this year we are? Why didn't you ask Edouard about it?"

"Not that I suspect Edouard of anything, but I decided to show it to the DREET agent and see if they think it has anything to do with counterfeiting."

"Too bad Daniel's not here to guide us. No doubt he could answer a lot of questions." Duncan rose and started gathering the papers he'd been reading. "You know, Dad, we should be working in his office. That's where all the records are going to be." Duncan stuck a binder under his arm and grabbed the stack of file folders with both hands. "If there's anything incriminating in the office, the sooner we find it, the better."

Philip glanced at his watch. "I'll meet you there in thirty minutes. I want to bring your mother up to speed."

"Works for me," Duncan said and headed to the vineyard office as Philip went in search of Genevieve.

TWENTY-SIX

I N THE PETIT salon, which had become her favorite retreat, Genevieve nestled in a faded paisley chair, and Becca sat cross-legged on a down-stuffed sofa. The fire threw warmth into the room and a pretty glow onto the frescoed walls. Just across the hall from the kitchen, the cozy room caught all the aromas, from baking bread to the smell of quiche bubbling in the oven.

Brainstorming about the Cité du Vin project, the two women talked non-stop, posing one idea after another until they had a roadmap of how to make The Art of the Vine exciting and successful. They'd start with a launch at Château Beaulieu and build from there.

Genevieve's phone vibrated its way across the table. She grabbed it before it could dance over the edge and saw Lillie's face on the screen. "You're back in Paris safe and sound I trust?"

"I am" Lillie's spirited lilt shot energy over the line. "Do you have a minute? I have news."

"Of course, and Becca's here with me. We've been throwing ideas for the Cité du Vin program against the wall to see what will stick. You should be here."

"I'm glad you said that. I'll be back sooner than expected. I just got off the phone with Elise Beaufoy, the Chairman of the Cité du Vin Foundation board. I can't begin to tell you how thrilled she was that you and Philip want to create a work-study program with them. Usually people who donate bags of money want to throw it at something glamourous, something flashy. The foundation has been wanting to do something like this for years." She paused to take a breath.

"That's excellent. I'm putting you on speaker so Becca can hear." Genevieve flashed a smile and filled Becca in.

"That brings me to my next piece of news. You're sitting down, right?"

"We are."

"They have a quarterly board meeting in just over a week. It was supposed to be in Reims with each Champagne house trying to top each other to impress Cité du Vin, but the hotel where the board was going to stay burned to the ground two days ago. If you can believe it, there's a California growers conference in Reims at the same time, and all the hotels are booked. So, guess what. They're having their board meeting in Saint-Émilion. It starts with a cocktail party on Thursday night and an all-day meeting on Friday, followed by a dinner. They've already booked a hotel in Saint-Émilion that can accommodate them, but they want you, Philip, and Duncan to join them for the cocktail party, meeting, and dinner. They want to highlight The Art of the Vine. Elise knows you're incredibly busy, having just arrived at Château Beaulieu, but the next board meeting is in Italy, and they don't want to have to wait six more months after that to get the program rolling. Would you three be able to attend?"

"Hmm," Genevieve's mind churned. "That's next Thursday?"

"Yes."

"How many people are we talking about?"

"There are fifteen on the board and some ancillary staff, so maybe twenty or so. And of course, Bernard and I will be there. What are you thinking?"

"Only twenty or twenty-five? That's nothing, Lillie. We'll host the cocktail party, meeting, and dinner here. We'll make the Champagne houses look like amateurs. We'll blow their socks off. Right, Delphine?" She grinned at Delphine, who had been standing in the doorway, listening. Delphine smiled at the energy in the room, then, remembering why she was there, said, "Lady Crosswick, you have a visitor. Monsieur Wang est ici."

"Kim Wang?" Genevieve's eyebrows arched. "What in the world…" she caught herself and lowered her voice. "Did he say what he wants, Delphine?"

"Non, my lady, but he did come with a beautiful bouquet."

"Well, in that case, show him in."

She said into the phone, "Lillie, we have to go. Text me the specifics and let's talk later today."

"You're brilliant, Genevieve. You, too, Becca. Bye."

"Well, that's exciting. I can't wait to tell Philip."

Genevieve pulled a tube of lipstick from her pocket and applied it without looking in a mirror. She smoothed her hair and was ready for Kim. "Becca, did you meet Kim Wang at Daniel's celebration of life? He sat next to me."

Becca shook her head. "I don't think so. Who is he?"

"His family owns Clos Peyra, the vineyard next door. He's seriously handsome," she said, lowering her voice to a whisper as he walked into the room.

What an understatement, Becca thought as she looked at Kim Wang's elegant, classic features.

Genevieve stood and extended her hand. "Kim, what a wonderful surprise."

Avoiding her hand, he pulled her into la bise, careful not to crush the bouquet he was carrying.

She heard Becca's hum of approval and shot her a look that said, "Stop it."

"For you, Genevieve." He handed her a stunning assortment of hydrangeas, lilies, roses and stock, a riot of purples, deep blues, and oranges, that smelled of spring.

"How lovely." She buried her nose in the blossoms. "You would have been welcome without such a beautiful offering, but if you're going to come bearing gifts, please, come often." She flashed a dazzling smile. "Delphine, would you mind putting these in water?"

"Certainement, my lady."

"Kim, I don't believe you met our dear friend, Becca Conway, when you were here yesterday."

Becca's stomach fluttered as Kim turned his velvet brown eyes on her.

He held her captive in his gaze for several seconds before he took her hand and brought it to his lips. "I would not forget such an encounter, I assure you," he said.

At a loss for words, Genevieve stood by watching until Delphine came to the rescue. "Monsieur Wang, voulez-vous boire quelque chose?" she asked, her voice formal and cool.

He dragged his eyes from Becca to the housekeeper. "Le Champagne serait parfait," he said in flawless French. He nodded to the bottle of Veuve Clicquot.

Within moments, Delphine returned with a glass, filled it, and extended it to Wang. "Monsieur."

Hearing an icy note in Delphine's voice, Genevieve made a mental note to ask her about it later.

"Will there be anything else, my lady?"

"Not for the moment, Delphine. Thank you." She gave the housekeeper an affectionate nod.

"Please, Kim, sit." She motioned to a chair near the fire. "To us." She raised her glass and the three drank.

"If I may," Kim began, looking at Genevieve, who smiled for him to continue. "My wife Jing and I would like you to join us for dinner Friday evening." He looked at Becca. "And we would love for you and your fiancé to join us, Mademoiselle Conway. We can make it quite a party."

Becca flopped back against the cushion. "How disappointing. David and I have to go to London Friday morning. May we have a raincheck?"

"Raincheck?" Kim's cocked his head.

"I mean, I hope you'll invite us again."

"Of course. It will be our pleasure. When you return, you and Sir David must come to the Clos."

"Too bad for you, Becca, but, Kim, we'd love to come. I look forward to getting to know our next-door neighbors."

"Excellent," he said. He drained his flute and stood. He smiled at Becca. "You will be missed."

Genevieve rose to see him out, chatting until they arrived at the front door. Kim wrapped his scarf twice around his neck and draped his coat over his shoulders. He turned to Genevieve, took her hands in his and asked, "How are you doing?" his voice filled with concern.

"Why do you ask?" Genevieve said, surprised.

He studied her for several seconds until he knew she was growing uncomfortable. "I'm just a concerned neighbor," he said at last, and released her hands. "Aren't you worried about Daniel's death?" His gaze was riveting. "Look after yourself. I wouldn't want anything to happen to you." Then, without warning, he flashed a broad smile. "Jusqu'a vendredi," he said.

"Yes, we look forward to seeing you on Friday," she said, glad he was leaving.

TWENTY-SEVEN

A FRIGID WIND WHISTLED through gnarly vines, warning tender buds not to make an appearance yet. Looking out at the wintery scene, Genevieve sipped her steaming coffee and scrolled through her calendar. She made two more entries, then looked up to see Philip stroll through the door, looking very continental in snug jeans, a black turtleneck and a scarf knotted through a loop around his neck. The sight of him still made her stomach flutter. A good sign, she thought.

"Good morning, darling." He kissed her. He kissed her again. "Mmmm. Coffee." He licked his lips, took her mug and gulped the steaming java. She watched with admiration as he took another swig.

"How can you do that? It's almost boiling." She grimaced, imagining his scalded mouth.

"It's not that hot," he dismissed, and ran his fingertips over her cheekbone. "You know, you're a real beauty," he said, lured by her green eyes. With his fingers under her chin, he tilted her face up, leaned over and covered her mouth with his. He lingered there until his body told him to stop or find someplace more private to continue. He could feel her smiling and pulled his lips from hers just enough to say, "You think this is funny? It's going to be hilarious if Delphine walks in here and sees what state I'm in."

His lips still on hers, her giggle turned into a throaty laugh.

"What's the big joke? What did I miss?" David asked, making his entrance and heading to the sideboard, where fresh pastries were waiting to be eaten. He piled a croissant and a pain au chocolat on a plate, then turned back to Genevieve, who was still giggling. "So? What's so funny?"

"It was nothing, David." She waved him off. "Philip just told me a joke and it made me laugh." She gave him a sly smile and pulled a tissue from her pocket to blow her nose.

"You're joining us for our conversation with Inspector Boucher, aren't you, David?"

"That's my plan." He put his plate and mug on the table, pulled out a pine armchair and sat. He took an enormous bite of a warm croissant and flakes sprayed the front of his hunter-green sweater.

Genevieve smiled at the crumbs littering his chest. "Good, isn't it?"

"Mmmm." He chewed, then swallowed. "Scrumptious. Worth the mess," he said as he picked pastry from his pullover and popped it into his mouth.

Philip refilled his cup from the French press. "I've got to go. Duncan's been in the vineyard office for an hour. We're trying to get through the files before the agent from DREETS comes tomorrow. Boucher will take up most of our afternoon today, so we're running out of time."

"What are you looking for?" David asked. "Is there any way I can help?"

"We're not sure what we're looking for, but whatever it is, six eyes are better than four. Come on."

"And they're off," Genevieve said to herself. As she watched them hustle out the door and stride across the terrace toward the vineyard office, she heard a growling in her stomach and realized she needed to eat. As if reading her thoughts, Delphine appeared with a new pot of coffee and a narrow tray of mini baguettes. "What are the chances I could have an omelet with mushrooms, olives and cheese?" she asked Delphine, knowing the chances were excellent.

"Lizette will have it done dans un moment. Fruit aussi? And what may I get you, Mademoiselle Conway?" she said as Becca walked in.

"Just coffee, please, Delphine." Becca sucked in her stomach. "I have to watch out for you and Lizette. You're treacherous with your fresh pastries and fabulous meals. She puffed out her cheeks.

"Madame, it would take many croissants before you have to worry about your waistline." Pleased with the praise, the house manager scooped up a tray of dirty plates and headed toward the kitchen. As Genevieve watched her leave, she marveled at how she and Philip had so quickly adjusted to having a small army of people care for their every need. It hadn't taken long to go from being self-sufficient to having most of their needs catered to.

"Becca." Genevieve took a sip of coffee and put down her cup before continuing. "You grew up in a very wealthy household. Did you always have a lot of staff to take care of you and your family?"

Before answering, Becca thought for several seconds. She draped her linen napkin in her lap and leaned her elbows on the table. "We did. When I think about it, I'm sure it was part of why I was such a mess for a long time."

Genevieve leaned forward, surprised.

"For years I was indulged and pampered. When I look at Émile, I see a lot of myself. Speaking of Émile, when will he get out of the hospital?"

"Funny you should ask. Henri went to pick him up about an hour ago. They should be back any time."

"I didn't hear what Émile's father said when Philip called to tell him his son had been poisoned. Was he furious?"

The shake of her head was almost imperceptible. Then, Genevieve said, "I was surprised by his comments, but Émile has been a problem for his parents for a long time."

Becca sat back in her chair. "What in the world did he say?"

"He said he shouldn't have been drinking while he was supposed to be working."

"Wow! That's heartless!" Becca snorted a laugh. "Compared to Baron de Sézanne, my parents were Mother Theresa and Gandhi. When Philip called him, was Émile out of danger?"

"He was. I don't think Philip dwelled on the fact that Émile could have died. My guess is he minimized that little piece of information. No need to worry the baron unnecessarily." She rolled her eyes.

"Wise thinking on Philip's part."

As if on cue, Émile ambled through the door carrying Genevieve's omelet and an array of fresh melon and raspberries.

"Well, speak of the devil. Émile, ça va?" Genevieve asked.

He smirked at her. "I am not as well as I would be if I had not been poisoned."

She couldn't help but smile. "I guess that's the last time you drink from a random bottle of wine," she deadpanned.

He set the plate in front of her. "You are correct." Having something more to say, he lingered, shifting from one foot to the other, then back again.

"Thank you, Émile." The dark circles around his eyes accentuated his ghostly pallor and he was even thinner than before he was poisoned. "We're happy you're out of the hospital and on your way to your old self. Lizette needs to ply you with lots of pastries so you can put on a few pounds." Still, he remained until Genevieve said, "Is there something else?"

"Yes, Lady Crosswick, there is." He studied the floor for several seconds. When he looked up, his eyes were moist. "Lady Crosswick, I want to thank you." His voice cracked. "The doctor said if you had not found me when you did, I could have died."

Genevieve's chair scraped on the floor as she stood. She clutched Émile's shoulders, then pulled him into a hug. His rigid body neither resisted nor surrendered. They stood in an awkward embrace, Émile's arms at his sides, until Genevieve decided she should let him go. As she released him, she felt his muscles relax.

He stepped back and gave her a stiff pat on the shoulder. He looked at her, then at Becca. "If there is nothing I can do for either of you, I should see if Delphine needs me."

But before he could escape, Becca moved in to give him a peck on the cheek. "Welcome home, Émile. We're glad you're back."

Crimson crept up his neck to the tops of his ears. "Merci," he mumbled, then turned and fled, passing Delphine as she walked back into the orangerie.

"What did you two do to that poor boy?" Delphine asked as she cleared plates and refilled coffee cups.

"We were just showing him we care," Becca said. "I think it might have been a bit too much for him." Her lips parted in a broad grin.

Genevieve rolled her spoon between her fingers. "He seems so vulnerable. I'd almost say sweet." She looked at Becca and Delphine for confirmation.

Becca nodded. "Sweet is the perfect word. Quite a change from the would-be art thief who tried to steal your Pollock."

"He's going to be fine," Delphine said with confidence. "The house staff is working him hard, but he's not complaining, and the vineyard workers are making him earn his place. That is as it should be." Her eyes softened. "And, I am happy to say, he is making friends."

Through the windows, they watched Émile lope across the terrace toward the vineyard, then turn as a young worker, about his age, called to him and waved. A lopsided smile plastered on his face, Émile waved back, and they walked together into the vines. With the sun brilliant in the winter-blue sky, the two were soon lost in its blaze. Watching them, Genevieve felt a glow of pride that she and Philip were helping this lad change the course of his life.

"My lady, may I get you anything else?" Genevieve's attention was pulled back into the orangerie.

"Delphine, could you please sit down for a minute?"

The house manager's brows arched. She hesitated for a heartbeat then said, "Mais oui," and sat on the edge of a paisley-covered dining chair.

"Yesterday, when Monsieur Wang was here, I got the impression you don't like him very much. Or perhaps I'm wrong." She studied Delphine's expression, but it gave away nothing. Waiting for a reply, she rose and picked up the carafe.

"Coffee?"

"Oui, s'il vous plaît." As Genevieve poured, Delphine folded her hands on the table. "You are perceptive, my lady. Or, perhaps I am too transparent." She draped her napkin over her knees. "I am not, as you Americans say, a fan of Monsieur Wang."

"And why is that?" Becca eased into the conversation.

"Alors, I can only say it is a feeling I have gotten over the years." Her eyes were glued to the napkin she was now twisting in her lap.

"There's nothing specific, no event, no one thing he has done to make you suspicious of him?" Genevieve looked at Becca, then back at Delphine. "Nothing?" she pressed.

Breathing a deep sigh, Delphine dropped the wrinkled serviette and locked Genevieve in her gaze. "If you must know, there are two reasons I believe Kim Wang is not the homme charmant he would like everyone to believe he is."

"Do tell." Becca leaned forward anticipating some great gossip.

"The first incident was when the Wangs had just moved into Clos Peyra. Monsieur Wang's father owns the conglomerate that bought the vineyard from the original French owners."

"I assume you were not happy about that."

"No one in Saint-Émilion was." Delphine sipped her coffee, wrinkled her nose at the cold brew, and shoved the cup away. "According to the potins, uh, the gossip, Kim was sent to make the clos more profitable and more prestigious. But, I am getting off the trail. Is that what you say?"

"Close enough." Genevieve bobbed her head, encouraging Delphine to continue.

"The Wangs had just moved into Clos Peyra, so I decided to take a basket of Lizette's pastries, some jams she had made, and, of course, two bottles of wine as a welcome gift."

"What a nice thing to do," Becca said.

"I walked through the headlands and alleyways from Château Beaulieu to Clos Peyra." Two blank faces looked at her. "A headland is the space at the end of a vineyard row and the alleyways are breaks between vineyard blocks, you know, rows of similar vines that are planted together in a block."

"Aha," the two said in unison.

"My point is that because I walked through the vineyard rather than drove, no one heard me coming. When I arrived, I knocked and the front door creaked open, so I eased into the foyer."

"This sounds like a murder mystery," Becca said, eyes wide.

Delphine patted Becca's hand. "I promise, I did not *see* Monsieur Wang actually murder anyone." She bit her lower lip. "But, I did hear an angry conversation, or I should say tirade."

Genevieve shook her head. "Your English is amazing, Delphine." Though Genevieve's French was excellent, she was in awe of Delphine's vast lexicon. "What is the French word for tirade?" she asked.

Delphine's lips twitched. "Why, tirade, of course," she said, which sent the three women into a fit of laughter.

As their hilarity dwindled, Delphine took a deep breath and blew her nose. "Let me finish," she said.

Becca couldn't stop giggling.

"All right, all right." Genevieve tried to look serious. "I want to hear the rest of your story, Delphine."

"And I want to *tell* you the rest of my story, my lady." Her amusement was gone, and she was sober again. "Être-vous prêt?"

Becca gave a thumbs up though she still giggled under her breath.

"Where was I?" Delphine thought for a moment then remembered. "Ah yes," she said, holding up her index finger. "I heard the tirade and had decided I should put the basket of pastries down and leave, when a few words caught my ears. I heard several men in a room. They seemed to be in a hot discussion. I had not met Kim Wang or any of the Wang family so I didn't know their voices, but I could tell that Kim's father was arguing with him."

Genevieve gulped from her water glass. "You don't speak Chinese, do you, Delphine?"

"No, of course not." Delphine shook her head. "They spoke French rather than Chinese, which I thought was odd until I realized there must be men in the room who only spoke French."

"Interesting." Two lines etched between Becca's brows. "What did they say?"

Delphine gazed into the distance, trying to recall what she had heard. "They were arguing about purchasing Château Beaulieu. Kim's father said if Kim couldn't make the deal, he must find another way to use Château Beaulieu's name." With her napkin, she dabbed the perspiration from her upper lip.

"What in the world did he mean by that?" Genevieve scowled then brightened, remembering something. "I may be able to answer my own question. When Daniel came to Paris, he said the Wangs have tried to buy the château several times. According to him, they wanted Château Beaulieu for something their own vineyard didn't have: a prestigious name."

Did you hear anything else," Becca asked.

"I did not. At that moment, Madame Wang appeared in the doorway behind me. She seemed to come from nowhere and I almost dropped the basket. Of course, I was embarrassed that she caught me écoute clandestine, I believe you say eavesdropping." Delphine's breath quickened as she relived the episode. "The madame was tres gentile, very kind, and took me into a beautiful little sitting room. She offered me tea, but I told her I had to get back to Château Beaulieu. I was anxious to leave. I don't know if Madame Wang told le monsieur I had overheard his conversation, but since that time, whenever he sees me he is very cool to me."

Deflated, Genevieve slumped in her chair. She wasn't sure what she had expected, but she thought Delphine's big reveal would be something more dramatic than overhearing a group of disappointed businessmen argue. She shivered and realized her cardigan had slipped off her shoulders and was gathered behind her. She wiggled it up her back and shoved her arms into the sleeves.

"It's chilly in here, isn't it?"

"Un peu, my lady. Would you like some hot coffee? This is cold," Delphine said, cupping her hands around the glass pot.

"Or tea, peut être?"

"I think I've had enough. Becca?"

Becca shook her head. "No, thank you. I'm fine. I want to hear the other reason you don't like Kim."

"I need to see if Inspector Boucher has arrived. But, Delphine," Genevieve and Becca leaned forward, eyes riveted on the housekeeper, "before I do, please finish." They had no idea what to expect but hoped for something more exciting.

Going against her rigid standards, Delphine poured cold coffee into her cup and drained it. "This would benefit from a shot of cognac," she mumbled. "What I am about to tell you is rather strange." The gold light streaming through the bank of French doors dimmed as the clouds swept across the sun. Her mood darkened with the fading light. "About six months ago, I took a lunch tray to Daniel. He was not in his office, so I left it on his desk."

"Before going back to the château, I decided to see if Henri needed anything. Knowing there was a new Lord and Lady Crosswick, he was here at the château rather than in Paris. He was going over every automobile to make certain they were all in perfect working order." She hesitated then went on. "I came around the corner of the garage and saw someone I believe to be Kim Wang put a rolled-up Persian carpet in the back of a Clos Peyra Range Rover."

Genevieve's brow furrowed. "Why did you say you saw someone you *believe* to be Kim Wang putting, a carpet in the back of his car?"

"I can't be certain, my lady, because he was wearing a hat and

I was quite a distance away."

Becca's eyes narrowed. "I'm sorry, Delphine; how is that significant?"

"That is significant, madame, because what if the carpet had a body rolled up in it?"

TWENTY-EIGHT

There was a long moment of silence while Genevieve and Becca looked at each other and then at Delphine.

"Delphine, are you suggesting that Kim Wang, a respected international businessman, and our neighbor, rolled a dead body in a carpet and tossed it in his Range Rover? That's what you're telling us?" Becca pressed.

"Oui, madame. A Persian carpet," she emphasized.

Genevieve mirrored Becca's look of disbelief. She was struggling to imagine that the house manager hadn't had a terrible dream. Or perhaps she had eaten magic mushrooms? Or had she been tipsy at the time? In Genevieve's mind, it was impossible that this man could do such a thing. "So, tell us, Delphine, what did you do next?"

Knowing her employer and her employer's friend thought she might be delusional, Delphine proceeded with care. "I can remember my first thought was to take a photograph on my mobile. I reached into my pocket, and it was not there. I could not photograph the man, and I could not call anyone if I got into trouble."

Surprised at the thought, Becca said, "Did you really think you might be in danger?"

Stiffening in her chair, Delphine narrowed her eyes. "Mademoiselle, would you not fear for your life if you were in the company of a man you thought had just murdered a man… or a woman?"

"Well, you weren't actually in his company, were you?"

Delphine rose from her chair, her jaw rigid, and began gathering napkins left on the table, brushing crumbs that had fallen from pastries. "I know what I saw," she said between clenched teeth. She was about to leave when Genevieve caught her arm.

"Delphine, please sit down. Try to understand what a surprise this is for Becca and me. To imagine Kim as a murderer is not easy. He doesn't look like a murderer, does he?" Genevieve flushed.

"And he's very charming," Becca added.

"We're just trying to process a shocking piece of information." Genevieve tugged on Delphine's arm until the house manager sat. "Please tell us what happened next."

Delphine's shoulders softened as she began to relax, but the clock ticked many times before she responded. At last, she said, "As you might imagine, I went straight to Daniel. I looked in his office, but he had not returned."

"Did you ever talk to Daniel?"

With her chin jutting, Delphine said, "Bien sûr, I reached him on his portable in Saint-Émilion and what he told me was surprising. He said the château had sold the carpet to Monsieur Wang. It had been in storage for years and the trustees of the estate wanted everything not in use," she pursed her lips and squinted, thinking, "mmm, liquated?"

Genevieve and Becca grinned at Delphine. "Liquidated," they said together.

"Philip and I know about the 12TH Earl's wishes to ensure his properties were efficient and self-sustaining, and that he ordered anything not in use to be," Genevieve paused and smiled at Delphine, "liquidated. Daniel's explanation about the carpet makes sense. Lord Crosswick and I appreciate what they did because Philip didn't inherit a heap of monetary perils. All the holdings are in sound financial shape." She cocked her head and said, "What did Daniel say about a body in the carpet?"

Delphine studied the border on the tablecloth. She looked up at Genevieve through her lashes. "I did not tell him. I started to, but then I thought he might think I was un peu fou, a little mad." She looked down again. "Perhaps he would have been right. Perhaps we'll never know."

TWENTY-NINE

Inspector Charles Boucher of the Bureau of Enquiry and Analysis, the BEA, woke at 5:25 a.m., five minutes before his alarm clock was set to jangle him from sleep. As he showered and dressed his rotund figure more carefully than usual, he felt a tickle of excitement in the pit of his stomach. Since he began investigating the mysterious incident of water in the tank of the 13TH Earl of Crosswick's Bombardier, he was starting every day with a renewed interest in his job.

For the last few years, as retirement loomed, the most important cases had been landing on the desks of younger officers. It didn't matter that he could dance circles around the rookies. They were coming out of universities having mastered mind-blowing technology. They were arrogant, dapper, and too flash. Charles Boucher was a slogger, but he had almost forty years of success under his belt and he was not going to let anyone else have this case. Besides, he had a crush on Lady Crosswick and he liked being around rich people.

By eight o'clock, he was in his wide leather seat, comfortable on the TGV from Paris to Bordeaux. The 340-mile trip would take two hours and twenty minutes. The commute from his home in the Paris suburbs to his office on the opposite side of the city could sometimes take almost that long. With fifteen minutes until departure, he made his way to the café car and indulged in a cappuccino and jambon et fromage croissant, lightly heated. There would be a car waiting for him at the station, and Lord and Lady Crosswick had invited him to stay at their château. He was looking forward to a night on thousand-thread-count sheets.

As the train slid out of Gare Saint-Lazare, Boucher slurped the last of his coffee. When he looked down, a field of flakes from his croissant covered his belly. If the lord and lady invited him to dinner, he'd have to do better.

He glanced at his watch, 8:27. He would be at Gare de Bordeaux-Saint-Jean by 10:45 or so. That would put him at Château Beaulieu around noon, perfect timing for lunch. "I bet they'll have something delicious, something traditional," he said to himself. He hoped there would be foie gras. The Bordelaise loved foie gras, and so did he. He could almost taste the rich, buttery delicacy. He leaned back against the headrest and licked his lips. It was going to be a spectacular twenty-four hours. Perhaps with luck he could stretch it to forty-eight.

"Dad, is this anything?" Duncan held up a copy of an email chain two pages long in French. "It was in this file marked 'Confidentielle'." In his other hand, he waved a blue folder. "Who in the world prints out emails?"

David snorted a laugh. "Wrinklies."

"Is that a shot at people my age, you pipsqueak?" Sitting at the desk, Philip peered between stacks of papers piled high. "What does it say, Duncan?"

"Dad, I can say with confidence that my French is no better today than it was yesterday. David, would you take a look at this?"

"Righto," he said, shoving himself off the floor with a grunt. He skimmed the paper, then scowled and looked at it again, reading slowly this time. "This might be something," he said, not taking his eyes from the page. He reached behind for a chair and sat.

"What is it, David?"

He held up his hand. "Give me a second here," he said, continuing to read.

Behind his desk, Philip stood, straightened his arms over his head, and groaned as he stretched. As he walked around the desk, he and Duncan locked eyes and his son shrugged his shoulders.

Philip sat on the edge of his desk and they waited. He looked at his watch and they waited. "What do you—"

David raised his hand again, demanding silence. Another two minutes dragged by.

Just as Duncan was about to go back to searching the files, David whispered, "Bloody hell. Bloody hell," he said again, louder this time.

"What is it, David?"

"Sit down, you two." His eyes dark as pitch, David looked from the papers in his hands to the two men waiting for his big reveal. "We need to have a French speaker confirm my translation, but this exchange is about a plan to buy Château Beaulieu and the need for another plan if the trustees won't sell."

Reaching for the pages, Philip said, "Let me see that, David. Who's it from?"

"I can't tell who sent or received the correspondence, but someone who knows tech would be able to tell."

Philip's eyes darted back and forth on the page. "What's this?" He pointed to a phrase and turned the page so David could see.

> *S'ils ne nous vendent pas, nous obtiendrons ce dont nous avons besoin d'une autre manière.*

David took the paper. "It says, 'If they won't sell to us, we'll get what we need another way'."

"That's what I thought it said. We'll share this with Boucher when he gets here." He glanced at the 19th-century bronze wall clock just as it pinged the first of twelve chimes. "By the way, shouldn't he be here by now?"

Deep in Philip's pocket, *Les Marseilles* announced a phone call. He fished in his trousers and pulled out his cell phone. Genevieve's picture filled his screen. "Hi, G. What's up?"

"Inspector Boucher just arrived. Delphine is showing him to his room. I told him we'd gather in the salon for drinks at twelve thirty, so you, David, and Duncan need to think about coming back to the house. I assume you're still in the vineyard office. Have you found anything interesting?"

"As a matter of fact, we have." He was still holding the emails. "It's good timing because Boucher might be interested in these."

"These what?" Genevieve's curiosity reached through the line.

"A couple of pages of emails."

"Sounds fascinating." Her sarcasm was hard to ignore.

Philip waved the pages in the air. "You just wait. This might be important."

"Clearly, you three are in a frenzy with your riveting emails and I bet you have a couple of wild texts, too, but you need to come back to the château, now."

"All right, all right. We'll be there. Give us ten minutes to wrap it up here."

"The timer's on, pal." And she was gone.

"Guys, we've got to…"

"We got it, Dad. The general has ordered the troops back to the barracks. Right?"

"Pretty much. Let's roll."

THIRTY

Cozy in an overstuffed chair just close enough to the crackling fire, Charles Boucher closed his eyes and sighed an appreciative "Mmmm," as he sipped his Kir Royale. He was the first to arrive in the salon and was not shy about making himself at home, with Delphine's permission, of course. It would be nice to have a foot stool, he mused, as his feet didn't quite touch the floor. He looked around for an ottoman.

"Inspector Boucher," Philip strode across the sun-kissed room, his hand outstretched.

Boucher scooched his bottom forward in the chair until his feet touched the floor. He popped out of the chair just in time to grab Philip's hand and pump it. "Lord Crosswick, it is un plaisir to be in your beautiful château. Merci pour votre hospitalite."

"It's our pleasure, Inspector. It makes sense for you to stay here. And I'd like you to meet our solicitor, Sir David Weatherington." He motioned for Boucher to be seated. "Lady Crosswick will be down shortly."

With a small tray with Kir Royales for Philip and David in one hand and a tray of hors d'oeuvres in the other, Delphine delivered the drinks, offered the appetizers, and was gone.

Anxious to hear what the inspector had discovered in the last few days, Philip was having difficulty waiting for Genevieve and Duncan, so he focused on small talk. "How was your trip, inspector?"

"It was wonderful, my lord. I love the TGV. I believe they have the best coffee in France."

"Are you serious?" David asked. "It would never have occurred to me that train coffee would be anything special. Good to know. Have you been to Bordeaux before?"

"Ah, oui. I was born in Libourne."

"Libourne! That's just a few miles away."

"So it is. My parents moved to Paris when I was a small boy, but for years I spent my summer holidays in this area with my aunt and uncle. They grew grapes for the wineries in Bordeaux and I would work in the vines."

"What a wonderful way to spend your summers." Images flashed through Philip's mind: of learning to leaf and prune and sucker, and the other important jobs that went into creating the perfect grape.

"I hated it," Boucher deadpanned. "I was miserable every summer. Would rather have stayed in school."

At a loss for words, Philip was grateful to hear Genevieve's voice.

"Inspector Boucher," she said. "How wonderful to see you."

Again, Boucher wiggled out of his chair and stretched to his full five foot three. Genevieve's handshake was firm and her hand silky. He held it a bit too tight and a bit too long and was embarrassed when she had to tug it from his grip.

"It's my pleasure to be here, my lady," he said, feeling heat in the tops of his ears.

"I trust your trip was smooth and uneventful."

"It was. I didn't give my briefcase to a stranger, if that's what you mean." Boucher chuckled and arched his eyebrows at Genevieve in what he thought was a charming flirt.

"You're much too clever for that," she vamped in return. "Duncan is on his way," she said as her son walked into the salon. "Speak of the devil."

"Sorry I'm late. I was on the phone with Julia, trying to solve the crisis of how Ella could stay on the swim team and still take dance and art. So many interests, so little time." The warmth filled his voice as he talked about his daughter. "Inspector Boucher, I'm Duncan Warwick, Lord and Lady Crosswick's son."

Boucher couldn't get out of his chair before Duncan was upon him. He craned his neck looking up at the Warwicks' son, who loomed over him, his hand outstretched. He could do nothing but offer his hand in return and try to meet the strength of the younger man's grasp. He was grateful that the handshake was brief. He admired the easy elegance of the younger Warwick and felt a quiver of jealousy. Why were rich people always attractive, he wondered?

"Have I missed anything?" Before sitting next to his mother on the sofa, Duncan tossed a log on the dwindling fire and the dry wood sparked into flames.

Genevieve patted her son's hand. "We were waiting for you."

"I understand you have news about the water in the Bombardier's fuel tank," Philip said, anxious to get to the point.

Boucher snuggled deep into his chair, happy to have the conversation in his court. He put his glass on the table beside him, hoping Delphine would notice it was empty. He reached into the inside pocket of his jacket and brought out the same small, scuffed notebook he had in Paris, but instead of the gnawed stub of pencil he had used before, he rolled an iconic black Mont Blanc pen lovingly between his fingers.

"First I must say, we in the BEA take incidents such as attempted murder very seriously."

Genevieve looked at Philip to see if the brutality of the words "attempted murder" had startled him. He seemed unphased.

"My team has been working very hard on your case, and we are making progress. We have found several things we would like to share with you, Lord and Lady Crosswick." He nodded at Duncan. "And, you, as well, my lord."

He saw his glass out of the corner of his eye. Somehow Delphine had replaced his empty flute with a fresh Kir Royale without him noticing. "She is stealth. We need her in the BEA," he thought. His observation made him smile.

Turning his thoughts back to business, he flipped his notebook open and studied it for a moment, using his Mont Blanc as a stylus to focus on each line. "Alors," he said, and looked up from the pad, his eyes sparkling. "J'ai trois chose…" He shook his head. "Pardon. En anglais, oui? He apologized and shifted to English. "I have three things of importance to tell you."

"Excellent," Philip said, encouraging the inspector to get on with it.

With his hand fisted, he held up his thumb. "First, we have

information about the mystery of water in the gas tank. With the help of our counterpart in the UK, the AAIB, the Air Accident Investigation Branch and their surveillance cameras, we know who watered your jet fuel."

"They had some decent video?" David asked. "That's a lucky break."

Genevieve shot forward in her chair. "Does that mean you know who did it?" She held her breath.

"Oui," Boucher said.

Philip and Duncan leaned forward, shoulders tense.

"Who did it?" Philip asked through clenched teeth. "Who tried to kill us?"

Looking back at his notebook, Boucher flipped a page forward. "His name is Lee Bowen. He is a minor voyou." He rolled his eyes to the ceiling. "What is the word en anglais?"

"Thug." Delphine had again slipped into the salon to freshen drinks and pass hors d'oeuvres.

The inspector started at her voice. "Merci, madame," he said to her retreating back. "She is quite something, hein?"

"Yes, she's quite something, indeed." Genevieve was anxious to keep Inspector Boucher on track, which was a challenge. "Tell us more about Lee Bowen, the minor thug," she pressed.

Unable to resist his third Kir Royale, he took a drink and then popped a tiny morsel of warm pastry stuffed with goat cheese into his mouth. "Delicieuse," he said, then hummed as he chewed.

Philip stood and walked to the fireplace. He warmed his hands then turned to Boucher. He was finding it difficult to keep his annoyance in check. "If you don't mind, inspector, could you please concentrate on sharing the information you came over three hundred miles to give us. So far, the little you've told us could have been shared in a phone call."

"Mais oui, my lord. I, uh, I apologize for getting off the paths."

"I think you mean track," Philip muttered.

"Hein?"

"Off the track. Getting off the track, man!" Philip almost shouted. He raised both hands in apology. "I'm sorry, Boucher. I'm a little on edge."

"But of course," Boucher smiled. "Who would not be on edge with people trying to kill them and trying to steal their expensive painting and their fine wine poisoning people?" His lips were pursed as he said, "Rohh la la," and shook his hand as if he had burned himself. "Quelle pagaille. Everything is quite a mess, is it not?"

"What do you mean when you say our wine is killing people? Are you talking about Daniel LaGrande?"

"Oui, I am."

Philip squeezed his eyes closed, massaged his neck, then opened his eyes. "How do you know about that? We haven't talked about our suspicions with anyone but the local police."

"Ah, my lord." Boucher's grin revealed deep dimples in his chubby cheeks. "I know everything, everywhere."

David rolled his eyes, impatient.

With a toss of his head, Boucher laughed and waved his hands in the air. His smile faded. "But, sadly, that is not true. If I must tell the truth, I have friends here. When I knew I was coming to see you I called a childhood ami, Frederick Picard, who is le Chef de la police municipal in Saint-Émilion. I wanted to find out if he had any information that could help our investigation. He informed me that Émile de Laudre had been taken to the hospital when he became ill from drinking poisoned wine, the same bottle from which Daniel LaGrande drank just before he died." As if remembering something, he blinked twice, then wrote for a moment in his little book.

He sucked in a breath and let it out, looking over Philip's shoulder with a vacant stare. "There are too many…" he paused, searching for the right word. "Unsettling, is that a word?" He shifted his gaze to Philip, who nodded in confirmation. "There are too many unsettling events to be unrelated."

Duncan slumped back in his chair. "You're suggesting, Inspector Boucher, that there is a thread connecting everything that has happened, from the watered fuel to the poisoned wine?"

"Baahh, oui," Boucher said, again pouting his lips, one brow arched. "It is more sensible than believing that each event is unique, n'est ce pas?"

Genevieve's eyes narrowed as she considered Boucher's theory, and staring into the fire, Philip replayed the inspector's words, wondering if they made sense.

For a while no one spoke, then David said, "But why would anyone be doing these things? Do you think there's a crazed maniac who randomly chose the Warwicks to attack?"

A mischievous smile twisted the inspector's lips. "Non, I do not believe there is a crazed manic stalking the Warwick family, but I do have a theory," he said, but went no further.

Four pairs of eyes stayed riveted on Boucher, waiting for him to go on.

They waited. The crackling of the fire and ticking of the brass pendulum clock bounced off the walls of the salon while the inspector sat in silence. With each tick of the clock, the tension in the room thickened. He rolled his Mont Blanc between his thumb and forefinger, studying the titled trio in front of him.

His nerves fraying with each breath, Philip was willing to wait no longer. He stood, walked to the fireplace, and turned. He drew himself to his full height, looming over Boucher, who sunk back into his overstuffed chair.

Philip's voice was even, but his eyes blazed. "Inspector, what are you playing at?" He stepped toward the officer.

Startled by Philip's sharp tone, Boucher burrowed even further into his cushion. "I promise, my lord, I am not playing at anything," he said and put up both his hands in defense. "I am simply offering a hypothesis."

"Then offer it," Philip snapped. "What do you think is going on?"

Genevieve and Duncan exchanged glances. His family had always known Philip to have an occasional flash of temper, but he was never so quick to anger as when he thought his family was in peril, which seemed to be happening too frequently since inheriting his title and wealth.

Boucher motioned to Philip to sit back down. "My lord, my intention was not to upset you and your family. Rather, my intention was to give you an opportunity to offer any thoughts you might have on all that has happened. It is remarkable how much people recall when they have time to consider events." He spread his hands wide. "Apparently, nothing comes to mind at the moment so I shall tell you my conjecture. Please, my lord, be seated. I promise I am as concerned as you are about the safety and well-being of your family."

"I doubt that very much, inspector." Philip's voice still had a cautionary edge. "But by all means, go on."

Boucher had been hoping that Delphine would appear and offer more of those little salty nibbles. He felt a gnawing in his stomach and worried it would begin rumbling. As if answering his prayers, the house manager appeared in the doorway.

"Excusez-moi, Lady Crosswick, mais le déjeuner est servi."

Genevieve stood, glad for the break in the tension. "Merci, Delphine. Gentlemen," she motioned toward the foyer. "Shall we go into lunch and continue the discussion?"

Boucher salivated at the thought of the delicious lunch to come. He scooched forward in the chair until his feet hit the floor. He drained his glass and set it on the coffee table.

David extended his hand. "Inspector, it has been most interesting. I have another commitment, so I'll say goodbye. Lord Crosswick will keep me informed of your progress."

"It has been mon plaisir, Sir David," Boucher said, then in a gentile gesture he crooked his elbow and offered it to Genevieve. She slipped her arm through his and they ambled across the foyer, into an intimate salon overlooking the vineyard.

As he walked into the beautiful room with a stunning table set for four, Boucher felt both a rush of pleasure and a sense of being out of place. These feelings clashed so loudly in his head, he was sure everyone could hear the clamor.

Genevieve patted the back of an upholstered dining chair. "Please, inspector, sit here, next to me."

He grinned, held her chair as his mother had taught him years ago, then eased his bulk between the delicate walnut arms of his chair. He watched Genevieve drape her napkin over her lap, snatched his from the table, unfolded it and laid it across his knees.

"Inspector Boucher, did I hear you say you are from Bordeaux?" Genevieve filled the room with small talk until the first course had been served and they could get back to the serious business at hand.

As he responded to Genevieve's query, Boucher leaned toward Lady Crosswick, taking in her elegant scent.

Duncan and Philip exchanged a wordless understanding that they must keep Boucher on track. He seemed distracted by the trappings of Château Beaulieu and by Genevieve herself. Duncan found it annoying that the rumpled police inspector was puppy-dogging his mother. Philip found it amusing.

Chloé placed the first course, smoked salmon, at each person's place and left a tray of small, warm baguettes on the table. When she was finished, she stood by the door.

Deep in conversation about Boucher's childhood in Bordeaux, Genevieve didn't realize Chloé was still in the room. She heard Philip clear his throat, looked up, and saw her lingering in the doorway. "Is there something else, Chloé?" Genevieve said.

"Ah, non, my lady." She dipped into a small curtsy and eased out of the room.

"Let's get back to your thoughts on the case, shall we, inspector?"

Philip commanded. He rose, pulled the bottle of white Bordeaux from the cooler and filled each glass.

Boucher gazed lovingly at the wine, pale gold liquid sparkling through the facets. "Si jolie!" he said, eyes filled with delight.

"All right, inspector." Philip was willing to wait no longer. "You were about to tell us your theory that all the events since we arrived in France are connected."

"All except the painting prank. I can say with assurance, Émile de Laudre is not a mastermind in an international ring of art thieves."

Everyone around the table smiled.

"I'm sure we can all agree on that," Duncan said. "But how do you think the fuel and Daniel's poisoning are linked?"

His mouth full of fish, it was a moment before Boucher could answer. He wiped his lips and enjoyed a long drink of the delicate Bordeaux. At last he answered. "First, the AAIB can confirm that Lee Bowen was caught on CCTV watering the fuel. He flew later that day from Leeds Bradford to Paris on a RyanAir flight." He slid another bite of salmon into his mouth.

"Merde," Philip mumbled Genevieve's favorite word under his breath. Here they were again embroiled in a mess, a dangerous mess.

"Dad?" Philip felt Duncan's concerned gaze on him. "I'm all right, Duncan. I just can't imagine why someone would want to kill us in a plane crash. Or kill us at all, for that matter." He leaned back in his chair. "I'm sure there's more to this theory, inspector."

"There is, my lord." Boucher tore an end from a baguette, slathered butter across the moist crumb and bit off a too-big bite.

He was the only one eating. The other three were picking at their salmon with little interest and waiting with amazing patience for him to continue. When his mouth was almost empty, he went on. "It is my understanding that, over the years, the Wang family has made several offers to buy Château Beaulieu. Is that correct?"

Philip bobbed his head. "We were unaware of the offers before Daniel told us. As I'm sure you know, the Chinese have been interested in the French wine market for years. They were buying châteaux at a rapid pace for a while, then the pace slowed, but now they're back at it. I'm also sure that you're well aware that Château Beaulieu is not for sale. Not now, and not in the foreseeable future."

Boucher nodded. "Je comprehend. And that makes my point stronger."

Genevieve scowled. "What do you mean?"

Boucher looked around the table. "D'accord, if someone wants to buy your vineyard and you do not want to sell it, how can they get it?"

Duncan sat forward. "You mean if you are a person who doesn't let morality get in the way?"

A light flashed in Philip's eyes. "That would explain the email we found that said if they couldn't buy Château Beaulieu, they would get it another way." Philip couldn't believe what was happening

Surprise jolted Boucher forward in his chair. "Vraiment? You have this email for me?"

"Yes, of course."

Duncan shook his head, skeptical of the idea. "I suppose

you kill the people who own it and buy it out of the estate. But wouldn't it be difficult to kill all the heirs?"

"Certainement, but you can frighten enough of the heirs so they might be happy to have a few more euros in their bank account and go home, n'est ce pas?" He narrowed his eyes at Duncan. "If your parents had been killed in a plane crash on their way to France, would you have come here to be the managing director?"

"How do you know about that?" Philip said, startled that Boucher knew of the family's plans for Duncan to take over Château Beaulieu.

Boucher snorted, "My friend on the Saint-Émilion police force told me." He shrugged. "He, how you say, gets about."

"Gets around," Philip said. He stabbed a small piece of salmon and brought it toward his mouth. Halfway there, he froze. His eyes went wide, and he smacked his forehead with his palm. "Of course. Of course. Your friend heads the Saint-Émilion police force. I talked to him yesterday."

Boucher's brows shot up, his Cheshire cat smile stretching from ear to ear.

"I asked him to check the bottle of wine Madame Duveau was drinking when she died."

A smirk had replaced Boucher's broad grin.

"You know, don't you? Tell me. Was Madame Duveau poisoned?"

Boucher shook his head, "No," and opened his mouth to speak, but instead a belch popped from his parted lips. Clutching his napkin, his hand flew to his mouth. He looked down at his plate, then up into Genevieve's eyes, which danced with amusement.

"Oh, my lady, excusez moi."

Stifling a giggle, Genevieve patted his hand. "Please, inspector. It's all right. Quite flattering, really. I'll tell Lizette you loved her salmon." He would carry the embarrassment with him for some time, she was sure.

Disinterested in the inspector's unease, Philip refocused the conversation. "Are you sure her bottle of wine had no traces of poison?"

"The police lab found no traces of poison in the bottle. They have confirmed she died of natural causes."

Genevieve brought her wine glass halfway to her mouth. It hovered there for a moment while she stared out the French doors. "Let's go back further, before Madame Duveau. Why would anyone kill Daniel?" She took a drink and held it in her mouth for a moment before swallowing it. "And you're not suggesting, are you, that someone in the Wang family has set all this in motion?"

Chloé came in and began removing the first course plates from the table.

Using an expression the Warwicks were learning to expect, Inspector Boucher pooched out his lower lip and vibrated a little farty sound, followed by, "Oh la la." He shrugged one shoulder and went on. "I am not yet prepared to say that. It could be many people together, or one person alone. It might be someone in Paris or someone here, or in Bordeaux. There are so many possibilities, but I don't believe it is anyone in Angleterre. We have retrieved Lee Bowen's mobile records. He was not clever enough to use a burner phone, so we know the morning of the fuel incident, he made three calls to an untraceable French number.

With the dishes removed, Chloé set down the tray on the buffet and poured more wine.

Pondering all the possibilities, Genevieve felt as if her head were about to explode. "Who in Paris would be involved? Could it be anything to do with the foundation?"

His glass refilled, Duncan took a swallow and then another. "What sense would that make, Mom? I think the inspector's idea makes the most sense: that all this has to do with wanting the vineyard."

"Look, inspector, this is all speculation, isn't it? No other evidence exists, except for the footage of Lee Bowen messing with the fuel tank and a few phone records, does it?" Philip's patience was wearing thin, and he could feel another headache creeping into his skull. "After lunch, we'll go to the vineyard office, and you can see the email I mentioned."

"Ah, bon." Boucher held up his glass in a salute before he drank.

"And," Philip continued, "since you seem to know everything else that's going on around here, I must ask you. Are you aware an agent from the DREETS is paying us a visit?"

The surprise on Boucher's face was gratifying and Philip smiled. "Aha!" he said and pointed across the table at the inspector. "You didn't know that, did you?"

Boucher could feel a crumb at the corner of his mouth. He scooped it off with his tongue, then said, "Non, my lord. I did not." He cleared his throat and drank from his untouched water glass.

"But one must ask, why are they coming to Château Beaulieu?"

"I have no idea. I suppose we'll all find out when they arrive tomorrow."

Chloé picked up the tray of plates and slipped from the petit salon. In the kitchen, she left the tray on a marble counter and slipped out the side door to the courtyard between the château and garage. She needed to make a phone call and she needed to make it now.

THIRTY-ONE

Everything Parisian had style, she thought, even the rain. When it drizzled, it sprinkled with the softness of a gentle caress. When it poured, it raged like a diva, demanding center stage. At the moment, the diva was out of control, pelting the windows at Maison de Laney so hard it was difficult to hear John Coltrane, her favorite, playing softly in the grand salon. Clarisse Morier squinted, looking through the French doors out into the garden, trying to see any signs of spring through the sluicing rain. She sipped her boulevardier cocktail, then ran her tongue over her lips, enjoying the spicey, bitter flavor left behind. Her brows drew together as she thought about the week ahead. Besides all the other things crowding her schedule, she had to direct the event for Cité du Vin at Château Beaulieu. Delphine could manage the mechanics, but only she could bring the style necessary to impress such a prestigious institution.

She felt her phone vibrate, reached into the pocket of her trousers and frowned when she saw the face that filled the screen.

"Oui?" she snapped. "Qu'est-ce que c'est?"

"We might have a problem." The voice on the other end of the line was controlled.

Madame Morier waited.

"As we discussed, it will be chaos here. You need to come to the château earlier than planned."

She noticed the rain was no longer sheeting down the windows and a rainbow had painted itself across the sky.

"There's no need to panic," she said. "This is not the first time I have managed such a situation." She punched *end call* and threw back the two fingers of blood-red boulevardier left in her glass.

THIRTY-TWO

By eight o'clock everyone in the household was already up and bustling. Everyone except Inspector Marcel Boucher. He was luxuriating in the guestroom where he hoped to spend several more nights. Why would he want to return to his tiny Paris apartment with its single bed, cramped kitchen and bathroom so small he could sit on the commode and wash his hands in the sink? He stretched, pulled the sheets up to his chin and rubbed the silky linens between his thumb and forefinger. He would love to live like the Warwicks. He thought about the conversation during lunch yesterday and wondered how solid his theory was. He was certain the fuel issue and Daniel LaGrande's death were related, but he was unsure who was responsible or why the events had occurred.

Startled by a gentle knock on the door, he tugged the sheets under his chin and sat up before he said, "Entre."

Chloé nudged the door open with her foot. "Bonjour, inspector," she said, carrying in a tray of coffee, croissants and little pots of jam and butter, which she set on the bedside table. "Voulez-vous quelque chose d'autre?"

He couldn't imagine wanting anything else. "Non, merci. C'est parfait." He remembered her from yesterday. Her face was fresh and pretty and her big eyes were surrounded by thick lashes Boucher thought were fluttering at him. Without any more conversation, she turned and left, pulling the door closed behind her.

He swung his sturdy legs over the edge of the bed and scooted closer to the breakfast tray. Saliva pooled in his mouth as the aroma of the warm pastries wafted into his nostrils. As he poured coffee from the French press into a porcelain cup, an image of Chloé danced in his mind. She was there yesterday pouring wine, pouring water, pouring coffee, removing, serving. Was she ever not in the room? Perhaps they should be more careful to speak only when she wasn't around.

"Perhaps you are getting carried away," he said aloud. "Perhaps you are becoming un peu paranoïaque, eh?" With that, he decided he'd better get moving or he'd miss all the excitement.

Downstairs, David and Becca were ready to leave for London. Henri tucked several bags into the trunk of a deep blue Jaguar XJ, then stood at attention by the open passenger door.

"I'm sorry I won't be here for the meeting today." David and Philip shook hands. "Call me after you talk to the DREETS agent. You know you can always reach me on a video call."

"I'll let you know what this visit's all about. I can't imagine why he's coming, but we'll know soon."

"You're sure you don't want me to stay?" As the Warwicks' attorney, David felt uncomfortable leaving if he might be needed.

"Absolutely not. You need to get back to the firm." Philip slapped him on the back. "Believe me, I'll send up a red flag if we need help on this side of the channel."

"Thank you both for being here this week." Genevieve gave David a peck on the cheek and squeezed Becca.

Becca held Genevieve by both shoulders. "Good luck with the Cité du Vin meeting. Let me know if you want to kick around anymore ideas before then. You're going to have such fun."

Concerned about the time, Henri urged the couple to finish saying their goodbyes. "Sir David, we should go if you don't want to miss your flight."

"Of course. Of course."

Duncan gripped David's hand and pulled him into a hug. "See you soon, mate."

Becca's eyes glistened with tears as she slid into the back seat.

"Why are you crying?" David asked. "Blimey. Women." He shook his head and Genevieve punched him on his arm.

"Ouch." David eased in after Becca, and Henri closed the door behind him.

Genevieve motioned for David to roll down the window. "You be nice to your beautiful bride-to-be." She pinched his cheek. "Or you'll have to deal with me."

"Anything but that," he yelled as they drove off.

The three stood and waved until the car was well down the allée, then trudged up the front steps. Philip pushed open the front door and stood aside to let Genevieve and Duncan enter. He followed them in and stopped short when he saw Inspector Boucher coming down the stairs looking as dashing as his stout body would allow. In navy-wool flannel trousers and a Breton navy-and-white striped sweater, he needed another ten inches to pull off the look. But to his credit, his navy scarf was perfectly draped around his stubby neck.

"Why inspector, how smart you look." Genevieve's smile was genuine. "Are you ready for some breakfast?"

"Ah, oui, my lady. The girl, uh Chloé, brought coffee and croissants, but I would not say non to an omelet." He beamed at his beautiful host.

She took his arm and, wrinkling her nose at his heavy cologne, guided him toward the petit salon where they had lunched the day before. Looking back at Philip, she said, "I assume you and Duncan will be in the office. Did you tell me the agent is coming at ten o'clock?"

"Yes. He sent a text this morning confirming."

"I'll get the inspector settled and be in to help. I won't be long."

"See you in a minute." Grateful that Genevieve was taking care of Boucher, he and Duncan strolled down the hall and back out into the crisp morning. "Do you think the inspector is getting a little bit too comfortable here?" he asked his son as they walked across the terrace.

Duncan smiled and took a beat before answering. "I don't know about that, but I'm pretty sure he's trying to supplant you as lord of the manor."

Philip stopped mid-stride and looked at Duncan before realizing his son was teasing him. "Smartass," he said, giving him a withering look. They chuckled together as they walked through the office door, and braced themselves for what might blindside them next.

THIRTY-THREE

Two people awaited them when Philip, Genevieve and Duncan entered the salon at ten o'clock. A youngish, raw-boned woman of average height stood ramrod straight in front of the fire, holding a coffee cup in one hand and matching saucer in the other. Her hair was pulled into a tight bun at the nape of her neck and her navy suit was severe and well cut, the narrow skirt hitting just below her knees.

A head taller than the woman, the man's posture was less rigid than hers. He seemed more casual, more relaxed. Dressed head to toe in black, he wore his uniform with as much style as one could and held his hat in both hands in front of him.

"Bonjour?" Philip said. Surprised by the fact that there were two people in their living room, not just one as he had expected, his greeting sounded more like a question than a welcome.

"Bonjour, Lord Crosswick."

Philip offered his hand, searched the man's eyes and said, "I assume you are Jules Lambert?"

"Oh, non, my lord. He stepped to the side and swept his hand toward the woman. "Ici, est Agente Lambert."

She set her coffee cup on a small table and moved in to shake Philip's hand, her lips parting with the beginning of a smile. "It happens all the time," she said in English with just a trace of French accent.

Striding forward with outstretched hand, Genevieve offered a warm greeting. "I'm Genevieve Warwick," she said, "and this is our son, Duncan."

"Lady Crosswick," the fellow said, with a sharp nod. "I am Frederick Picard of the municipal police." He turned to Philip and Duncan and gave another snappy bob of his head. "Lord Crosswick, we spoke on the phone about Madame Duveau."

"Yes, I remember. It's good to put a face to a voice."

The second Boucher hit the doorway, his voice bellowed across the salon. "Freddy! Freddy, mon Dieu! Qu'est-ce qu'on fout ici?"

French zipped back and forth, fast and furious between the two old friends. They bear hugged and slapped each other on the back.

Though Philip and Genevieve didn't catch every word, they knew the razzing was edgy and the sort of banter only two old friends could share.

Just as Agent Lambert was about to break up the reunion, Inspector Boucher backed away from Picard. "Pardon, pardon," he said, and addressed the Warwicks. "As you might have guessed, I had no idea Freddy— er, uh, Directeur Picard, would be coming today. Quelle chance!" His smile stretched from ear to ear.

"What a nice way to begin our meeting," Genevieve said, motioning everyone to be seated. "Please, there is coffee on the sideboard. If you would like anything else, don't hesitate to ask."

"The hospitality here is spectaculaire," Boucher said, flaunting his guest status.

Genevieve arched one brow at Philip, amused how comfortable the inspector was.

"Now, if you don't mind, Lady Crosswick and I are anxious to find out the purpose of this meeting." Philip crossed one leg over the other and straightened the crease in his trouser leg.

"I am certain you are." Agent Lambert took control of the conversation. "My lord, my lady," she nodded at Philip and Genevieve in turn, then flipped open a red leather notebook. "Earlier this year on January 14th, we received an anonymous telephone call from a man who said he believed Château Beaulieu was involved in a counterfeit, uh, shall we say, scheme?" She leaned forward with her elbows on the suede-covered arms of her chair.

"What does that mean?" Philip's brows drew together, and his mouth curved down, not quite certain what to make of what he had just heard.

"I don't understand," Genevieve said, confused. "Are you suggesting we're selling fake wine?"

Lambert raised her palms toward Philip and Genevieve. "Non, non, non," she said. "Let me start again. The person who made the phone call suggested that, without your knowledge, a perpetrator may be using elements of Château Beaulieu's winemaking capability for nefarious purposes."

He shrugged his shoulders. "I don't get it. Who could be using our winery without our knowledge, or the knowledge of our vigneron? And how would they be using it?"

Genevieve pushed out of her chair and walked to the sideboard, her hands shoved in the pockets of her burgundy wool pants. She turned to Agent Lambert and said, "I'm sure you know the story of our recently inherited wealth, which includes this château and its vineyard." She poured a cup of coffee and walked back to her chair. "This is our first experience as owners of a property that's part of such an important industry." She set her coffee on the walnut table next to her chair and sat. "Though we love to drink wine, we are novices in this world of creating a great vintage. One of our strengths as entrepreneurs, is that we always appreciate what we don't know. Assume we know nothing about counterfeit wine, which is true, and start from the beginning."

Lambert's cool blue gaze rested on Genevieve, admiring her composure. "Let me start by telling you that wine fraud is an enormous business. Some estimate it to be a three billion euro gouge in the side of the industry."

Surprised, Genevieve's mouth formed a silent "O" at the enormous number.

"DREETS is a wide-ranging directorate, and I won't bore you with the details of everything it covers. Fraud is our responsibility." Lambert stopped to take a drink of coffee. "There are two challenges when we encounter fraud. The first is, though wine is synonymous with France, its production is a tiny part of our GDP, just one percent."

"Really?" Duncan said, voicing everyone's amazement. "Only one percent?"

"Yes. As a result, wine counterfeiting is a low priority for our directorate and the police have little interest in it. In fact, if we had not had a direct call tipping us off, if Château Beaulieu were not a prominent producer and you were not a titled owner, we would not be here."

"Interesting," Philip said. "And the other challenge?"

"Ah, oui." It was the first French she had used. "The other challenge is that in the illustrious wine regions like Burgundy and Bordeaux, many of the more exclusive châteaux refuse to cooperate."

"Why?" Genevieve couldn't imagine any owner not wanting to root out counterfeiters.

"They don't want anyone to know about the frauds. By telling no one, they feel they are protecting their good name, when, in fact, they are allowing inferior product to reach the marketplace under their label." She threw a smile around the room. "We are grateful that you are allowing us to pursue this." She leaned back and folded her hands in her lap. "And, of course, there was the attempt on your life and the death of Daniel LaGrande, all of which are possibly connected to a wine fraud, so the case becomes quite interesting for departments other than ours."

Though they had talked several times with Inspector Boucher about a connection between all the events, until just now it had all seemed quite far-fetched.

"What a mess," was all Philip could say. "What a fucking mess." He looked at Genevieve, searching her eyes for anything that would tell him what she was thinking. What he saw were questions.

"Okay, Agent Lambert, how is someone using Château Beaulieu to counterfeit wine?" Genevieve said.

"Ah, yes." She nodded. "We see fraud in one of three forms." Her thumb popped up as if she were approving of the ways wine could be counterfeited. "First, counterfeiter's fake bottles and labels. You may have heard of Rudy Kurniawan."

"Rudy Kurniawan! I've heard of this guy." After listening quietly to Agent Lambert, Duncan sparked to life. "A good friend of mine in New York bought some of his Romanee-Conti about a year before he was arrested."

"Which friend?" Philip was curious.

"James Ridgeway. You and Mom met him a couple of times when Julia and I were still living in New York. Now that he knows the wine is fake, he thinks of the bottles as a piece of history. An expensive piece of history, for sure." He looked at Lambert. "Kurniawan's scam was all about creating bottles that looked authentic and filling them with bogus wine, right?"

"Vraiment," Boucher said, anxious to get into the conversation.

"He moved millions of dollars of fake wine before he was caught in 2012."

Duncan was on the edge of his seat now. "Didn't he stupidly forge some Clos Saint-Denis from Domaine Ponsot, labeling them with dates that were way before any recorded production from that domain?"

"I am impressed," Lambert said. "You know a lot about Monsieur Kurniawan. So you understand how faked bottles and labels are used to counterfeit wine?"

Everyone in the room nodded, even Boucher and Picard.

Lambert raised her index finger, so her thumb and pointer

looked like a gun. "The second way: counterfeiters use authentic bottles and labels, fill the bottles with inferior wine and sell at the price of the fine vintage. This is more difficult than printing fake labels because genuine bottles and labels are difficult to come by." She took a deep breath, then continued. "That brings us to the last way of counterfeiting wine. If you sell bottles of wine which are authentic but have been damaged by excessive temperatures and you do not disclose the damage, you can be charged with fraud. Under that same category is any wine that is enhanced with chemicals to conceal that it has deteriorated or to increase its sweetness. That kind of fraud can only be detected by analyzing the bottle's contents." She picked up her coffee and drank several sips before putting the gold-rimmed cup back in the saucer. "You now know more than you ever wanted to know about counterfeiting."

"Thank you for the education, Agent Lambert. If you had to guess," Philip said, "what kind of fraud are we involved in?"

She pressed her lips together and shook her head several times. "At the moment, we cannot be certain there *is* counterfeiting involving Château Beaulieu. We must determine that first."

As Genevieve's mind began to wander and her gaze swept around the salon, she smiled at the fire crackling on the hearth and marveled at the view through the windows and beyond the terrace. Grapevines stretched as far as she could see, down the hill and beyond the next rise. She couldn't imagine a more fairytale existence. Everything was perfect—everything except the fact that someone was trying to kill them and steal their wine, maybe their vineyard. She felt her spine stiffen and her jaw clench. It was going to be a cold day in Hell when the Warwicks allowed anyone to take over their lives and harm their family. And according to the forecast, the temperature was not falling. In fact, it was going to get very, very warm.

THIRTY-FOUR

NOBODY DELIVERED A song like Zaz. Her throaty voice blasted "Je Veux" through the speakers, filling the car with energy and making it impossible for Edouard to do anything but join her belting out the lyrics, off key and at the top of his lungs. "Je veux d'l'amour, d'la joie, de la bonne humeur." He slapped time to the beat on the steering wheel and mimicked her kazoo during the chorus. He loved Zaz. Who didn't?

As he turned left off D122 onto Rue du Palat, his pulse revved. He never tired of the approach to Château Beaulieu. After a quarter kilometer, the low, ancient stone walls gave way to row after row of dormant vines, looking like arthritic knuckles. They waited for the earth to warm and the sun to kiss their sleeping buds awake. But before the vines woke, those who cared for them, who nurtured and loved them, would soon begin palissage, the art of trellising the tender shoots. Of the hundreds of tasks necessary every year to bring the perfect grape to its peak, Edouard loved palissage the most. It was an intimate act between the vigneron and his vines. It was the act of spreading the leaves to make certain the sun and the wind could caress every crevice, every surface. If palissage were done well, the vines could flourish and those responsible would be rewarded with a good, perhaps even a great vintage.

After another kilometer, he clicked on his left blinker and pulled into the long driveway that announced Château Beaulieu. Before opening the gates, Edouard sat for a moment savoring the view. Elegant and understated, the château dominated the gentle rise of the earth on which it sat with an undeniable presence. He had been here only three years, but he knew this was where he would be for the rest of his life. This was his vineyard, his château, his soil. He knew how much Daniel had loved Château Beaulieu and in three short years the managing director had infected Edouard with that passion.

He punched in the code. The gates crept open, and he eased the dark green Range Rover under the linden trees. He knew the story about Philip George Winston Laney, the 9TH Earl of Crosswick, inheriting Château Beaulieu from his French wife's family. Lucky bastard. And now this new earl was here to take over. There had to be continuity. The vines knew if their caretakers loved them or if they were just a trophy. Depending on how you cared for them, they would give you everything or they would give you nothing. If the Warwicks didn't give him free rein over the vineyard, the vines would know.

By the time Edouard arrived at the house, he had talked himself into an unpleasant mood, worried that the Warwicks were not going to value him. He was young, but this was his life, his passion. He was already an award-winning vigneron, but his greatest achievement was that Daniel LaGrande had placed the future of Château Beaulieu in his hands. "Dammit," he said, slamming his palm on the dashboard. "The Warwicks better appreciate me." He threw open the car door and jumped down from the seat.

"Edouard," Delphine's voice cut across the courtyard and he turned to see her waving him to come to the house.

"Merde," he said under his breath. He opened the back car door, grabbed his jacket off the seat, and slammed the door harder than he intended.

Delphine's brows shot up and Edouard knew he needed to tuck his irritation into his back pocket.

"Lord et Lady Crosswick sont dans le salon avec l'agente de DREETS. Vas-y tout de suite."

When Delphine commanded, everyone followed her orders, including Edouard. He would join them in the salon, but he wasn't going to be happy about it.

He slumped against the thick molding in the doorway, unnoticed, until Duncan got up to throw a log on the fire and saw him. "Edouard! Great. You're here. Just the man we need."

Surprised by the warmth in Duncan's voice, Edouard's mood lifted ever-so-slightly.

"Come, sit over here." Genevieve patted a spot next to her on the loveseat. "There's coffee on the sideboard."

Again he was taken by surprise. He raised his hand. "Rein, merci. I need nothing."

Introductions were made all around before Edouard sat down on the edge of the loveseat.

"Agent Lambert," Philip said, "would you please fill Edouard in on our conversation? I would imagine you can skip the rudimentary education on wine counterfeiting. As Château Beaulieu's vigneron, I'm sure he has a sophisticated knowledge of such crimes."

Lambert offered a concise recap of the previous hour's conversation and ended with, "Is there anything you can think of that the caller could have been talking about?"

While the agent spoke, Edouard sat with his arms folded across his chest. He stared at the floor, listening for any tone of accusation, but there was none, and his tension began to ease. When she was finished, he relaxed into the loveseat and said to the agent. "First let me ask a couple of questions, if I may."

"But, of course."

"I take it you have no indication who made the phone call or where it was made from."

She shook her head. "Non."

"And there have been no further calls?"

"Non."

"I see," he said, a smug smile tugging at his lips.

"But there is one important piece of information I have yet to share, Monsieur Comte." Agent Lambert flashed a cocky smirk of her own and everyone in the room waited. She reached into her cordovan leather briefcase and pulled out a piece of paper in a plastic folder. "We received this last week." She walked to Philip and handed him the sheathed stationery.

A quoi de droit,
Vérifier les commandes de bouteilles
pour Château Beaulieu
rapport aux chiffres de production.

In an instant, Genevieve was up and looking over Philip's shoulder. "A quoi de droit." She looked at Lambert. "To whom it may concern, right?"

The agent nodded.

"Verify the commands of the bottles?" Confused, Genevieve's brows drew together.

"Allow me." The agent took the paper and read. "To whom it may concern. Check the bottle orders for Château Beaulieu against production figures." She returned to her seat and set the paper on her lap. "What do you think that means?" She looked around the room at four blank faces.

"I don't understand," Duncan said. "Is this suggesting that we might have purchased more bottles than we need?" He screwed up his face. "I mean, wouldn't that be smart to have extra bottles, so if you break some in production, you don't shut down the bottling line?"

Agent Lambert started to reply, but Duncan interrupted her with another thought. "Or are they suggesting we have ordered fewer bottles and we're diverting our wine into someone else's bottles? Why would we do that?" His mind was spinning.

Lambert started again, more forceful this time. "We need to go through all the papers and computer files in the vineyard office. We can either bring in a forensic team or box everything and take it to our headquarters."

"What's your preference?"

"It is best if we stay in the vineyard office and perhaps if we could have a little area where we can organize any evidence we find," Lambert said. "If we are here, we may have ready access to the staff if we have questions, may we not?"

"Everyone will be at your service." Philip looked at their vigneron. "Edouard, will you please tell the vineyard staff that they may be questioned by the DREETS agents and that Lady Crosswick and I would appreciate their cooperation?"

"Of course. I shall make certain everyone is available." Edouard drummed his fingers on the arm of his chair, wondering where this was all going.

"Of course, we shall keep Inspector Boucher and Director Picard informed of our findings." Lambert inclined her head toward her two colleagues. "If you have no objections, the team will come on Monday. And, my lord, please keep the office locked until then."

"Of course. In fact, Edouard, could you go lock it right now? Do you know where the key is?"

Already heading toward the door, Edouard said, "It's in the office, of course."

"Before you go, Monsieur Comte," Agent Lambert called out. "What did you do when you learned that Daniel LaGrande was killed by a poisoned bottle of Château Beaulieu wine? Did you take any precautions to confirm that the methanol wasn't in any other bottles?"

Edouard spun around. "Of course I took precautions. We have strict protocols when there is suspicion that any of our wine is tainted, and we followed all of them. I can say with certainty that the poison was limited to Daniel's bottle." He turned to Philip. "You don't think for a minute that I would allow you, Lady Crosswick, or anyone else to drink our wine if I wasn't sure that it was pure, do you?"

"Of course not, Edouard. I would never question your commitment to Château Beaulieu." Philip walked with him to the French doors. "I know you'll make sure the office is secure." He opened the terrace doors and patted Edouard on the back as he sent him on his way.

Turning back to Lambert, Philip asked, "You'll be heading the task force, won't you?"

"I shall."

"Is that a long commute for you?" Genevieve asked.

"Non," Lambert replied. "I live on the west side of Bordeaux so it's a pleasant drive to Saint-Émilion." She gathered the few things she'd taken from her briefcase and put them back in the exact same place from which they came. When she was finished, she stood and extended her hand. "Thank you for your cooperation."

Philip shook her hand. "Thank you for pursuing this, Agent Lambert. If we have a counterfeiting issue here, we want to get to the bottom of it as quickly as possible." He put his hands in his pockets and gazed out the French doors for a moment before looking back at her. He nodded at Genevieve and Duncan. "We three are out of our element in this situation. We'll do everything we can to be supportive, but I don't believe we're going to be much help in connecting the dots."

"But, my lord, that is our job," Agent Lambert said, and headed for the door.

In the kitchen, Chloé finished polishing the last copper pot and hung it back on its hook on the rack over the island. She plucked the earbuds from her ears and shoved them deep into her apron pocket. The tiny microphone she had stuck under the coffee table in the salon had done its job. She hadn't missed a word and had a lot of information to pass on. She smiled at the thought of the big payday that was about to come her way.

THIRTY-FIVE

With the morning gone, Genevieve sat in the petit salon with a bowl of onion soup, a baguette, and a slab of unsalted butter. She combed her fingers through her hair then rested her elbow on the table and cradled her head in her hands. Digging her fingers into the muscles of her neck and shoulders, the tension stored there made her wince. She squeezed the bridge of her nose and decided a quick nap would be the smart strategy. Philip, Duncan and Edouard were reviewing the morning's revelations and plotting plans for Duncan to meet tomorrow with Elise Beaufoy in Bordeaux at Cité du Vin, so now would be the perfect time to sneak away. Exhaustion from stress was the worst, and, since arriving in France, their lives had been packed with one stressful event after another. Small wonder fatigue was about to bury her. She took a last spoonful of her soup and dabbed her chin with her linen napkin.

She dragged herself up the stairs, down the hall to their bedroom, and collapsed onto their bed. Breathing a great sigh, she tugged a celadon cashmere throw up to her chin in one smooth motion before falling into an instant, deep sleep.

When lips nuzzled the back of her neck, she inhaled Philip's warm, woodsy scent.

"Mmm," was all Genevieve could manage.

Looming over her, Philip tugged gently on her shoulder, rolling her from her side to her back. He kissed her softly on her eyelids. "G," he whispered.

"Mmm?" she said again.

"It's almost five o'clock."

"Hum?" She forced her eyes open. "Did you say it's almost five o'clock?" Her voice was hoarse.

"I did." He sat down on the edge of the bed and brushed a wisp of hair from her cheek.

She scrunched her eyes closed, opened them, blew a puff of air from her cheeks and propped herself up on her elbows. "Wow. I just wanted to close my eyes for a minute and four hours later, I'm still comatose. I think I could sleep forever." She leaned into Philip and grazed his lips with hers. "I had a dream about Charlotte," she said, watching his eyes for a reaction.

For a moment Philip was confused, then it dawned on him who Genevieve was talking about. "How is our dear, dead Charlotte?"

"Considering she's almost a hundred and seventy-five, she looks remarkable."

"Did she have any sage counsel for us about all this mess happening here at her venerable château?"

Genevieve shoved herself into a sitting position and rubbed her hands over her face. "I don't know if I'd call it sage counsel, but she did throw a glass of wine in the air, and it evaporated. Then *she* dissolved into a billion tiny stars." She shrugged, smiled and said, "I don't think you can call that advice, do you?"

"I don't think so. Not unless it's some coded message." He stood and ruffled Genevieve's hair. "Listen, cute girl. You need to get your very nice butt out of bed and come talk to Delphine. She needs guidance about what's going to be served to the Cité du Vin Board and when and how much—you know, she has a lot of questions, none of which I could answer. Well," he corrected himself, "I could have given her answers to every question, but they wouldn't have been the right answers." He beamed at his tousled wife.

As he turned to leave, Genevieve whacked him on his bottom with a pillow. At that, he turned, grabbed his wife with one hand and began tickling her with the other until she was screeching and weeping with laughter. "I'm bigger than you are, and you know I'll always win, right?"

"Stop it, Philip! Stop it!" She wheezed.

He gave her one more tickle in the ribs, then stepped back. "Nothing better than a good tickle, is there?" He grinned and he pointed at her as she cocked her arm to heave a small, decorative pillow at him. "I wouldn't if I were you," he said, still grinning.

She lowered the cushion and harrumphed her way off the bed. "You don't play fair."

"Pardon me? As you know, all's fair in love and war."

"Was that love or war?" Genevieve asked as she straightened the bed and slipped into her shoes.

"Both, I guess. Can I tell Delphine you're on your way?"

"Of course, you meanie," she laughed. "I'll be right down."

Genevieve could hear Philip whistling James Brown's "I Feel Good" all the way down the hall.

THIRTY-SIX

THE MORNING WAS already getting away from him as Duncan gulped the last of his coffee. "I need to get in the shower before I go. Dad, which car do you want me to take?"

"I don't care. Text Henri and ask him. Never mind. You go shower. I'll talk to Henri. Do you want something flashy or something practical?"

Duncan cocked his head. "What do you think, Dad?"

"I'll see what I can do. God, isn't this fun?" Philip said, punching in Henri's number.

"Yup," Duncan said as he jogged off.

"Henri, Duncan has a meeting at Cité du Vin in Bordeaux this morning and needs a car. He wants to drive something exciting. What would you suggest?" Philip was silent, listening to Henri's suggestions. "Whoa. You're kidding. We have that? By all means. That's the car he needs to drive. Thanks, Henri." He listened a moment. "I'd say in about twenty minutes. Perfect." He clicked off and grinned at Genevieve. "This is when I don't mind all the hassle that comes with all of this." He swept his hand around the room."

"I knew you'd come to your senses. I was pretty sure you wouldn't want to give it all up."

"The jury's still out on that, G," he said, worry replacing his smile.

Ignoring his response, Genevieve said, "Sounds as if Henri is bringing something spectacular to the front door." She popped a plump strawberry into her mouth.

His excitement bubbled back. "Wait until you see it. Just wait."

She grinned at her husband, who had turned into a teenager before her eyes.

"You will not believe this car. I've got to go to the garage and have Henri show me everything we own. We've been here almost a week and we haven't had a moment to explore this grownups' amusement park." He sat back and stabbed a piece of quiche.

With his shirt unbuttoned, his shoes in his hand and his hair still dripping, Duncan flew back into the room. "I just checked the traffic. There's an accident on N89. I just called Elise and left a message that I might be late. You know we're meeting to set the schedule for The Art of the Vine."

Philip nodded. "I do."

"According to Elise, the word is getting out and already potential students are requesting applications for the program. Pretty exciting, isn't it?"

"It is, but you need to slow down," Philip warned. "The last thing you need is to get in an accident or get a ticket. Besides, the car you're driving will get you there in a nanosecond."

Duncan sat down to put his shoes on. As he tied his laces, he looked up at his dad with an excited smile. "What does Henri have for me? Something cool?"

"I'm not telling. I'll just let you be surprised when you open the door. We seem to have some amazing cars. Who knew?" Philip snorted a laugh.

Duncan buttoned his shirt, pulled a navy collared sweater over his head, ran his hands through his hair and considered it combed.

When Duncan and Philip opened the front door and walked out onto the terrace, Henri was leaning against a tangerine-colored masterpiece.

A long low whistle announced Philip's pleasure.

"Wow," was all Duncan could manage.

Henri hefted himself off the car and pressed the pop-in handle that opened the driver's door.

For a moment, Duncan had forgotten he was in a rush. "What are we looking at, Henri?" he asked.

A smile stretched across Henri's face, which was unusual, for such a serious man. "You are looking at a Ferrari Purosangue, my lord. Château Beaulieu's name was put on the waiting list when they first began taking orders. It was delivered two weeks ago, just before you got here, Lord Crosswick." He motioned to Duncan to come closer. "I know you don't want to be late for your meeting, but I need to run you through a couple of things."

He pulled on an inch-long plastic fin that appeared to be part of the shoulder line. There was a soft sound of a motor and the back door powered open. "In case someone needs to ride in the back seat, you should know how to open the rear doors."

"Good thinking, Henri. I would never have discovered that little lever. It could have been embarrassing to shoved Elise

Beaufoy through the window." They laughed at the image. He glanced at his watch. "I'm sure there's a lot I need to know to fully appreciate this machine, but the immediate question is, what do I need to know in order to drive to Bordeaux and back?"

Henri took him through the rudimentary operation of the flashy Purosangue and finished with a few cautionary words. "Remember, this car is a V12 and has 725 horsepower. It will not let you forget that it is a thoroughbred. It lives to run fast, so be gentle, be cautious. But above all, have fun."

"Thank you. Thank you for this." He gave Henri a quick smile that said he was ready to get on the road.

"Hurry back," Philip raised his hand. "I mean, come home safely."

Duncan flashed a thumbs up to his dad. He looked on the dash, on the column, on the console, and saw no start button. Henri pointed to the bottom of the steering wheel and Duncan pressed a touch-sensitive spot. The V12 awakened with a sharp bark, then settled into a gravelly purr.

"That was fun," he said.

The door closed with a satisfying thunk and he was ready to go. In the pit of his stomach, a flutter of terror caught his attention. His shallow breathing and sweaty palms confirmed that he was afraid to press on the gas, but pressing on the gas was the only way to make the car go forward. And he had to move forward to get to his meeting. His jaw tightened and the ball of his foot met the firm pedal. He applied the tiniest bit of pressure. Nothing. He pushed more firmly, and the engine whined. Embarrassed, he realized the car was still in park.

Out of the window, he saw his father standing with his arms crossed, and one hand over his mouth. Duncan could tell he was laughing. He could see Henri's shoulders shaking as he chuckled.

"Good god, man, get a grip," Duncan said to himself.

He pushed the switch on the center console from park into drive and, mustering his courage, eased forward. Nothing broke or bent or cracked. He was encouraged and pressed firmer on the gas until he was moving down the driveway at a snappy thirty kilometers an hour. He stopped at the end of the allée. Before moving on to Rue du Palat, he looked both ways several times. At last, he made the turn. Though he had owned several nice cars, they had all been clunkers compared to this. He was driving a dream.

His confidence built and so did his speed. On his right, Clos Peyra flashed past. Duncan smiled knowing he and all his neighbors were anxious for the coming months when the vines would begin to grow, and the châteaux would buzz with activity.

As he approached Château Pitique, he was confused to see a large draft horse charging between the vines, hurtling toward the stone wall that separated the fields from the road. He marveled at the power of the Percheron, hooves pounding against the frozen earth, broad shoulders rippling with each galloping stride. Then, in an instant, awe turned to fear. A man in red ran behind the horse, urging it forward. Shouting and thrashing a crop back and forth above his head, the man's eyes were wide and wild in his crimson face, his mouth distorted with each violent insult he screamed at the stallion.

The horse was now so close, Duncan could see the breath

snorting from its nose. His foot hovered over the brake pedal and an image of his crushed Ferrari flashed in his mind.

The horse took two mighty strides and flew over the low wall, landing just in front of the speeding Ferrari. Duncan yanked the steering wheel to the left and the horse thundered in front of the Purosangue, missing it by inches. The motor screamed as the car sped toward the stone wall. He wrenched the wheel to the right, and barely avoided crashing into the barrier before careening back onto the pavement. Slamming on the brakes, he screeched to a halt, his heart roaring in his ears and his breath stuck in his chest.

His head jerked to the right and watched the horse gallop up the vine-covered hill toward Clos Peyra. He flopped back in his seat, gripping the steering wheel with both hands. Out of the corner of his eye, he saw the man in the red barn jacket streak up the hill toward Chateau Pitique.

What in the hell had just happened? Glancing in the rearview mirror, Duncan saw a car approaching. He needed to move. He was unharmed and hoped the Ferrari was as well. Mentally he crossed his fingers and eased his foot on the accelerator. Nothing banged or rattled. The engine still had that exquisite, throaty growl and nothing seemed to be out of alignment. "Thank god for that," he said.

"Turn right in twenty-five meters, onto D122," the GPS lady said in a distinctly British accent, and Duncan laughed out loud. "Well, damn. Why didn't you say, 'Keep calm and carry on?'" he asked his robotic companion, then clicked off the GPS. "Change of plans. Elise Beaufoy and Cité du Vin, you'll have to wait."

His palms were slick with sweat and his heart still beat in his ears. One at a time he wiped his hands on his jeans. He made a U-turn and headed back to Château Beaulieu. As he relived each detail of what had just happened, it seemed clear that someone had tried to kill him, or at the very least, tried to frighten him. If they wanted him dead, they had failed. If frightening him was their goal, their plan was a wild success. The niggling fears that had caused him to delay his family's arrival, had just proven well-founded.

As he turned down down the driveway toward home, his pulse began to quiet. He was anxious to talk to his dad and, for the moment, would keep the bewildering event between the two of them. There was no need to terrify his mother. There'd be time for that later.

THIRTY-SEVEN

Genevieve was putting the final special touches on an oversized card she was going to send to Alex and Ella. She had printed several small photographs of the château and pasted them on the inside. One more bright cutout flower between Alex and Ella's names on the front, and it would be perfect. She held up the card, admiring her work. Her fingers, sticky from the glue, picked up everything she touched. She shook her hand, but the tissue on the tip of her finger waved in the air like a flag of surrender. She tried pulling it off with her other hand, but shreds stuck to those fingers. "Soap and water," she thought, and went to the kitchen in search of help.

Normally a hub of activity, today the kitchen was vacant and silent. At the sink, Genevieve shoved the hot water lever with her elbow. She rubbed her hands under the stream. When she depressed the pump on the soap dispenser, she heard a moan and thought it came from the plunger. She hit it again. The moan was louder, followed by a breathy, "Oui! Oui!"

"I don't think that's the soap dispenser," she said under her breath. She grabbed a towel from the rack and wiped her hands as she crept toward the pantry. The door was almost closed. She stood for several seconds, listening to what were decidedly the sounds of sex, trying to decide whether to interrupt the amorous encounter or creep away.

"It's my kitchen," she decided. "If anyone's going to frolic in here, I think it should be Philip and me." She cleared her throat, then cleared it louder. The sounds stopped. "Hello," she said. No reply. "Excuse me. Who's in the pantry? I'd prefer not to come in."

She heard a flurry of startled whispering, then silence, then the rustling of clothes being pulled on or rearranged. "Un moment, s'il vous plaît. Un moment."

Genevieve thought she recognized the voice as Chloé's but wasn't sure. She backed up to the kitchen island, leaned against the wooden countertop, and waited. Finally, the door opened and indeed, Chloé stood between the bright sun streaming into the kitchen and the shadows of the windowless pantry. Rather than embarrassed, she seemed irritated, defiant. Behind her was a man. A young man.

"Excuse-moi, my lady." Chloé jutted her chin. "I suppose I should apologize for being amorous when I should be working, but…" Her voice trailed off. She pouted her lips and shrugged. "Quand l'occasion se presente, when opportunity knocks, one must answer."

Genevieve was more annoyed by Chloé's attitude than her actions. "But, Chloé, did you seize the opportunity, or did you *make* the opportunity?"

Chloé rolled her eyes and sighed.

"At any rate, please introduce me to your opportunity."

Chloé stepped to the side. "Pourquoi pas?" She gestured for the fellow to come forward, and Genevieve could see that he was, in fact, young—and gorgeous. His shirt was misbuttoned, and his pants zipped halfway. Chloé nodded at him. "This is George…" she stopped, realizing she didn't know his last name. "This is George," she said again, but did not go on.

"Well, George George," Genevieve said, "it's interesting to make your acquaintance under these circumstances. I don't recognize you, so I assume you don't work at Château Beaulieu. Where are you from?"

Chloé translated. "He does not speak English," she said. "He works at Château Pitique, the château just beyond Clos Peyra."

"Does he, now?" Genevieve gave them both a withering stare. "Do you invite all your boyfriends to the pantry, Chloé?"

Looking like a frightened rabbit, George stood stone still but his eyes darted back and forth between Chloé and Genevieve.

"How often do you have sex in the kitchen?"

For the first time, color rose in Chloé's cheeks. "Oh, my lady. This is the first time, and I assure you, it won't happen again."

"And I can assure you, if it does, you won't find yourself in this kitchen again, or anywhere else at Château Beaulieu. In the next few weeks, there will be two young children at the château, and I guarantee they are much more precious to me than you are. If I have to worry for one second they might come upon you and old Georgie here," she jerked her thumb toward the boy who was sweating from terror, "in a compromising position in the kitchen, the garden, the garage…" She cocked her head and let the image speak for itself. "I would suggest George leave, and you," she arched her brows at Chloé, "get back to work."

Though he spoke no English, George knew he'd been given his cue to make a run for it. He shoved his arms into his red barn jacket and scurried out the door.

THIRTY-EIGHT

Unsure what Jing Wang would be wearing, Genevieve changed her clothes three times. Dressed and ready to go, Philip sat by the fire in their bedroom, reading a report on this year's anticipated grape yield. Each time Genevieve emerged, Philip glanced up, said, "That's nice," then looked back at his papers as his wife huffed back into the enormous closet to try again.

"G, we've got to go," he said, as he checked his watch. "Fashionably late is one thing, but we're getting close to being rudely tardy."

"I think this is it." He heard her muffled voice from deep in the dressing room.

"Tada." She twirled into the room, the ankle-length skirt of her red cashmere dress billowing out with each turn. The wide bateau neckline swept from shoulder to shoulder and allowed her hair to swish back and forth, grazing her collarbone with each turn of her head. A belt of the same fabric with an ornate gold buckle, nipped in her slender waist. "Worth the wait?" She struck a pose and threw a sultry stare at Philip.

"Always," he said, heaving himself out of the chair and patting her butt as he walked by her to pick up his jacket. He pulled it on, turned to her, and said, "Get your shoes on and let's go. I'll meet you downstairs."

"So much for dazzling the man," Genevieve said. "Not exactly the reaction I was hoping for." She caught a glimpse of the clock on her bedside table. 7:45. "Oh, merde! We were supposed to be there at seven thirty."

When they rang the doorbell at Clos Peyra, they could hear the clock from within gong eight times. A few seconds passed, then a minute. Just as Genevieve was about to press the button again, the door flew wide and there stood Jing, her long, jet-black hair parted in the middle, cut blunt and swaying behind her. An inch shorter than Genevieve, the two were wearing the same color red, but instead of a dress, Jing was wearing a strapless, wide-legged, form-fitting jumpsuit. Around her neck was a thick, eighteen-karat gold collar that hugged her neck like the one-piece suit hugged her slim hips.

"Bonjour! Bonjour!" she said. Her cheeks were flushed, her smile broad, and the smell of vintage red wine whispered on her breath. She pulled Genevieve into the two-story foyer, before giving her la bise. While Genevieve handed her coat to a maid in black, Jing shifted her attention to Philip, bestowing welcoming kisses on him. That done, she linked arms with each of the Warwicks and propelled them into a huge salon with a fireplace crackling at the far end. On either side of the hearth sat a man and a woman, both with flawless porcelain skin glowing from the flames. They were so still and perfect, Genevieve thought for a moment they might be statues. But then they rose together and stood like royalty, waiting for Philip and Genevieve to approach.

"Come, come," Jing laughed, tugging them along. "Meet our friends." They stood in front of the young man who greeted her with a boyish grin. He was more cute than handsome, a bit chubby and shorter than Genevieve, who couldn't resist the mischief in his eyes.

"Han, this is Lord Crosswick." She presented Philip like a prized possession. "And this is Lady Crosswick." She pulled Genevieve forward. "Lord and Lady Crosswick, this is our friend, Han Shou, but we call him Hank. He and his family own Château Pitique, just across the road."

"Hank, we sort of met at our party in Paris. You're a friend of Bernard Reines." Philip extended his hand but didn't mention the scuffle between Bernard and Daniel. "Good to see you."

"Lovely to see you again," Genevieve said, grasping Hank's hand with both of hers.

"I understand the party was quite a success," Hank said. "Bernard told me there were several large donations made that evening."

Jing turned to the beauty standing on the other side of the fireplace. "And this is Hank's wife, Lian."

Her hands folded in front of her, Lian nodded. The corners of her mouth lifted, but the smile didn't quite reach her eyes.

Genevieve grinned at Lian. "I'm sorry you weren't with Hank in Paris, but I'm delighted to meet you now. It's time we start getting to know our neighbors. We've been here just over a week and haven't had a moment to breathe."

"We were at Daniel LaGrande's beautiful celebration but

had to leave the moment it was over." Lian spoke so quietly that Genevieve had to lean forward to hear her. "I'm so sorry I didn't have a chance to introduce myself. Han's parents were here from Hong Kong. They do not like to be left alone, so we had to rush home."

"I thought I saw you in the crowd," Genevieve said, taking Lian's hand in hers. "We'll start our friendship this evening. Shall we?"

This time it was Lian's eyes that smiled when she said, "I would very much like that," and gave Genevieve's hand a squeeze.

"Where's Kim?" Philip turned to Jing.

"I'm right here," he said as he strode into the room carrying two open bottles of Pétrus. He placed them on a sideboard, then made a beeline for Genevieve. He took both her hands in his and said, "Bonjour, ma belle," followed by a kiss on each cheek.

"Philip," he said, offering Philip his hand then giving him a hardy pat on the back as if they were old friends. "Bonjour, mon ami. You met our neighbors?"

"We did." Philip smiled. "We appreciate the invitation this evening. Since we got to Château Beaulieu, we haven't had a second to relax, so this is a real treat."

Kim walked back to the sideboard and began to fuss with the wine glasses. "Well, you two, you can be certain that our mission tonight is for you and Genevieve to enjoy yourselves. To that end, we're going to start the evening by indulging in a couple of bottles of Pétrus. I hope you don't mind that we're drinking this little merlot rather than a divine Château Beaulieu cab." He nodded to Philip as he began to pour.

At the thought of preferring even his château's best wine over a glass of Pétrus, perhaps the most sought-after red wine on the planet, Philip laughed out loud. "I'm offended, Kim, but I'm sure I'll get over it by the time I finish the second glass. Thank you for this," he said, accepting the proffered Conterno glass, its sexy hips tapering into a long neck that captured the exquisite nose of the purplish-ruby ambrosia. Philip swirled the wine, enjoying the beauty of the light peeking through the rich color. He stuck his nose into the neck of the glass and was rewarded with notes of cedar, dark chocolate, blackberries and the richness of leather. As he waited for Kim to propose a toast, he anticipated how the bouquet would translate to the palate. He caught Genevieve's eye and shared an intimate smile.

When everyone held a glass, Kim stood in front of the fireplace looking very much like a master of the universe, dashing in a narrow-cut green velvet dinner jacket, white tieless shirt and sharply creased black pants. "Thank you, dear neighbors, for joining us this evening," he began. As he spoke, he cradled his wine glass between his hands. "We are the lucky ones. We have passion for our work, we have good friends, and we have Pétrus." Polite laughter rippled through the small crowd. "Pétrus in the glass is a beautiful thing, but Pétrus on the palate is heaven. To heaven." He raised his glass, closed his eyes and took a noisy slurping sip. The others followed suit.

"Ganbei," Hank mumbled.

"Santé," Jing offered in a cheerful voice.

Without toasting Lian drank, and Philip and Genevieve said, "Cheers," in unison.

Only once before had Genevieve and Philip enjoyed this legendary wine. Less than six months ago when they arrived in New York City to begin claiming Philip's inheritance, the law firm handling the estate, Holmes Fitch Smythson Morrow, served it upon their arrival. No doubt, the pricey wine was added to their legal bill for that month. The Pétrus was exceptional then, and it was exceptional now.

Genevieve took a second taste, enjoying the silky finish on her tongue. "This is very special, Kim. Thanks for sharing, you two."

"I'm sure you've all heard the stories about how much counterfeit Pétrus there is in the world." Kim remained standing in front of the fire.

"I don't know about this." With her new interest in counterfeit wine, Genevieve leaned forward. "Tell us more."

Kim swirled his glass. "According to reports, there is more Pétrus drunk in Las Vegas every year than their total production. That is to say, there is a lot of counterfeit Pétrus around."

The lines between Genevieve's brows deepened. "Is this true or is it urban legend?" She put her wine glass down and joined Kim at the fireplace. "Are you saying counterfeiting Pétrus is a huge problem or are a lot of wines counterfeited?"

"I would say it is not a big problem at all," Hank said, and drained his glass.

Kim's first glass of wine was almost gone. "You're wrong, Hank. Wine counterfeiting is a massive fraud. Not only does it encompass the most expensive wines," he held up his glass, "but it is a problem all the way down to bodega wines like Yellow Tail, with plenty of fraud in between."

Color rose in Hank's round cheeks and, much to everyone's surprise, he banged his glass down on the table next to him. "If it's such a big problem, why doesn't anyone do anything about it?"

Genevieve's pulse quickened. She had paid attention yesterday, when Agent Lambert lectured them on counterfeit wine, but that had seemed more of an academic discussion. Hearing Kim's story and watching Hank's temperature rise at the introduction of the subject made it more realistic.

"We might have a counterfeit issue at Château Beaulieu." Genevieve started to share their conversation with DREETS, then stopped. She looked at Philip for confirmation that it was all right to continue. He hesitated a second, then nodded. "An agent came from DREETS yesterday. Do you all know what that agency is?"

"Of course," Kim and Jing said. Hank gave a small shrug of his shoulders. Lian said nothing but seemed disinterested.

Genevieve went on. "They received an anonymous note urging them to check our bottle orders against our production. What they're insinuating is that there are more bottles of Château Beaulieu being sold than we are making. They're coming back Monday to start a full forensic investigation."

Kim went from guest to guest, pouring a second glass of wine. "Are you worried?"

"We don't know enough to be worried," Philip said. "If someone is filling our bottles with their wine, where is it being sold? According to Agent Lambert, Hong Kong is the biggest importer of Bordeaux wines followed by mainland China, then the US, but I'm sure you already know that. We, on the other hand, are just coming up to speed."

The woman who had taken their coats stood in the doorway, brows raised at Jing. "Ah, I believe dinner is served," Jing said, sweeping her arm in the direction of the servant. "Florrie will lead the way."

"Please bring your wine. There is more in the dining room, but we don't want to leave any behind." Kim laughed, but his tone was serious.

Kim offered Genevieve his arm. She took it, and they chatted about Clos Peyra as they made their way to dinner. It was an interesting building that had changed and grown over the course of hundreds of years. The front of the house, the salon, dining room, and large library were in the newest wing of the clos, which was only a hundred or so years old. The frescoed walls were a soft, burnished bronze, a stunning background to the many contemporary canvases that hung throughout the first floor.

As they walked into the dining room, Genevieve heard herself gasp. The room was a movie set. The ceiling sparkled with hundreds of tiny lights, muted to a glimmer. A single candelabra with twelve candles lit the intimate round table, set for six. Two identical candleholders sat on the sideboard. The room glowed like a sunset. Flames flickered off faceted glass, and cream-colored porcelain reflected the warmth of the stars in the ceiling.

Kim led Genevieve to a dining chair opposite the sideboard with the candelabras. Above the buffet hung a long Impressionist canvas. While everyone else was being seated and chatting away, Genevieve stared at the painting of green leaves, rippling blue water, pink and yellow lilies, all emerging from the thick brush strokes that defined them. She squinted, hearing none of the conversation. She sensed a joke had been told and people laughed, but still she couldn't drag her attention from the canvas.

"G," Philip said. "G," he said, louder. "Are you okay?"

Genevieve shook her head to break the trance. Her mouth hung open until she could gather herself. Finally, she said, "Kim, Jing, is that really a Monet?"

"You like it?" Jing beamed.

Eyes wide, Genevieve nodded. "Of course."

"It's a fake. A counterfeit, if you like. Good, isn't it?"

She squinted, disbelieving. "It's amazing."

Jing leaned forward. "It's a very good copy, but it's quite dim in here." Everyone but Genevieve laughed. "The mind sees what it wants to see, doesn't it?"

"Hmm," Genevieve hummed. "I suppose it does."

"It's rather like the Pétrus," Kim said. "If you think you are drinking a twenty-thousand-euro bottle of wine, who's to say you're not?"

He squeezed Genevieve's hand. She left it there a moment, then slipped it from his grasp and put it in her lap. Kim was beginning to unnerve her.

Kim didn't notice, and pressed Philip to continue the conversation they were having before dinner was announced. "Tell me more about the counterfeiting at Château Beaulieu. By the way," he interrupted himself, "did your lawyers tell you we've been trying to buy Château Beaulieu for years? My god, your people are tough. They've been unwavering."

Philip's smile dazzled. "That's as it should be, don't you think? They knew that my late cousin, the 12th Earl of Crosswick loved the château. It has a long family history. Not as long as Clos Peyra's before your family bought it, but long, nonetheless. Of all our properties, Château Beaulieu and Wilmingrove Hall, our family seat in England, are the two estates we'll never part with."

Two servers put small bowls of soup in front of each guest. Kim rose to bring another bottle of wine from the sideboard and refilled his guests' glasses himself. When he finished, he set the bottle on a silver wine coaster at his place.

"Kim, why are you so interested in Château Beaulieu?" Genevieve decided to ask.

"Prestige," he said. "I know. We Chinese have always built for the centuries ahead, but we millennials do not have the patience of our ancestors. And my father has not given me the luxury of patience. Clos Peyra has potential. I believe in another generation it will be a fine vineyard, but my father wants Clos Peyra to be a superior château in the next five years. That will be difficult without adding a property that is already revered. Château Beaulieu is a perfect match. Your château is everything we want ours to be, and it is all of that now."

The words rang in Genevieve's ears. They were almost the exact words Delphine had overheard years ago when Kim and his father were arguing.

"Do you think you can ever make the vintage of your dreams, Kim?" Hank spoke for the first time since they sat down to dinner.

"Of course I do. But I need the time to do it. No amount of

money can overcome a lack of time." His words were passionate, then lightened when he said to Hank, "What the hell are you doing over there at Pitique? You seem to be happy growing wine for the corner shop except for the little specialty dessert wine you're fooling around with."

"You're making a dessert wine?" Genevieve asked. "Tell us about it."

"It is wonderful." It was the first thing Lian had said during the entire dinner.

A light sparked in Hank as he started sharing the details of his project. "I have some second wine grapes that—"

"Second wine grapes?" Genevieve interrupted him. "I don't know what those are."

As he spoke, Hank became more and more animated. "These are grapes that will not be used for the Grand vin, or the first label. A second wine is a wine produced with grapes from younger plots, which means they are not as mature. At Château Pitique, we have no great terroir, thus we have no great grape." Eyes dancing, Hank looked at each of the dinner guests. "Unlike Clos Peyra, no amount of time will turn us into a great vineyard. So, I am purchasing second-growth sauternes grapes from a vineyard about an hour from here. Over the last couple of years, I have been experimenting with this grape and at last have created a dessert wine that I believe has a bright future in the Chinese and US markets."

"How can we try this new wine?" Philip said, always anxious to support entrepreneurs, particularly when they were local.

"You're in luck," Jing broke in. "We're serving it this evening with the crème brulée."

"This is our lucky day." Genevieve beamed at Hank, enjoying his bubbling enthusiasm. "It must be expensive to create a new wine," she commented, "especially when you can't use the grapes from your château."

Hank looked down at his plate, his exuberance dwindling, replaced by discomfort. "As Kim said, we are selling some mediocre Château Pitique wine to the corner shops in the UK and some bodegas in New York, but it has been a challenge. Sometimes, in order to succeed, we must do things we would prefer not to."

When he looked up from his plate, Genevieve saw worry in his eyes. She reached over and patted his hand. "Let's try some of this magical concoction of yours, shall we?"

Jing summoned the servers, who whisked away dinner plates and replaced them with crème brulée, tiny French strawberries piled on the side, topped with a sprig of mint. Servers brought in tulip glasses and set them at each guest's place, next to the glasses left with traces of Pétrus.

With Kim's encouragement and great flourish, Hank held up a long, slender, octagonal bottle. He sliced the sleeve with the foil cutter then inserted the helix off center, pressed in and turned the corkscrew. When he eased the cork out of the mouth of the bottle, there was a satisfying pop. Applause erupted around the table and Hank's lips crept into a self-conscious smile.

"What are you calling this ambrosia?" Genevieve said.

He turned the label toward everyone. On an elegant cream

background, the words Château Pitique, La Vie Douce were written in gold, with the burgundy CP logo scrolled at the top of the label.

"Hank, I love the name. The Sweet Life." Genevieve offered her glass, anxious to try the wine.

Hank accommodated by filling hers first, then proceeded around the table. When everyone's glass sparkled with amber liquid, Hank held up his glass. Before he toasted, he held the gaze of each person around the table, then said, "To the sweet life and all my friends who dwell here," he said with tenderness.

Though Philip was not fond of dessert wine, when La Vie Douce hit his palate, he couldn't help but smile. It was like drinking the fragrance of orange blossoms with a soft rose finish. He'd never had anything like it. When he looked across the table at Genevieve, he knew she was having a similar experience.

Genevieve took a tentative sip. She licked her lips, then took a longer draw, grinning as she swallowed. "Hank, this is delicious. Well done. Philip, don't you think we should serve this at the Cité du Vin dinner?"

"Absolutely." Philip set down his empty glass. "Uh, apparently I like it, Hank—very much." He was delighted when Hank poured more La Vie Douce into his glass. "Where are you in production?"

Hank radiated energy as he talked about his plans. "We are about to bottle the first small batch, all of which will go to local restaurants and bars. If we get a good response from this first blend, we will have another ready to go in two months. The next round will go to wider distribution. My father wants us to ship to

Hong Kong, then to mainland China, but I want to concentrate on the French market first." His face clouded. "He is pressing me to make a success of the vineyard." He glanced at Kim. "It is no secret that I have botched my life up more than once and the pressure from my father to succeed is enormous. So, I am doing whatever I must." His smile was back, but not as sparkling as before.

"For what it's worth, I think you have a winner here," Philip said.

"How many bottles can we get for a large dinner party next week?" Genevieve shared their plans for creating a work-study program at Cité du Vin, then said, "Hank, this would be a spectacular way to showcase La Vie Douce. This is the board of directors of Cité du Vin. What better group to dazzle?"

"How many people will be at the party?"

"There will be about twenty or twenty-five." She took another drink. "I'm in love with this." A lightbulb went on. "I just remembered. Bernard will be here for the meeting."

"He called yesterday and said he was coming. We're going to spend time together on Sunday after everyone is gone." Hank thought for a moment. "If there are twenty people, I would say two cases should be enough." He looked very young when he said, "I appreciate you serving La Vie Douce to such a prestigious group. It would give my wine a real boost if they like it.

"We're delighted to do it, Hank. The wine is quite special," Philip said. "Two cases should be more than enough, but there's nothing wrong with having some left over. It sounds as if it'll be tough to get for a while, which is a smart strategy."

"That is the plan. We hope to create a big demand for La Vie Douce and keep supply low for a while. That way we can increase production slowly and gradually eliminate the other things we're doing." He studied his hands. "I look forward to that day," he said, as he twisted his napkin.

From somewhere in the house, they heard twelve deep bongs from the longcase clock.

Genevieve shoved her sleeve over her watch. "I can't believe it's midnight." As soon as she knew the time, she realized how tired she was. "Philip, we should be going."

As if the clock signaled the end of the evening, everyone stood and began to move into the foyer and toward the door.

As they stood waiting for their coats, Genevieve and Jing discussed when they could get together again, while Lian looked silently on.

The three men huddled together outside on the front steps in the crisp night air. Seizing the opportunity to speak to them before Genevieve came out, Philip said, "The strangest thing happened earlier today, Hank. Duncan, my son, was driving by your château and a horse jumped from your vineyard, over the stone wall, and almost onto his car. He swore someone in a red jacket was urging the horse over the wall and onto the road. Do you know anything about that?"

"Oh my god, Philip! That was your son? Is he all right?" Hank said, eyes wide with concern. "One of the horses got out this morning and was running through the vines. We have a new, inexperienced stableman who tried to get him back to the barn, and rather than get him under control, the idiot startled the horse and he nearly collided with a car. I am so very sorry."

Philip's eyes narrowed as he studied Hank. "So you knew about this?"

Hank put his hand on Philip's shoulder. "We've been worried all day about what happened but couldn't find out who was driving the car. I am just grateful your son is all right."

"What was that about a horse almost colliding with Duncan?" Genevieve asked as she came out of the front door.

"Nothing, G. I'll tell you about it later." He slid his arm around her waist and nudged her toward the stairs.

Pulling back, Genevieve gave Philip a sidelong glance and was about to ask another question when she saw him shake his head at her. "Thank you for the delightful evening, Kim," she said instead. "And, Hank. We'll have one of our fellows pick up the two cases of La Vie Douce on Monday. Just text us what we owe you and where to pick it up."

"I shall be at a meeting in Bordeaux all day on Monday, so I appreciate your man collecting the cases. They will be ready and waiting."

Genevieve gave him a kiss on each cheek then leaned in to offer the same to Kim.

"Next time we'll do this at Château Beaulieu."

The moment they were in the car, Genevieve turned in her seat to Philip. "What was that all about? What in the world did a horse have to do with Duncan?"

Philip told the story as Duncan had shared it with him earlier in the day, ending with, "Duncan said the Purosangue handled it like a dream."

Stunned, Genevieve had nothing to say for several seconds, then she found her words. "I don't give a crap that Duncan loves the car! First, why am I just hearing that our son was almost killed by a neighbor's horse jumping on his car?"

Philip opened his mouth to speak.

Genevieve held up her hand. "Did you believe Hank when he said the horse was just wandering around in the vines? That's ridiculous!"

Philip kept his eyes on the road but felt the fire of Genevieve's words.

"Don't you think there are too many near-disastrous accidents threatening this family? Why have you kept this a secret all day? Does Julia know?"

He pulled onto the long lane leading to Château Beaulieu, slowed, then stopped the car at the broad front steps. He unclipped his seatbelt and took Genevieve's hand in his. "I should have told you." He turned her wedding band around and around on her finger. "But Duncan and I didn't want to frighten you and Julia." He could just see the outline of her head in the dark but heard her snort at the idea. "We decided to wait until we talked to the local police."

"Did you call them?"

"We did."

"And?"

"They said they would look into it. I asked to speak to Frederick Picard, you know, Boucher's buddy, but he's in Spain until Monday."

"What did you think about Hank's response?"

"He seemed genuinely concerned." Philip held her hand in the dark. "But, he said something that made no sense. He said they've been trying to figure out all day who the driver was so they could contact him and make sure he was all right. I can say with assurance, there is not another tangerine-colored Ferrari Purosangue in the neighborhood, perhaps not in Bordeaux, maybe not even in France. How in the hell did they not know whose car their horse almost crushed?"

Genevieve said nothing, but Philip could hear her breath quicken.

"And the other thing. I've been trying to figure out what the motive would be. What would anyone have to gain by injuring Duncan?"

"Maybe whoever it was isn't trying to injure Duncan but rather frighten our family. Who would like us to give up Château Beaulieu and go back to England or the US?"

They looked at each other through the darkness. "Kim Wang," they said.

THIRTY-NINE

WITH RAIN PELTING the windows and the wind howling through the trees, Sunday morning was made for snuggling deep under the covers.

When Philip, Genevieve and Duncan surfaced, they found the perfect rainy-day breakfast waiting. Lizette's pain perdu, which the three agreed was the best French toast on the planet, was accompanied by fresh orange juice, bloody marys, mimosas, and steaming coffee.

The rest of the day was as lazy as the beginning. Though Philip, Genevieve, and Duncan made several attempts to work on projects, as the sky turned purple then darkened to black, the three were still nestled in Philip's study in front of a dwindling fire where they had been most of the day. Someone needed to toss a log on, but no one had the energy. Genevieve slipped her feet out of her shoes, lifted them into Philip's lap, and gave him a pleading smile, hoping he would massage them.

"I desperately want to go to bed, but I keep thinking about everything that's happened since we got to France, and I'm so exhausted I can't move."

"Ah, ma cherie, let me recount our adventures," Philip grabbed Genevieve's foot, and, began to count. He wiggled her big toe. "On our trip from England to Paris, the engines cut out on the Bombardier, we plummeted, the engines started, and we landed." He moved to her next toe. "A naughty intern at the family art museum tried to extort five million euros from us by stretching a giclee print over an original Jackson Pollock. He was easily found out, but instead of sending him to jail, we took him under our wing and are now employing him here at the vineyard." Genevieve's middle toe was next. "Daniel LaGrande, Château Beaulieu's GM for nearly forty years, is presumed murdered by poisoned wine just before we arrived." Genevieve squealed as Philip tickled the bottom of her foot before moving to her fourth toe. "A close friend of Daniel's warned me that Daniel had told her something very serious before he died, then she died the next day. We thought she was poisoned, but the evidence said no? And last but not least…" He held up Genevieve's foot and wiggled her little toe. "We believe someone tried to make Duncan crash yesterday while he was passing Château Pitique." He raised her foot in victory. "Tada. There you have it, folks. The Warwicks' big French adventure all on one foot."

"Sorry, Dad. We need the other foot."

Philip's brows drew together. "What did I forget?"

"Threatening notes, a stolen briefcase, and the counterfeiting of our wine."

Philip slapped his forehead. "Of course. The counterfeiting may be the one thing that ties all of this together. Except maybe for Émile's five-million euro prank."

"Aah, yes, the one event that may be an isolated incident," Duncan said. "Émile and his prank seems to be unconnected to the other events. He's a chronic screwup who, much to everyone's surprise—"

"And delight," Genevieve added.

"—seems to be finding his way under the firm hand of the staff here." Duncan took a drink of coffee. "I can tell you one thing. That lucky bastard's doing something I'd like to be doing," Duncan said.

"What's that?" Genevieve thought a moment, then clapped her hands. "Oh, I bet I know. He's helping Henri in the garage. That's it, isn't it?"

"It is." Duncan nodded with a sheepish grin.

"But, Duncan, we own all those fabulous cars." Philip pointed out the obvious. "Isn't it better to drive them anytime you like and have someone else take care of them?"

Duncan thought a moment, then aimed his index finger at his father. "You make a good point, Dad. I'm still getting used to our family's ridiculous wealth."

"Good. I'm glad. I'm not interested in anyone in this family becoming one of the entitled rich. We need to do all the good we can with this fortune." Genevieve drained her Cognac glass, put it on the side table and said, "That's the end of my lecture, folks. And now, I'm going to bed. I'll leave this brain trust to solve the problem of who's counterfeiting our wine and why they're trying to kill us all." Genevieve kissed the top of Philip's head and blew a kiss to Duncan.

"I'll be up in a flash," Philip said.

The two watched Genevieve drag herself out the door. "Duncan," Philip said. We don't need all this money. We struck it rich a long time ago with the women we chose."

FORTY

Bleary-eyed, Duncan sat slump shouldered, head in hands, untouched cold coffee and a croissant in front of him. Just as his mind wandered toward a fuzzy dream, Philip slapped him on the back.

"Good morning," he said. "Rough night?"

"You could say that. I didn't sleep for one second. After your recap of events, I couldn't shut my brain off. I can tell you one thing. I'm glad Julia and the kids aren't coming until all this is over."

"No question. That was the right decision." Philip looked at his watch. "Agent Lambert and the gang are due here any minute. Do you feel up to meeting with them?"

Never one to shirk his duty, Duncan raised an eyebrow. "Of course, Dad. What's your best guess? Do you think they're going to find anything?"

"Beats the hell out of me, but someone's trying to hurt our family and quite possibly Château Beaulieu, so we'll keep at it until we find out who it is. Maybe Lambert's team can unearth something, maybe they can't. After last night, I have my own suspicions."

Duncan leaned forward. "What happened last night?" He gulped his cold coffee and cringed.

As if on cue, Chloé entered the petit salon, a French press in one hand and small tray of croissants straight from the oven in the other.

"Lord Crosswick," Chloé said. "Your guests have arrived and are in the salon. Shall I tell them you will join them when you are finished with breakfast?"

"No, Chloé." Philip was already shoving his chair back. He grabbed a croissant, tore off a piece and shoved it into his mouth. "Come on, Duncan. It's showtime."

When Philip and Duncan arrived, the small army of DREETS agents was milling around, some admiring the salon, some admiring the view. Jules Lambert strode across the room to meet the two Warwick men, hand outstretched.

"Bonjour, my lords," she said, all business and without any preamble. "If you can show us to the vineyard office, we are ready to begin."

"By all means." Philip led the way.

After yesterday's unrelenting rain, today sparkled. The entourage left the salon through the French doors, looking like a little parade as they crossed the courtyard, careful to avoid lingering puddles here and there. Walking three abreast, Philip and Duncan tried to make small talk with the DREETS chief, but Agent Lambert was focused on the task at hand. Her mission was to find any clues to support the accusation that Château Beaulieu was the victim of counterfeiting. When they pushed through the door to the vineyard building, Émile was staggering through the door at the other end of the hall, carrying two cases of wine at a time into the tasting room.

"Émile, why don't you use a hand truck?" Philip yelled to the struggling young man.

He jerked his head in acknowledgment. "It's okay, my lord. There are just a few to bring in. This is what Delphine asked me to pick up from Château Pitique."

Philip flashed a thumbs up and slid the key into the office door. "This door has been locked since you asked us to secure it on Friday," he said to Lambert. As they stepped into the room, a smell filled the air: a combination of leather, red wine and remnants of rose lilies left from Daniel LaGrande's celebration of life a week ago. It was hard for Philip to believe it was just seven days since they had said goodbye to Daniel. So much had happened in a week.

"What do you need from us, Agent Lambert?" Duncan asked.

"I believe we have everything we need," she said, then reconsidered. "Is there a safe?"

Philip thought for a moment, looked around the room then said, "I don't know." He held up one finger. "Give me a second." He tapped in a text, hit send, and kept his eyes on his screen. Almost immediately his phone pinged a response. "Edouard, our vigneron, said there is a safe. He's on his way."

While they waited, Lambert organized her team. Every piece of paper in every file had to be read and cataloged. Every computer file had to be evaluated, and every email read to determine if it was nothing or one of the many brushstrokes that would help to paint the total picture. It was going to be a long, tedious day and Agent Lambert was anxious to get it underway.

Within five minutes, Edouard was through the door, muddy from trellising the vines. As he walked into the room, his dirty boots left perfect tread prints on the brick floors. When he saw what a mess he was making, he winced at Philip and backed up two steps before Philip said, "Don't worry about it, Edouard," and waved it off. "Where's the safe?"

"La bas." He pointed across the room to a still life painting of a bottle of wine, grapes, and a candle.

"Behind the painting?" Philip asked.

"Oui."

Lambert found a latch under the frame on the left. It swung away from the wall on its right-hand hinges. "Et voila," she said. "And the combination?"

Edouard called out the numbers and Lambert rotated the dial as if she had done this many times before. With the final number, Philip and Duncan heard a click and looked at each other, excited to see what would happen next. Lambert pulled the lever and the thick door eased open. She peered into the safe, blocking everyone else's view. She reached in and pulled out a small stack of euros, which she handed to Philip. Next came a few letters and some papers. "And that is all," she said. She rifled through the stack and stopped when she came to a thick cream-colored envelope with *Lord and Lady Crosswick* written in elegant script on the front.

"This appears to be for you, Lord Crosswick."

Confused, Philip took the proffered letter. "Why would there be a letter for me in the safe?" He studied his name on the envelope. "This looks like Daniel's handwriting. He wrote a thank you note to Genevieve and me after he stayed with us in Paris." A lump stuck in his throat as he looked at the script of a dead man.

"If you could open it, it might be helpful. Perhaps there is some useful information, something that will shed light on our investigation."

"Of course." Philip looked around for the best place to sit down. "Uh, yes. I should open it."

Lambert put her hand on Philip's arm. "My lord, why don't you and your son go to the château and read the letter? Call me when you're finished, and we'll go over it together. We'll get on with things here."

"Let's do that, Dad." Duncan put his arm around his father's shoulders and urged him out the door. "Do you want Mom to join us?"

"Yes, of course."

When the three had gathered in the salon, Duncan handed his father a letter opener. Philip slipped it along the fold, slicing it open. He pulled two vellum sheets from the envelope and held them up so Genevieve and Duncan could see Daniel's elegant hand. He pulled his glasses from his sweater pocket and began reading.

> *My Dearest Lord and Lady Crosswick,*
>
> *I am not certain how I have come to this moment in my life. I have always treasured honor above all, so the dishonor I have brought upon myself is more than I can bear.*

I cannot undo my treachery of the last three years, when I provided bottles and labels to unscrupulous men who stole the prestige of my beloved vineyard and used it to sell their inferior wine as that of Château Beaulieu. I beg your forgiveness.

When I met the two of you in Paris, I realized for the first time that what I was doing was unforgivable. I realized I had not just compromised myself, but I had betrayed your trust and the trust of generations of the House of Crosswick.

My shame is overwhelming and, though there are others involved, I have no one to blame but myself. I cannot return from this dark abyss of shame, so there is nothing for me to do but say adieu.

Please know my love for Château Beaulieu and its soul is in my dying breath.

Daniel LaGrande.

FORTY-ONE

A BANK OF ANGRY clouds drifted across the sun and plunged the bright salon into shadows. Philip stared at Daniel's note for a long time before looking at Genevieve. "I don't understand. What's he saying?"

Genevieve left her chair and walked to Philip. She tugged the letter from his fingers and reread it in silence. When she was finished, she put her hand on his. "I think he's telling us that he's been involved in counterfeiting wine for the last three years." She held the papers up and swallowed hard.

Duncan blew air from his cheeks. "I didn't have the good fortune to meet him, but from everything I've heard, no one would expect this of him, would they?"

"No." Philip shook his head. "No, they wouldn't. The idea that Daniel LaGrande would do something dishonorable and jeopardize Château Beaulieu's reputation is…" Philip searched for the right word. "I guess I'd have to say, shocking." He took the letter back from Genevieve. "Here, where he says, 'I cannot return from this dark abyss of shame, so there is nothing for me to do but say adieu,' is he saying he's going to commit suicide?"

Genevieve blinked and a single tear slid down her cheek. "I don't know any other way to interpret it," she said.

"Ahem," Agent Lambert cleared her throat as she stood in the open door to the terrace. "Excuse me, my lord." She was wearing plastic gloves and holding folders. "We have uncovered a few things I think you should see."

Philip motioned to Lambert. "Come in, come in." He thrust Daniel's letter at the agent. "You think you've discovered something. Wait'll you see what we have." He could feel his bewilderment at Daniel's treachery simmering into anger.

"Is there something interesting in the note?" Lambert pulled her glasses from her pocket and put them on before looking at the pages.

"Oh, I would say so." Philip's mind began to race. "According to Daniel's letter, he's been involved in counterfeiting Château Beaulieu wine for the last three years." He paused, thinking. "Could he have been behind the water in our gas tank? Could he possibly be the one who tried to kill us?" He choked out a laugh. "If we were dead, he'd continue his reign over the château. In fact, it wouldn't surprise me if he and Kim were in cahoots. Together they'd have both properties." As he spoke, he paced back and forth in front of the windows, his fury building. "Kim has made no secret of how much he wants Château Beaulieu." He stopped to stare out at the vineyard, his fists clenched at his sides. "It's a good thing he killed himself. If he hadn't, I might have killed him myself when I found out what he was doing."

"Philip, stop it!" Genevieve pushed herself from her chair and crossed to him in three rapid strides. "What is the matter with you? The man made a terrible mistake and was so fraught with remorse that he didn't feel he should live." She grabbed her husband's shoulders and squeezed them hard. "I don't believe for one minute Daniel had anything to do with the fuel incident. He said there were other people involved in this," she fluttered her hands, "whatever it is."

Agent Lambert had read the note twice. The first time she skimmed it. The second time she read each word, looking for clues. "Lord Crosswick, could you please sit down?" She had the commanding voice of a headmistress and Philip sat. "With Daniel's suicide note and these files, we now have some excellent clues." She laid two folders on the coffee table in front of her. "It is as if Daniel LaGrande laid out a map." She held up one folder. "This is the file of emails you gave me last week, between Daniel and someone receiving Château Beaulieu bottles and labels. When our technical people delved into who was on the email chain besides LaGrande, they found an IP address in Hong Kong—or at least routed through Hong Kong—and one in Paris." She slapped that file closed.

"Paris?" three surprised people said.

"Yes. It appears someone in Paris is a piece of this puzzle." She held up the second folder. "LaGrande kept excellent records of purchase orders and shipping documents. This next piece of information may or may not be important." She shifted in her chair. "When this all started, LaGrande changed bottle manufacturers. For over a hundred years, Château Beaulieu bought bottles from VOA in Albi, about three hundred kilometers from here. Three years ago, he switched that business to a Chinese bottle manufacturer. We just spoke to the managing director of the French factory. He said they did everything they could to save the business, but LaGrande could not be persuaded to stay with them. It is likely his partner pressured him to make the switch because he either owns the Chinese bottling company or they could get a throwback."

"A kickback," Philip corrected.

"You are sure? Kickback?" Lambert's brows drew together.

Philip nodded.

She went on. "For the last three years, he has ordered seventy thousand bottles from the new purveyor. Fifty thousand have been shipped here to Château Beaulieu for your annual production, and twenty thousand shipped to a storage facility just outside Libourne. He did the same thing with your labels. When we did an online search we found that the warehouse holding the bottles and labels is owned by a Chinese mega-corporation with an import-export business as part of their holdings. One of our agents is there now to see if we can find out more information." Agent Lambert sat back in her chair and paused to let the information sink in.

Genevieve was the first to break the silence. She leaned forward and held Lambert's gaze. "You're saying that Daniel was providing bottles to someone who was filling them, probably with an inferior wine, then selling them under our label."

"That's what we've pieced together so far, with LaGrande's help." She waved the second folder, then laid it in her lap. "It seems he wanted to make certain you would be able to solve this riddle. We appreciate his posthumous help."

"But you have no idea who his partner was in all this, do you?" Philip's curiosity was overcoming his anger.

"The evidence is pointing its finger, but we have a few more facts to confirm before we have the total picture." Lambert plucked off her reading glasses and tucked them into her purse. "And one more thing I must tell you. Inspector Boucher called me over the weekend. He discovered that Lee Bowen, the man who put water in your jet fuel, worked for the Wang family until recently."

"I guess that answers the question of who Daniel's partner was, doesn't it?" Duncan said.

"No," Genevieve gasped. "That's not possible. Kim has been so nice to us since we got here. How could anyone try to kill you, then turn around and invite you to dinner?"

Duncan snorted. "Mom, you're not that naïve. There are millions of euros at stake here." He jerked his head at Lambert. "What would you say? How much money is involved in counterfeiting twenty thousand bottles of Château Beaulieu's best wine?"

"It depends on where it is being sold, but if it is shipped to China, the wealthy Chinese business class would pay fifteen hundred euros a bottle for a fine wine. That's thirty million euros a year. The Chinese are just developing their palates, and they are in love with prestigious labels, so it's an easy sell and a huge revenue stream worth protecting at all costs."

A chill shot through the room as Philip, Genevieve and Duncan heard the realities of what was at stake.

"Do you think the threat of being caught and imprisoned

would be reason enough to take drastic action, like maybe causing a Bombardier jet to fall out of the sky?" No one could miss Genevieve's sarcasm. She stood up and walked to the sideboard, poured a glass of lemon-infused water and drank half of it.

"No doubt," the agent said. She stacked the folders on top of each other, picked them up, and tapped the bottoms on the coffee table to align them. When she stood, her lips were pressed together in a grim line.

"What's next?" Philip asked.

"My office needs to double check the evidence we've gathered. We need to wait for a few other pieces of information to be confirmed, then, if everything checks out and it continues to support the Wang family as the counterfeiters, we shall plan a search of Clos Peyra in conjunction with Directeur Picard. That could happen as soon as Wednesday, the day after tomorrow."

"You think you'll have enough evidence for a search warrant," Genevieve said more as a statement than a question.

Confusion flashed across Agent Lambert's face, then, in an instant, disappeared. "Ah, oui, the American search warrant. We do not have such a restriction. If there is belief a law is being broken, we may enter someone's property. Practical, eh? In this case, we have more than enough suspicion to launch a full, what you call, search and seizure."

The Warwicks exchanged mystified looks, trying to understand the whirlwind that was beginning to spin around them.

"Agent Lambert." Duncan shook his head as if to clear his thoughts. "If you find confirmation at Clos Peyra that Kim is the one involved with Daniel in the counterfeiting, what will the charges be?"

Lambert pulled her shoulders back, her eyes dark with concern. "From what we suspect at this moment, the charges will be multiple and serious. Besides the counterfeiting, there will be charges of international fraud, wire fraud, wine fraud, mail fraud, and, of course, conspiracy to commit murder." She walked toward the door. Before leaving, she turned back to the group. "These next few days will be busy here, at Château Beaulieu. I'm sure the Wangs will not cause you any problems. They are aware we are investigating, so they will want to, as you say, keep a low profile. But, Director Picard will have a car and officers at your front gate, and if anything unusual happens here at Château Beaulieu, please let me know immediately. Anything at all." She started to leave, then stopped once more. "Please share this information with no one. Absolutely no one." Finally, she opened the door and dashed across the terrace, leaving three people reeling.

"Wow, that's a lot to digest." Duncan's voice was barely a whisper. "I don't even know where we begin."

A ping announced a text on both Philip's and Genevieve's phones. Genevieve plucked her mobile off the table beside her chair and Philip pulled his from his pocket. "You've got to be shitting me," Philip said.

"What is it?" Duncan asked.

Genevieve looked up from the screen. "It's Kim asking if there's anything he can do to help with the Cité du Vin meeting."

"Yeah, there are two things he can do," Duncan snarled. "He can stop counterfeiting our wine and he can stop trying to kill us."

FORTY-TWO

For the rest of the day, the vineyard office hummed like a beehive. Directeur Picard arrived with a team that fingerprinted everything in sight, but soon abandoned the effort, realizing it would be impossible to identify the many prints on every surface. Phone calls were made. Responses came ringing back. While the officers and agents dug in every crevice for any undiscovered bit that would help support their case, Lambert and Picard set up headquarters in the tasting room. On the massive oak table, where wine lovers often gathered to treat their palates to some of the finest wine in the world, papers were laid out in meticulous order in hopes they would confirm the rapidly evolving theories. All evidence was pointing to the Wang family as the perpetrators of all the crimes that had been committed against Château Beaulieu and its owners.

Lambert massaged her temples. This was a huge case for her. If she wanted to continue her climb up the chain of command, she had to get it right. Just a few more questions to answer before she had an airtight case and would feel confident going ahead with searching Clos Peyra on Wednesday or maybe Thursday.

She leaned her head against the back of her chair, stared at the ceiling, and reviewed the evidence one more time, looking for holes in her theories.

"Agent Lambert." She jumped at Picard's voice, then shook her head as she laughed. "I forgot you were here," she said.

"Deep in thought, hein?"

"Oui."

Picard picked up his pen, ready to write. "If you would, s'il vous plaît, give me the list of loose strings we must tie up. I love that American phrase."

Lambert snickered. "I believe what you meant to say is loose ends we must tie up."

"Ah, oui. That's the phrase." Picard chuckled at himself.

"Allons," she said, and flipped through her notepad. In rapid French, she repeated the list. "We need to know who wrote the note warning Lord Crosswick that there was danger at Château Beaulieu. We need to know how it got into his briefcase. We have to figure out who intercepted the note on the train. How in the world did they know it was there?" she said, and looked at Picard, hoping he would have an explanation. He did not.

She went on. "We have to clarify the Paris connection. You said your people are working on that, oui?"

"Oui. Our tech people are getting close, in fact I expect to hear from them any time. They shouldn't have a problem pinpointing the IP address from the emails." Picard's phone pinged a text and he glanced at the screen. "Tech says another hour and they should have the IP address," he said.

"Ah, bon." Lambert sat back in the wooden chair and tapped

her pen against the edge of the table. "One thing that is bothering me. I want to know what happened to Lee Bowen. He came to France and disappeared. Call Inspector Boucher and see if they have the credit and bank card search results back."

"I'll also ask if they checked video surveillance." He punched in his old friend's number, and it went straight to voice mail. Picard left a message with his questions and ended the call.

"Excuse me." Philip stood in the doorway.

"Lord Crosswick, please come in." Lambert nodded toward a chair. "Join us."

Philip walked to the table and swept his eyes over the pieces of evidence laid out. "You've gathered a lot of information, haven't you?"

She said nothing, but her pride was evident.

Philip held up his phone. "I was just looking through the photos on my phone for something Genevieve wanted and ran across the picture I took of the note that was in my briefcase. Did you two know about that?"

"Yes, of course," Picard said. "Inspector Boucher shared that with us."

"I looked at it closely and I believe it's Daniel LaGrande's handwriting. If you compare it to his suicide note, I think you'll agree. It seems he wanted to warn us of what was going on and wanted us to understand there was more ahead."

"I have the suicide note here." Agent Lambert leaned across the table and picked up the paper sheathed in plastic. She laid it next to Philip's phone. The writing on the photo and Daniel's final note were from the same hand. "I'd say you're right. That would explain how it got into your briefcase. Either he slipped it in there when he was at your home for the party, or he asked someone to do it for him. That would be easy enough." She made a checking off motion. "That's one question answered."

Picard's phone vibrated. "Ah, bon," he said when he saw it was his tech team. He looked at Lambert and Philip and pointed to the screen as he answered. "Picard." He listened. "Oui. Oui. Vraiment? Non." His eyes widened. "Non," he said again, drawing out the word in disbelief. "Vraiment? Eh Bien. Merci. D'accord."

Philip and Lambert waited for Picard to tell them what he had just heard.

"Well?" Philip said.

Picard plopped into his chair, slack jawed. "The IP address was traced to a computer at the Laney Musée des Beaux-Arts."

FORTY-THREE

PHILIP THOUGHT HE had misheard. "What did you say, directeur?"

"You heard me correctly, my lord. The IP address is from a computer at the Laney Musée des Beaux-Arts… in Paris… your musée."

Philip looked as if he'd been slapped, his mouth open, his green eyes huge as saucers. "How…" he stopped. "Jesus, how is that possible?"

No one answered.

The sound of wood scraping on brick pierced the silence, as Philip pulled out a chair and crumpled into the seat. His head, cradled in his hands, felt heavy as a stone.

Agent Lambert and Directeur Picard could hear Philip muttering under his breath. They looked at each other, wondering what to do next. As Picard was about to speak, Philip slowly raised his head, his eyes on fire.

"All right," he seethed. "We're going to find out who at the LMBA is involved in this and we're going to make them sorry they ever started this little venture." He stood and leaned on the table. "Directeur, what do we need to do to discover who the Paris link is? Do you want me to call Lillie Langdon and talk to her?"

"Non, non, my lord," Picard cautioned him. "Please leave this to us." He waved his hand between Lambert and himself. "Our people still have papers to go through. Our hope is that there will be a clue somewhere in the file: a name, a reference, something that will tell us who at the musée is involved and what their role is."

With the devastating news about the LMBA connection, Philip was filled with new questions. "You know we're about to host a meeting and dinner for the Cité du Vin Board of Directors. Should we call the meeting off?"

Lambert uncrossed her legs and leaned forward, her elbows on her knees. "I think it's best if everything continues as planned. We want to surprise the Wangs. The moment we discover who the Paris connection is, that's what we'll do."

Picard nodded. "We have looked at who is attending the meeting and see that Mademoiselle Lillie Langdon will be here. She is the directrice of your foundation, oui?"

"Oui."

Philip sat forward and rolled his shoulders, trying to work out a kink between the blades. He hesitated a moment, then asked the question he feared. "You don't think Lillie could be the Paris partner, do you? That would be devastating to Lady Crosswick and me." He felt a lump rising in his throat.

"I'm afraid until we know definitely, we shall remain suspicious of everyone." Picard tapped his pen on his pad. "There are few people in this world who would not be tempted by a part of thirty million euros. Wouldn't you agree, my lord?"

Philip stared through Picard and didn't respond.

"And Bernard Reines will be coming? He is the directeur of the Laney Musée des Beaux-Arts?" Picard continued.

"He is." Philip thought for a moment. "I don't remember if I told you that Bernard is a friend of Hank Shou, who owns Château Pitique. Hank's family hosted Bernard when he was on a fellowship at the China Academy of Art in Hangzhou. They've been friends for at least ten years."

Picard jotted some notes, then looked at Philip. "You had not mentioned this." His brows arched. "Is there anything else you might not have shared with us?" Still clutching his pen and notebook, he laid his hands in his lap and waited.

Philip wasn't sure how to respond. "My apologies, Director Picard. This is all very new to us. Before Agent Lambert brought the counterfeiting to our attention last Friday, we thought we had just two problems: a fuel issue, and a dead managing director." With every word he spoke, Philip felt energy leaking from his body. "We've barely spent any time here at the château. We're just getting to know our staff and we don't know our neighbors or the community. We have no idea what we know or don't know. Please keep asking questions and see if they prompt any answers." He stood and looked down at Picard. "If there's nothing else, I'll excuse myself."

As he left the tasting room, fatigue nearly drowned him. He glanced at his watch and couldn't believe it was only two o'clock. The day felt much older. When his stomach rumbled, he realized, not only was he exhausted, but starving as well, so he trudged to the kitchen. Throughout his sixty-four years, he had found there were very few problems that couldn't be solved with a good sandwich.

FORTY-FOUR

ON WHAT SEEMED to be the longest day of his life, Philip was in bed by nine thirty, propped against piles of pillows with a chocolate-brown duvet tucked under his arms. His eyelids drooped, and a rerun of the day played on a loop in his head as a French game show droned on television in the background. He had yet to tell Genevieve about the LMBA connection. He was dreading that conversation, but it would have to happen soon. Everyone would arrive tomorrow for the Cité du Vin meeting.

His body relaxed into a sleepy freefall, then snapped back to consciousness when he heard Genevieve call goodnight to someone as she opened their bedroom door. Though she was quiet, her energy shouted through his drowse. He could feel her bustling around the room—folding, plumping, straightening—until finally she bent over him and kissed him on his forehead. He reached out, grabbed her by her arms, and swung her across his body onto the bed.

She shrieked with surprise that rolled into laughter. "My god, you startled me," she choked out. "I thought you were asleep."

Free from his covers, Philip loomed over her, no longer tired. "Aha!" he said. "Thinking I was asleep, you tried to steal a kiss, didn't you, my pretty?" He cackled like the Wicked Witch from Oz.

As she waited to see what her husband would do next, Genevieve giggled, her eyes holding his as the tension mounted.

He lowered his head until their noses were almost touching. She blinked.

He blinked. "I have news," he said.

Still playing their amorous game, she ran her tongue around her lips. "News?" she said, her voice husky. "What kind of news?"

Philip kissed her on the nose, then sat back against his pillows. "News you're not going to want to hear." His playful tone was gone.

Totally confused, Genevieve rolled onto her side and propped herself up on her elbow. "Are we still playing a game, or do you have something serious to tell me?"

"I have something serious to tell you." Philip sighed. "Are you ready for this?"

She shoved herself up and sat cross-legged. "Good god, Philip. You're scaring me. What is it?"

"Picard's people traced the Paris IP address." He stopped.

Genevieve strained forward. "Philip," she said through clenched teeth. "Tell me."

He reached out, took her hand, and squeezed it. "The computer is at the Laney Musée des Beaux-Arts."

Genevieve's face was blank. She sat still as a rock, staring at Philip as if she hadn't heard him.

Then her hand began to fidget in his. He watched her expression as his words began to sink in. A flicker of understanding sparked in her eyes. Her gaze left his and looked over his shoulder at nothing, then came back, locking his eyes with hers.

"Okay," she said at last. "I guess that means someone at our museum is trying to do us harm." She snorted in disgust. "I guess I should say they're trying to kill us and steal our wine. And that someone could be Lillie." She sniffed. "Is that about it?"

Philip raised her hand to his lips and kissed it. "That's about it," he said.

FORTY-FIVE

Tuesday could not have been more chaotic. Madame Morier arrived from Paris to help with the Cité du Vin event. She and Delphine were knee-deep, struggling over who was responsible for what. Genevieve popped in and out of the fray, trying to referee until, at last, she realized that their hostile tone, plentiful hand gestures and endless stream of aggressive French was their way of working together.

Lillie and Bernard would arrive on the TGV this afternoon. They would both stay at the château. Their job was to ensure that at the end of the board meeting everything for The Art of the Vine was in place and the program was ready to roll out.

Though Philip had assured Genevieve Cité du Vin would not turn down the enormous endowment they were offering, she was determined to show the board what an asset the Warwicks would be as partners. Always well-polished, every nook, cranny, doorknob, windowpane, brass hinge, carpet fringe, wood floor, and French door at Château Beaulieu shone with an extra luster. With everyone bustling to create a perfect event, energy bounced from floor to ceiling and back again.

For the next two days, Château Beaulieu was a beehive, buzzing with preparations from morning until well into the evening.

By early afternoon on Thursday, Genevieve's vision was perfectly executed and even she was satisfied.

At Saint-Émilion's elegant Hotel de Pavie, board members were arriving and settling into their rooms before making their way to Château Beaulieu. The invitations waiting for them were not specific about what to expect, but the mystery only served to heighten their excitement.

> *Please join us at Château Beaulieu, today at*
>
> 17:30
>
> AS
>
> *The Saint-Émilion Jurade welcomes the Cité du Vin Foundation Board with a special tribute.*
>
> PHILIP AND GENEVIEVE WARWICK

By five forty-five, everyone had gathered in the salon and a flute of Veuve Clicquot bubbled in each person's hand.

Stunning in a cabernet-red silk jacket and narrow-cut trousers flared from the knee, Elise Beaufoy stepped from the crowd to acknowledge Philip and Genevieve.

"Lord and Lady Crosswick," she gushed, her taut face attempting to smile. "On behalf of the Cité du Vin Foundation Board, I must thank you for your hospitality in hosting our meeting, and for your magnanimous gift to Cité du Vin." Her hands fluttered as she spoke. "By creating The Art of the Vine, you will change the lives of many young people by giving them a place in the magical industry of French wine. Merci beaucoup for allowing our foundation to be a part of this magnificent project." She pulled Genevieve into la bise and blew a kiss across the room to Philip.

Appreciative cheers and claps filled the salon until Philip tapped his Champagne glass to quiet the crowd. "Thank you, thank you," he began. "Présidente Beaufoy and members of le Fondation pour la Culture et les Civilisations du Vin Board of Directors, welcome. Genevieve and I are thrilled you have gathered here at Château Beaulieu as we explore The Art of the Vine and how, together, we'll make this program a reality. But, before we get down to the hard work of creating something from nothing, we have a treat for you. You are all familiar with the Jurade, a group tasked in 1199 by Richard the Lionheart to guard the quality and health of the vines of Saint-Émilion, planted by the Romans and nurtured to this day. This afternoon the Jurade will honor you with their traditional pipe and drum parade, usually seen only twice a year. But today they make an exception just for you, La Cité du Vin Board of Directors. With that introduction, please refill your glasses before Genevieve leads you out to the front steps."

The group followed Genevieve through the foyer, flooded out the front door and onto the wide limestone porch. Those who had seen the parade before buzzed with excitement, thrilled at knowing what awaited them. Those who had not, bubbled with anticipation.

Philip snaked his way through the swarm of bodies and down the stairs to Genevieve's side, where he handed her a faceted flute.

"Ooolala," she said, and sipped, the bubbles tickling her nose.

"Your attention, please," she said, but couldn't be heard over the din. "May I have your attention, please?" She raised her voice, but to no avail. Without warning, Philip let loose an earsplitting whistle that silenced the crowd. "Ah, thank you, Philip." She flashed him a grateful smile. "For the next few minutes, please focus your attention on the far end of the lane and listen carefully."

Even as she spoke, a faint note like thunder rolled in the distance. "Listen," she said, putting her hand to her ear.

The sound grew louder by the second, bass drums booming a rhythmic warning. Then, the whine of the bagpipes began. Twelve pipers, four abreast, turned onto the lane followed by more than a hundred members of the Jurade of Saint-Émilion, their crimson robes swaying to the pipers' music. The haunting tune crescendoed with every step they took toward the château, drones of the bagpipe holding the moaning, low note, the chanter playing the melody.

The bass drums rumbled, and the snare drums trilled their

relentless beat, driving the marching pipers forward. The wail of the bagpipes grew louder and louder until the spectacle was in front of the electrified crowd. As they played the last notes of the melancholy song, the pipers parted and the jurats strode through the aisle.

The first jurat stepped forward. "Lord Crosswick," he bellowed. "I have a decree for the Board of Cité du Vin."

"Of course, Jurat Manoncourt," Philip said. "Présidente Beaufoy, if you please." He motioned for Elise to come forward.

On her four inch stilettos, she teetered down the three broad steps, then, with full pomp and circumstance, the head of the brotherhood began. "Presidente Beaufoy, we wish to extend an invitation for the revered Board of Cité du Vin to join us as our honored guests for the Jurade festival in June and the Ban des Vendanges in September." He handed Elise a rolled-up parchment, tied with a red ribbon, secured with a red wax seal. He kissed both her cheeks. "Now," he said, looking at Philip, "I believe there is wine to drink." And the crowd let out a mighty cheer.

On the other side of Saint-Émilion, at police headquarters, Agent Lambert, Directeur Picard, and Inspector Boucher, who had returned the night before, were in the eye of the storm. While activity swirled around them, they methodically placed the final pieces in the puzzle, the last of which they discovered an hour ago. Stuck to the back of one of the last files they had pulled from the cabinet was a yellow post-it note, written in Daniel's hand. Dated two months ago, the note was a reminder to call his Paris partner, with a name and phone number. Now that they had the last link in the chain, a small team of municipal police prepared for the arrest of a local citizen. They inspected their pepper spray, batons, and handcuffs, bantering back and forth, trying to keep their adrenaline under control.

It was rare in Saint-Émilion for the police to deal with serious crime. A loose dog nosing through an upended garbage bin, the occasional graffiti painted on the side of a house, or a drunk teenager who had to be helped into the back of a police car and driven home was the height of adventure in the pretty, medieval town. For most of the squad, tonight would be the pinnacle of their law enforcement careers, and they could hardly wait for the directeur to give them the order. Their nerves jittered knowing it was mere moments before they were out the door and on their way.

FORTY-SIX

Beautiful at any time, the tasting room dazzled as the scene of the Cité du Vin opening cocktail party, with the late afternoon sun filtering through the wall of French doors. As the natural light waned, hundreds of candles would cast their glow throughout the room. There were no traces of Lambert, Picard, and their teams. Their boxes and papers had been displaced by sparkling glasses, bottles of fine wine, and a stunning display of hors d'oeuvres.

The Jurade and Cité du Vin guests made their way from the front of the château, across the courtyard and into the vineyard building. As the crowd filtered in, a jazz trio played and the fragrance of lilies and peonies sweetened the air. Spirits were high after the grand introduction to the evening, and the crowd was enjoying themselves as they chatted, nibbled scrumptious morsels, and waited for the wine to flow.

Earlier in the day, Émile had brought in eight cases of Château Beaulieu's best and arranged a case on the table ready to be uncorked. Philip found Jurat Manoncourt in the crowd and caught his eye. He motioned to the portly man with a bushy white mustache and rimless glasses. The Jurat wove his way through the crowd to Philip.

"Oui, my lord. Are we ready to uncork the ambrosia?"

"We are," Philip said, just as his phone vibrated in his pocket. He held up a finger. "Just one minute." He glanced at his screen and saw the text from Directeur Picard.

We are leaving for the search and seizure, it read. *Update soon.*

Philip heard himself gasp and felt blood rush to his head.

"Is everything all right?" Manoncourt asked.

"I'm fine," he said. "Champagne in the afternoon always gets to me." His smile was weak but convincing. "Give me just a couple of minutes and we'll get on with it, shall we?" Before the Jurat could respond, Philip plunged into the crowd in search of Genevieve. When he found her, she, Elise Beaufoy and Lillie were in deep conversation. "G, I need to speak to you for just a minute."

"Hi." Lillie kissed Philip on the cheek. "Find me when your husband's finished with you," she said to Genevieve. Lillie grinned, slid her arm through Elise's and joined a trio of board members who were drooling over the tempura coconut shrimp.

"What's going on?" When she looked at Philip, Genevieve knew something was amiss.

He pulled his phone from his pocket and showed her the screen.

"So, this is happening," she said. "They're on their way to Clos Peyra?"

"It looks that way. I've got to get back to Manoncourt. He needs to uncork this wine and get it flowing." He took her hand.

"Come with me," he said, and pulled her with him back to the tasting table. "Are you ready, Monsieur?"

A nod from the jurat assured Philip that he was more than ready. Philip looked at the trio of musicians and motioned for the drummer to give him a flourish. With the room quieting, Philip cleared his throat before he spoke. "Mesdames et Messieurs. We would be fools if we did not impose on Charles Manoncourt, the First Jurat of Saint-Émilion and one of the preeminent wine authorities in Bordeaux, to uncork the first bottle of the evening and pass judgment that it is worthy of this special gathering."

Claps and cheers thundered through the room. With great ceremony, Manoncourt sliced the foil then screwed the worm into the cork until the bootlever was in a perfect position to make the first pull. He twisted it in just a bit further and slid the cork out. Another round of applause erupted from the crowd. Genevieve handed the jurat a sparkling crystal glass with a generous bowl and tapering neck, perfect for their elegant Château Beaulieu grand cru.

As Manoncourt poured then swirled the wine, Genevieve realized she was holding her breath. His nose delved into the glass in search of the beautiful notes created by the marriage of merlot and cabernet franc. It lingered there too long. He lowered the glass, took a breath, exhaled, and again plunged his nose into the goblet. Genevieve and Philip watched as the jurat's eyes darted back and forth. At last, he lowered the glass again, smiled an uncomfortable smile, swirled the wine one more time and took a slurpy sip. In an instant, he turned his back to the crowd and spit the wine back into the glass.

"Monsieur Manoncourt, q'est que c'est? What's the matter?" Philip's eyes bulged. He grabbed a glass and splashed wine into it. What he tasted was a red worthy of Two Buck Chuck.

"Perhaps the bottle was not properly stored, my lord. Shall we try another?" The jurat bit his lower lip.

Philip had already cut the foil on another bottle and handed it to Manoncourt to uncork. "Genevieve, find Émile," he said. She was already texting him.

The second bottle was no better, nor was the third. By the time Émile arrived they had opened five bottles, all of them worthy of a corner shop in a beer-drinking town.

"Émile, where did you get these bottles of wine?"

He shrugged. "These were with the bottles of La Vie Douce Delphine told me to pick up yesterday from Château Pitique. There were two cases of dessert wine. When I was loading them onto the truck, I saw six cases of our grand cru on a pallet in the corner of the warehouse. It seemed odd to me that they would be there." Anxious he had done something wrong, his words tumbled out. "Delphine didn't say to pick up the grand cru, but I assumed they were ours. I asked the guy on the shipping floor and he said to take them. Is there something wrong? What's the matter with it?"

"It's not our wine," Philip said flatly. "They are our bottles, filled with someone else's inexpensive wine."

Sensing something was amiss, Delphine made her way from across the room to Philip and Genevieve. "Bad wine?" she said.

"Looks like it." Philip was unsure how much to reveal. "Until we figure this out, could you get more Champagne from the cellars?"

"Of course, my lord. Consider it done."

"Philip!" Genevieve said, tugging on his sleeve. "You know what this means? This means Kim isn't the counterfeiter, it's Hank. We need to text Picard."

Philip pounded on his phone, then hit send. He and Genevieve watched his screen, but there was no response.

"Call him," she said.

He called, but it went straight to voicemail. He tried Lambert with the same result.

"We need to go to Clos Peyra." Butterflies fluttered in Genevieve's stomach. She wasn't sure if they were from excitement or fear; maybe both.

"We can't let Picard arrest Kim," Philip said. "We need to tell Duncan so he can manage things here and keep the party going." As he and Genevieve shot out of the tasting room, he texted Duncan to meet them at the garage.

Within minutes, they were in a Cotswold-blue Jaguar XKE, waiting for the garage door to open. When Duncan tapped on the window, Philip and Genevieve almost jumped through the roof.

"What's going on?" Duncan said, anticipating the emergency had something to do with the events at the clos.

"We've got to get to Clos Peyra," Philip said, his voice clipped and urgent. "Picard and Lambert are about to raid the Wangs, and they're not the counterfeiters."

Disbelief flashed across Duncan's face. "You're kidding."

Philip brought Duncan up to speed as fast as he could, anxious to get on the road. "Hank must be the counterfeiter. Don't tell anyone. Delphine and Manoncourt are the only people who know what's going on and we want to keep it that way. Get wine from our stock and keep everybody happy. We'll be back as soon as we can."

"But, Dad—"

"We've got to go," Philip interrupted. He put the car in gear and roared out of the garage.

Though their mission was urgent, Philip couldn't keep a smile from his lips. He accelerated and the XKE hugged the road as he banked into the corners. He turned down the narrow lane that led to Clos Peyra, expecting to see police cars and lights flashing, but the only car in front of the house was Kim's BMW.

"That's strange, isn't it?" Genevieve leaned forward, straining against her seatbelt. "Didn't you expect to see cars and lights and lots of police? Where is everybody?"

Philip slowed to a crawl, then stopped twenty yards from the house. He pulled out his phone, scrolled to Picard's text, and read it again, this time aloud. "We are leaving for the search and seizure. Will update you soon."

"He doesn't say they're coming here to Clos Peyra, does he?" Genevieve searched the message for a clue to what was happening.

While he was staring at his screen, Philip's phone vibrated, and a text popped up. "Han Shou in custody. On our way to CB," he read aloud. "What the…" he said as he looked at Genevieve.

She shook her head and held up both palms, confused. "How did they figure that out?"

"If they're on their way to Château Beaulieu, we'd better get moving," he said. He smashed the clutch to the floor and threw the gearshift into first. Gravel spun beneath the wheels as he gave the engine too much gas. They shot around the circular drive and back down the lane. Philip stopped just long enough to see there were no cars coming, then gunned the engine onto the main road. Within three minutes they were racing down their driveway. As they approached the château they noticed three unfamiliar Citroëns.

"Cops," Philip said as he slammed to a stop. "Why in the hell have they come here?" He threw open his door, grabbed the door jamb and grunted as he pulled himself from the low-slung car. By the time he was around to her side, Genevieve was already up the stairs and opening the front door.

In the tasting room, bona fide bottles of Château Beaulieu were being emptied at a rapid clip. Laughter, chatter, and music filled the space, and everyone was having a wonderful time, oblivious to the police drama rumbling nearby.

Lillie's animated conversation captivated two Cité du Vin board members while Bernard smiled at Lillie's ability to engage everyone, from pauper to king. He was about to detail how The Art of the Vin work-study program would fill the void that was growing more critical by the year for vineyard owners, when he felt a vice grip on his left shoulder and an iron grasp on his right wrist. A man's voice was almost a whisper in his ear. "Bernard Reines, you are under arrest," the man on the left said. "Just come quietly. We have Hank Shou in custody and he'd very much like for you to join him."

Fear flooding through him, Bernard looked around for Lillie, but she had eased off into the crowd and left him on his own.

The two officers kept a firm grip on Bernard as they pushed

him toward the door. They looked like three friends perhaps going out for a smoke. No one noticed that he was leaving. No one cared.

Realizing that his masterful counterfeiting scheme was about to come crashing down, panic seized him. As they stepped out of the tasting room, Bernard mustered all his strength, broke out of the officers' grips and charged down the hall, head lowered and fists pumping, just as Émile emerged from the storeroom carrying an armful of wine bottles. Bernard smashed into Émile, knocking them both off their feet. Bottles flew into the air and crashed on the brick, spraying shards of glass and splattering wine everywhere.

Terrified that he had injured his former boss, Émile jumped up and pulled on Bernard's arm trying to help him. "M— M— Monsieur Reines, pardon, pardon. Je suis désolé." He pulled his shirttail from his waistband and tried to mop wine from Bernard's face.

Bernard slapped Émile's hands away. "Éloigne-toi de moi espèce, d'idiot," he snarled, fisting his hand, ready to punch Émile. But before he could strike, the two officers pulled his hands behind his back and cuffed him. This time, the officers weren't as polite. They yanked Bernard to stand and held him firmly.

"I wouldn't call Émile an idiot, I'd call him a hero," Duncan said, standing in the doorway. "I came into the hall just in time to see you stop this counterfeiting son-of-a-bitch from getting away. Well done, Émile." He stuck out his hand and pulled the confused young man off the floor.

"Je ne comprends pas. I don't understand." Émile looked at his former boss, who was now wine-soaked, disheveled and handcuffed.

Duncan put his arm around the young man's shoulders. "Émile, for the last three years, Bernard has been the head of a small group that counterfeited millions of euros of Château Beaulieu wine." Duncan felt Émile's body stiffen and a guttural laugh roll from his throat.

"I am not surprised." He glared at Bernard. "From the moment he suggested I cover the Pollock with the giclee, I knew he was full of… I think you say, larceny."

"Wait a minute." Duncan dropped his arm from Émile's shoulders, stood back and studied him. "I thought you got the idea when you read his manuscript."

"That's what he told me to say if I got caught, but I never read his book. He paid me five thousand euros to play the prank on Lord and Lady Crosswick." He shrugged. "It wasn't a lot, just pocket money, but I thought it would be fun. He assured me that even if they traced the joke to me, I would not be in trouble." He smacked his forehead with the heel of his hand. "As he said, I was an idiot to trust him. It wouldn't surprise me if he did other illegal things while heading up the LMBA."

"Well, my friend, Bernard is in custody, and you are the one who stopped him in his tracks." As he gave Émile a pat on the back, he saw his parents at the other end of the hall, his father on the phone and his mother striding toward the strange scene.

Genevieve walked to within inches of Bernard and drilled into his eyes for several seconds. "Thank god it was you." Still staring at him, she shook her head. "I guess the LMBA wasn't enough. Was it just about the money?"

Rather than meet Genevieve's withering gaze, he looked past her.

"Thank god it was you," she said again. "You, we can lose, but we would have been devastated if it had been Lillie." She turned to Émile. "And thank you for saving the day, Émile. You keep surprising us." She stretched up on her tiptoes, kissed his wine-spotted cheek, then licked her lips. "Love the vintage," she said, and beamed at him.

Philip shoved his phone into his pocket as he joined the group. "That was Directeur Picard," he said to Genevieve. "He, Lambert, and Boucher will be here later to brief us, but it seems we have the real prize right here. The mastermind, the puppet master, the genius behind the scheme." He turned to Bernard. "Hank is selling you down the river, my friend, and according to him, you're the one who insisted that Genevieve and I fall out of the sky and die in a French cow pasture. There are so many things I want to say to you, Bernard, but sometimes, a simple gesture says it best." At that, Philip drew back his arm and, for the first time in his life, he punched a man and heard the satisfying crunch of a broken nose.

FORTY-SEVEN

By the time Agent Lambert, Directeur Picard, and Inspector Boucher arrived at Château Beaulieu, the party in the tasting room was over. Where the Jurade had marched en masse and in precision with the pipers to begin the afternoon, they now wandered and wobbled in small groups down the long allée, leaving jollier than when they arrived. The Cité du Vin board members and their entourage piled into hired cars that would return them to Hotel de Pavie, where they would refortify themselves for tomorrow's meeting. Thanks to the discrete handling of events, no one was the wiser about the swirl of police activity just outside the tasting room.

Now the three officers and three Warwicks gathered in Philip's study. The circles around Lambert's eyes suggested sleep had not been her friend over the last few days and judging from Picard's rumpled, spotted shirt, Genevieve was sure he had not been home recently. But Boucher was pert and perky, happy to be at Château Beaulieu and back in Genevieve's company, no matter what the occasion.

"I'm assuming you have a lot to tell us." Philip looked at Lambert and Picard sitting on a sofa, and Boucher by the fire in the down-filled chair he loved.

"We do," Picard said. "Much of it you know, but there are some things that may come as a surprise. Inspector Boucher, would you like to begin?"

Delighted to be the center of attention, the BEA Inspector began. "As you know, we determined some time ago that Lee Bowen was responsible for watering your fuel tank."

"As I recall, Lee Bowen worked for the Wang family. Wasn't that one of the fingers pointing at Kim?" Genevieve said.

"It is true. At one time, he worked for Kim Wang's father in England. According to Hank, he asked Kim to recommend a man in the UK who could help him with a few things. That's how he got Bowen's name. We had no trouble tracking him to France. It got more difficult after that, but through tracing his credit cards we discovered he had rented a car. With that information, we used surveillance camera footage to follow him to Château Pitique. No doubt he came here to receive his payment. The day after he was here, the car was found at the airport parking lot. We think he had access to a new identity, a passport under another name, and left the country." He paused, looked over the top of his glasses and smirked. "He is not worth the resources it would take to find him. He is, as you would say, small onions."

"Small potatoes," Philip corrected. "He's small potatoes." Philip was teeming with questions. "What about Daniel's note in my briefcase? And who were the people who beat you to the train?"

"Ah, oui. A good question," Boucher said. "When LaGrande was in Paris for the party, he asked Madame Morier to slip the note into your briefcase. He wanted to warn you of the danger that lay ahead. Bernard overheard him ask for Madame Morier's help and arranged for his people to intercept the note."

"But how did—"

Boucher put up his hand, anticipating Philip's next question. "Lord Crosswick, Bernard tapped your phone as soon as he knew you and Lady Crosswick didn't die in a plane crash."

"Holy crap," Philip seethed. He snatched his phone from the side table and threw it into the fireplace. He blew the air from his cheeks and slumped back in his chair.

"Jeeze, Philip. Was that necessary?" Genevieve scowled at her husband.

He mumbled something under his breath.

Taking that as her cue, Lambert picked up the story. "When the Shou family bought Château Pitique three years ago, Bernard convinced Hank that counterfeiting Château Beaulieu wine and shipping it to China would be easy and very profitable."

"That makes sense," Genevieve frowned. "Bernard and Hank were old friends and I imagine Bernard knew Hank was under pressure from his father to make a quick success of Château Pitique. What a perfect opportunity for Bernard, but why he would risk so much—his prestigious position in the art community, his freedom—to be involved in such a thing?"

"Ah," Lambert sighed. "Hank offered some interesting insight. Though Bernard is well educated, he does not come from a wealthy family. According to Hank, he always loved fine things, and as director of the LMBA he was always surrounded by the best of everything, but none of it was his."

"So rather than work hard and earn the lifestyle he lusted after, he decided to steal his way to wealth."

"You are exactly right, Lord Crosswick."

"Take it from someone who knows, it's better to inherit lots of money." Philip laughed at his own joke.

Lambert gave Philip a moment to enjoy himself, then went on. "The other important piece of the puzzle was Daniel LaGrande. They needed Château Beaulieu bottles and labels, which Daniel could easily get for them. The challenge was to get him involved." Agent Lambert looked at the three Warwicks to make sure they were following. They all nodded.

Lambert continued. "You all know about Daniel's nephew, Paul, who borrowed a hundred thousand euros from his uncle." Again, everyone nodded. "Paul told Madam Morier that his uncle had saved him from financial disaster." She looked up from her notes. "Interesting pillow talk, I would say. Later, in one of her gossipy chats with Bernard, she told him Daniel had loaned money to Paul."

Before Lambert could go on, Genevieve jumped in: "So Bernard suggested to Daniel that supplying bottles and labels would be an easy way to refill his coffers…"

"…and it wouldn't do Château Beaulieu any harm," Duncan finished.

Agent Lambert smiled. "Exactly. According to Hank, Daniel was fine with the arrangement until he learned that Bernard had ordered Lee Bowen to water down the gas in your jet. That was too much for him."

Genevieve's eyes flashed. "I would hope so."

"Apparently Daniel found out about Bernard's fuel tank order at your gala in Paris," she went on. "Hank said they had quite a row. Did you know anything about that?"

Genevieve stiffened as she remembered the scene at Maison de Laney. "So that's what their argument was all about!"

Philip and Genevieve gaped at each other.

"When Daniel died, Hank was stunned by his death and feared Bernard had killed him. When he heard it was suicide, he was relieved," Lambert added.

Genevieve thought for a minute, then asked, "Was Madame Morier involved in any of this?"

"No. It appears she knew nothing about Bernard and Daniel's scheme."

"And, just to confirm, Lillie wasn't a part of it, was she?" Genevieve held her breath.

"Non."

She exhaled. "I'm so glad."

"Chloé, however, is another story." Picard spoke for the first time in a long while. "Hank paid her to spy on the household. I doubt that she reported anything important, but, nonetheless, I am certain you will want to address that."

"Won't she be arrested?" Genevieve asked.

"Only if you press charges. And I'm not certain what they would be. Gossiping, perhaps?" Picard chuckled. "There is no indication that she was aware of the criminal activity, however George, her paramour, is a different situation. He has been Hank's bon à tout faire, I believe the English say dogsbody, for the last few months doing all his dirty work. We have him in custody. He was the one who chased the horse through the field and over the wall."

The Warwicks looked at each other, wondering what questions had been left unanswered. After a moment, Philip said, "What happens next?"

"We turn our evidence and our recommendations over to the magistrat de siège, the public prosecutor. That judge will decide whether or not to go forward with prosecution."

Duncan couldn't believe what he was hearing. "You mean it's not a foregone conclusion that Bernard, Hank, and their merry band will be prosecuted?"

"How is that possible?" Genevieve thundered.

"As I told you at our first meeting, it is difficult to entice the law to bring wine counterfeiters to justice." Agent Lambert looked resigned. "I believe, however, that because Bernard tried to murder you, the magistrate will be much keener." She gathered her papers, slipped them into her briefcase, and stood. "We shall keep you posted as the case moves forward. Thank you for everything, all your help and your cooperation. I hope we don't have the opportunity to meet again under the same circumstances."

Philip extended his hand to Agent Lambert. "I assure you, we won't hesitate to call you if we think anyone is fiddling with our wine."

"Directeur Picard." Duncan gave his hand a firm shake. "We now have close ties to our local police. Let's hope we won't need you often, but we know you'll be ready if we do."

Genevieve stepped to where Boucher was standing, waiting like an eager puppy. "And, last, but certainly not least, Inspector Boucher. You've been with us since we landed in France. We could say you are among our oldest French friends." When she held out her hand, Boucher caressed it in both of his. Duncan grimaced while Philip bit his lower lip, trying not to laugh.

"Lady Crosswick, je suis éternellement à votre service. I am forever at your service. You have but to call, and I shall be here." He brought her hand to his lips, kissed it, then bowed from his waist.

Genevieve looked across Boucher's bent back at Philip, who was stifling a chuckle.

Always gracious, Genevieve nudged Boucher from his bow. "My family and I are in your debt," she said, sliding her hand from Boucher's grip. "It's getting late, and we know you all have many things to do to wrap up this case."

She led them into the foyer and toward the front door where Delphine offered their coats. She gave Picard his jacket and held out Boucher's topcoat and scarf. He took his scarf and swirled it around his short neck, the last loop covering his mouth and nose. He shoved it down, hoping no one had noticed. He took his coat from Delphine and swung it around to drape it over his shoulders. As he took a step toward Genevieve to say a final farewell, his coat slipped off his shoulders, falling to the floor. Trying to look as suave as possible he bent down, scooped it up and slung it over his arm.

Picard and Lambert were already down the stairs and heading toward the police car as Philip stood with the door open. When the inspector realized he was the last one to leave, he grabbed Genevieve by the shoulders and gave her a final kiss on each cheek. "Au revoir," he said.

"Au revoir, Maurice," Genevieve said, and waved.

Philip closed the door, and they collapsed against it, howling with laughter.

FORTY-EIGHT

HER EYES STILL closed, Genevieve listened to Philip's slow, steady breathing. She thought about the yin and yang of yesterday—a welcoming event and auspicious beginning to their partnership with Cité du Vin amid the turbulent finale to their three-month-long series of mysteries. It was hard to believe that the party guests in the tasting room were oblivious to the capture and arrest of Bernard just yards away, but anyone who heard the crash of bottles as Émile smashed into Bernard would have assumed a server dropped a tray of glasses on the brick floor.

"You have to hand it to the French," Genevieve thought. "They never let anything distract them from superb wine and fine cuisine." In the words of William Shakespeare, "All's well that ends well," she mused. And today everything was going to end perfectly.

She looked at her watch, 7:15. Fifteen more minutes, then she would get up. She rolled toward Philip, slid her hand around his bare chest, kissed his shoulder and snuggled into his back. "It's meeting day," she whispered.

"Hmm," was his response.

She kissed his neck this time. "I said it's meeting day."

He took her hand and kissed the palm. "Go back to sleep. It's the middle of the night."

"It's almost ten o'clock. The board will be here any minute."

Philip pulled her wrist to his eyes and squinted. "It's 7:18. Aren't you exhausted after last night?"

"Like I said, it's meeting day. Lots to do."

He rolled onto his side so they were face to face. "G, you realize *we* are giving millions of euros to the Cité du Vin for a program that, for the next many years, will benefit hundreds of kids and many vineyards. We don't need to impress these people. The Jurade parade kicking everything off and the cocktail party last night were wonderful. You love doing these spectacular events, I know." He put his hand on Genevieve's cheek. "But, shouldn't Cité du Vin be dazzling us?"

Genevieve rolled onto her back and stared at the ceiling. "Let me ask you a question."

"Sure."

Philip saw a tear trickle from the corner of her eye and slide down the side of her face.

"G." Philip traced the damp path with his forefinger.

She turned her head toward him, her eyes sparkling from the tears that were about to overflow.

"What's going on?" Philip searched her face for a sign of what could be wrong.

"Since the jet incident, you've said repeatedly you're going to disinherit yourself," she smiled and sniffed.

He said nothing but remained locked in her gaze.

"With every new revelation, and there were many, you became more emphatic that we should resume our pre-inheritance lives. Now that this crazy mystery is solved, what are you thinking?" She sniffed again.

For what seemed like ages, Philip stared at Genevieve. She could read nothing in his eyes and had no idea what his response was about to be. She caressed the side of his face, but still he said nothing.

Her lips parted as she was about to speak, but before she could, he leaned forward and covered her mouth with his. It was a soft kiss, a gentle kiss, and it said everything. As he pulled back, Genevieve saw the answer in his eyes.

EPILOGUE

SPRING AND SUMMER raced across the calendar in a blur, leaving the chaos and madness of March behind. Now here they were on the edge of fall, watching the September sun streak the sky with yellow and crimson as it dipped toward the horizon.

The view over the vineyard could have been a painting. For miles, green vines waited in tidy rows, heavy with grapes ready for harvest. The red from the sky reflected on the leaves, the grass, the trees. Around a long table covered with a crisp white linen cloth that puddled on the stone floor of the terrace, the Château Beaulieu family lingered over the remnants of a late-summer dinner.

French and English flew around the table non-stop, and laughter pealed across the valley like church bells.

Unusually quiet, Philip and Genevieve sat, shoulders touching, their clasped hands resting on the table. Watching frisky Cooper chase Alex from one end of the terrace to the other, Genevieve couldn't imagine a more perfect tableau. Ella sat on Delphine's lap, frowning in concentration as the house manager showed her the fine art of creative napkin folding. They had turned squares of linen into a parade of whimsey as a rabbit, a swan, a fan, a star, and a bishop's hat marched down the center of the table. Ella was determined to fold a much-crumpled serviette into a unicorn but was having little luck.

Putting a flame to the last unlit candle on the table, Émile paused before moving to the lanterns scattered along the low, stone wall rimming the terrace. "Is this not a perfect evening, Lord Crosswick, Lady Crosswick?" he said, his face bronze and glowing from hours spent in the fields.

This was not the arrogant, lost boy who had attempted to extort money from Philip and Genevieve for their Jackson Pollock a mere seven months ago. Over the summer, he had worked hard under Edouard's keen eye. He was a surprising student, learning quickly and voraciously, and he seemed to be falling in love with Château Beaulieu and vineyard life. At least ten pounds heavier, much of that lean muscle, he was robust and clear-eyed, with an energy and ready smile that confirmed they had made the right decision to bring him to their château. Over the past months, he had become a trusted part of their lives.

At the end of the table, Duncan and Edouard sat in rapt attention while Henri regaled them with stories of the cars in the Château Beaulieu collection. "As interesting as the automobiles in the collection are," he nodded at Duncan, "the stories about, I believe you say, the ones that got away are even more fascinating. One day I shall share them all." He sat back and lit a Gauloise, inhaled, and watched the glow of the cigarette tip as he blew a long stream of smoke into the night.

A cheer went up when David emerged from the house, his arms filled with reinforcement bottles of mineral water and wine. He and Becca had come for the weekend and rounded out the exuberant group.

"So," Becca said, as David walked around the table filling glasses. "David and I have a rather enormous favor to ask of the Warwick family."

Conversation stopped and everyone on the terrace waited for her to continue. She looked at each expectant face, glowing in the candlelight. Even Alex and Ella leaned forward with anticipation.

She gave David a pleading glance, hoping he would jump in. "Don't look at me, darling. This was your idea."

"You're right," she said. "Philip, Genevieve, Duncan, Julia, and of course Alex and Ella, David and I have decided on our wedding date."

"It's about time," Julia said, raising her goblet.

Genevieve didn't miss a beat. "And you're going to have the wedding here, right?" She pulled her phone from her pocket and brought up her calendar. "What date are you thinking?"

"Oh, boy! Can I be a flower girl?" Ella was off Delphine's lap and at Becca's side in an instant, jumping up and down, curls bouncing around her sweet face.

Stunned that Genevieve knew what she was about to ask, Becca was speechless.

Genevieve scrolled forward through the months, then looked at Becca. "Are you thinking during the holidays?"

"How did you know? We were thinking December 20th. Would that work?"

Genevieve's smile was radiant. "That would be perfect." She leaned into Philip's shoulder. "That's *our* anniversary."

"Really?" Becca's eyes glistened.

"And, The Art of the Vine students will have completed the first half of their program, so we're having a party for them the week before."

"How's the program going?" David asked.

Philip's grin stretched across his face as he thought about what they had created in such a short time. "It's beyond what we could have imagined." He turned to look at Genevieve. "It's amazing what you can accomplish if you throw money at a project."

Genevieve squeezed his hand and smiled into the night.

"It makes all the hassle and mystery and danger worth it, doesn't it, G?" he said. "Didn't I keep telling you it would be crazy to give all this up?"

In response, Genevieve's full-throated laughter rang across the terrace and into the vines.

Philip glanced at his phone, checking the text that had just pinged. It was from Richard Durand, a well-credentialed and fastidious art historian they had hired to replace Bernard as the director of the Laney Musée des Beaux-Arts.

Lord Crosswick, I have found some paperwork that concerns me regarding two paintings that were sold to the Cité du Vin last winter. There is no emergency. Please call Monday. RD

Philip seized on the part of the message that said there was no emergency and drew his attention back to the magical scene whirling around him. For the first time since arriving in France, he was sure he and his family were heading down the right path, and after months of waiting to feel the spirit of his Laney ancestors at Château Beaulieu, tonight their essence surrounded him. The thrill of seeing The Art of the Vin in full operation with the promise of affecting many young lives in the future made everything they had been through worthwhile.

He tapped his wine glass with his knife and a dulcet tone rang out. "Your attention, please. I would like to make a toast to all of you. Everyone around this table is here because Genevieve and I cherish you. You are Château Beaulieu. As Duncan and Julia become the lord and lady of this grand Château, Genevieve and I know they will be successful because of all of you. With many exciting events to look forward to before the end of the year, let's enjoy each and every day in this very special place with you very special people. Santé."

"Santé," everyone responded, including Cooper with a loud bark.

La Fin

Did you enjoy

ART, WINE, AND CRIME?

Please leave fellow readers a review!

amazon.com/review/create-review/REPLACE

KEEP READING FOR A SNEAK PEEK OF

JONATHON WILLIAM WALLACE LANEY

The 12TH Earl of Crosswick

A Lord and Lady Crosswick Mystery Short Story,
Available Exclusively at tanalhboerger.com

AND SO IT BEGINS

I'M QUITE SURE my first memory is floating in moist darkness, waiting for something extraordinary to happen. And then it did. I remember my surprise at the waves that rhythmically ebbed and flowed. The longer it lasted the more it annoyed me and just when I decided I'd had enough, the biggest wave of all shoved me against an elastic band. Of course, I didn't know at that time what an elastic band was, but in retrospect, that's what it felt like. And then, another big shove through a small hole, and I was blinded by bright lights bouncing off white walls, white uniforms, white sheets, white faces. I think I was upside down, though, again, I have to say, I didn't know what upside down was. I whimpered, but when someone smacked my bottom, I gave them what they were asking for—a big, fat wail. I remember thinking, "What a set of pipes!"

That was 3 August 1921. I've been telling that story since I was four and every time I do, someone pats me on the head, well, not so much anymore, since I'm, well, dead, but they used to, and they would say, "What a funny story, you clever boy." I would roll my eyes knowing, even at four, that they didn't think I could possibly remember my time in the womb and my journey out into the world. But I did.

And I remember my mother. She always smelled of roses. When I was six, she told me that Rose Otto was her favorite perfume because my grandmother Lady Caroline, had given her a vial of the treasured scent on the day she married my father. Our family believes in tradition and Rose Otto was a tradition that began with my great-grandmother, the magnificent Charlotte Chaubert, the toast of Paris and London. According to my mother, who loved to tell a lively story, Charlotte was my grandfather's passion. Lord Philip adored her, denied her nothing, but in the end, the love of his life was taken from him far too soon.

Sometimes I wonder if I had heeded their story as a warning, could I have veered from the events that took my life down a path I did not choose, or want? It's a bit late to ponder these things, but sometimes my mind still goes there.

The London Times, August 6, 1921

THE COUNTESS OF CROSSWICK HAS BEEN DELIVERED OF A SON

The Countess of Crosswick was safely delivered of a son at 05:26, 3 August, at Columbia-Presbyterian Medical Center, New York City, New York. The baby weighed 7lbs 2oz.

The Earl of Crosswick was delighted to greet his first child.

Lord and Lady Crosswick will reside with their son, Jonathon William Wallace Laney, at their home, Margrave House, Kensington, upon their return to London.

And so I was announced to the world. An auspicious beginning, to be sure. A proper English babe wailing his way into the world, not in the serene, shaded lanes of Kensington, London, but into the noisy, brash streets of New York City, surely a harbinger of how I would live my life.

I'm not certain that my parents wanted more children, or actually any children at all. It seemed to me they were delighted with each other and would have been perfectly happy to live their interesting lives surrounded by artists and musicians rather than a brood of young savages. Regardless, I was the only savage they produced, and it suited me that they stopped at one, as long as I was it.

It was said that I was a bonnie baby, but that was my mother and my granny speaking. I doubt if my father said the same. I believe he preferred the attractive swirl of paint on canvas more than the red face of a newborn. He tended to avoid me in my early years until I could ride well enough to join him on The Hunt at Wilmingrove Hall, our family seat in Yorkshire. Or when I could give him a good run for his money on the chessboard. Then he began to take an interest in me and my development.

I had a nanny I loved nearly as much as I adored my mother, but my nanny was my friend and my mother was, well, someone I worshiped. She was a charming, brilliant, and stunning woman who never tired of bringing life and laughter into our home. No matter what I did, she delighted in it. If I colored a picture for her that was nothing more than a few scribbled lines on the paper, she would declare it to be the work of a burgeoning young talent. If I made a mudpie and insisted it was a plum pudding, she would pretend to eat it all and insist it was worthy of a Michelin star. She read to me. She tutored me in the vast and spectacular art collection that was my parents' pride and joy and because she loved it, I loved it.

And she told me stories. The night she told me the tragic tale of my great-grandmother, Charlotte, the wife of the 9th Earl of Crosswick, it was raining and cold. I was six. My mother and I huddled together on a small sofa in my father's study, which would one day be mine. I remember how cozy we were with a lap robe tucked around us and a fire crackling on the hearth. My hands cradled a cup of hot cocoa, and my mother kept stealing sips, smiling at me each time she did, a little cocoa mustache painting her upper lip. The smell of cocoa still reminds me of my mother. The smell of cocoa and Rose Otto.

"Your great-grandmother was a beauty," she began. "Everyone adored her, but no one as much as your great-grandfather." As she spoke, my mother's forehead nearly touched mine. Her voice was so quiet, I watched her lips to make certain I didn't miss any words. "It was your great grandparents' fortieth wedding anniversary, and this house was filled with guests who were here to celebrate with them." My mother's hand was cool on my cheek. "Everyone gathered at the bottom of the staircase, waiting for Charlotte to make her grand entrance. When she appeared, she was stunning in a shimmering silver dress with a train that curved around her feet. Even at sixty-four, she was breathtaking." My mother looked deeper into my eyes. "You have her eyes, darling boy." And she kissed the tip of my nose, then went on. "The 9th Earl raised his Champagne glass and said, 'To my magnificent bride of forty years. No one else has ever walked the earth, whom I could love as I love you.' At the end of the toast, the band struck up Charlotte's favorite song 'Oh You Beautiful Doll' and Charlotte blew a kiss to the Earl." My mother's eyes were glistening with tears. I didn't understand why she was crying. "When she started down the stairs, the toe of her shoe hooked on her gown's silver train. She tried to grab the banister but missed and tumbled head over heels down the stairs. By the time she reached the bottom, she was…." My mother's voice trailed off, but I understood.

"One day, darling boy, I'm sure you'll meet her," she said. I know my mother intended to comfort me, but when she saw my eyes, wide with fear at the idea that I was going to run into an old, dead lady, perhaps in the middle of the night when I got up to go to the loo, I'm certain she realized she had miscalculated. She quickly tried to recover, pulling me close, kissing my forehead, and laughing. "Don't worry darling. I just meant we'll talk about Granny Charlotte again, and the more we talk about her, the more you'll feel you know her."

I didn't believe her, and for the next year, I lived in fear of great granny jumping out of my wardrobe, every evening when I opened the door to get my dressing gown. Other six-year-olds were frightened of monsters or goblins. I was terrified of my beautiful, kind, dead great-grandmother. And then I learned, purely by accident, that Granny Charlotte was a ghost.

YOU ARE CORDIALLY INVITED

to step inside the 12TH Earl's world.

JOIN TANA'S NEWSLETTER TO DOWNLOAD THE WHOLE STORY, FREE:

WWW.TANALHBOERGER.COM

OTHER BOOKS BY TANA L.H. BOERGER

Money, Murder, Mayhem
Art, Wine, and Crime

ACKNOWLEDGEMENTS

"It takes a village," is not just an African proverb, but one of life's realities. Without my village, there would be no second book. Thank you to my two North Stars - my sister, Alana Davidson, and my husband, Tom Boerger.

Thank you to my cherished cheerleaders and morale boosters, Paul and Kay Zimmerman and Bucky Holmes.

Thank you, Karen Glaser for applying your clever mind and linguistic skills to keeping the English/French back-and-forth accurate.

Thank you to my editor, Rosie Walker, a fine writer in her own right and a spectacular artisan who consistently helps me craft the first draft of a meandering manuscript into a story worth reading.

Thank you Caerus Kourt, designer extraordinaire, for interpreting my novels and creating the perfect cover. You are a master.

And thank you to The Poison Lady, Luci Zahray, whose passion is poison and without whom I would never have known about the glories of methanol. You are a murder mystery writer's best friend.

And, finally, thank you to all of you who are falling in love with Philip and Genevieve Warwick, their family and friends and the wacky, treacherous, charming, unpredictable people who inhabit their glamorous world. Without you, what would be the point?

ABOUT TANA

Though Tana is an unapologetic Anglophile, she also has a passion for France. At fifteen she spent her summer studying French in Villard-de-Lans near Grenoble and fell in love with the French lifestyle. It wasn't long before she realized that her lust for Paris and Bordeaux, where *Art, Wine, and Crime* is set, would keep calling her back. She shares that passion and many others with her husband, Tom. When they aren't in the UK, France or someplace else wonderful, they spend their time in Sanford, NC and New Jersey with their amazing son and daughter-in-law, and their two fabulous grandchildren.

WWW.TANALHBOERGER.COM
f TANALHBOERGER

Printed in Great Britain
by Amazon